1000 METTLE FOLDS

CUT I: THE FALL

1000 Mettle Folds
Cut I: The Fall

Steve Gerlach
& Amanda Kool

2011

Authors' Note:
This story is a work of invention. As such, the places and names found within are predominantly fictional.
In some cases, the authors have used creative licence to suit their purposes.

To Lew, Marty, Mike and Barry
For the inspiration and fine malt whiskey.

Never tackle frail old men...

PROLOGUE

The knife drew across her remaining breast.

A slow, shallow cut, it sliced from the middle of her chest, upwards and across, flicking around her nipple, finishing high near her shoulder.

Not a killing cut. Not yet.

The skin folded apart, the edges curling slightly before the blood flowed, rolling down her chest to pool with the rest. The cut was methodical, exact.

There was pain, but it was distant, like the noises outside.

Blood smeared the blade of the knife, dulling its shine.

She was naked, helpless. There was time until she bled to death. They both knew it.

The knife moved further down, the tip of the blade lightly touching the skin of her forearm, balancing there for only a second before pushing down, slicing forward and cutting deep.

She didn't cry out. She was beyond voice, beyond resistance. Numb.

The blade cut deeper now, tearing skin and muscle, not stopping until it scraped hard against bone.

The time for screaming had passed. The fear had left her, as had her ability to fight this. She had only enough energy to breathe; slow, struggling breaths.

She managed to raise her head once, to look at the room around her. Her room, her private place. Some things she didn't recognise as the haze settled over her eyes. She could make out the suitcase, half packed, near the table that had been her father's. It was old and rickety. One of its legs was propped up by the only two books she owned.

She'd never read them. She couldn't read and only now did she think that was a sad thing.

On top of the table was a candle, burning brightly, but almost all gone now. Soon the wick would burn down, leaving the flame to gutter in a pool of yellow wax. It flickered as she watched; shadows dancing around the walls.

Her gaze moved slowly to the left. Her bed, the dresser, her window with the tattered pale blue curtains, the broken pane of glass that she would reach through to unlock her door. All so close and familiar; comforting. All of it covered in bright splashes of blood. Splattered and sprayed with it, smelling warm and fresh like meat left on the bench to thaw for the evening.

If only she'd never lost the key to the door.

If only she'd been able to make the rent.

Her worst fear was living on the street, being homeless and without shelter. But now that didn't seem so terrible.

She felt as if she was floating above it all, seeing it all from her ceiling. Her dresser, the fireplace, her bed...what *was* on the bed?

She almost didn't recognise herself as her gaze drifted along her body. She was lying down, her un-lacerated back safe against the old bedspread. What she saw couldn't be her. This gutted, exposed carcass...

It couldn't be.

A piece of...skin. Torn and ragged. A piece of her. Lying next to her left hand, a section, flung away from the butchery. On the small table by the bed, leaning to one side, was her other breast, flung there like an afterthought, left there like a discarded meal, torn and ravaged. Destroyed.

A large piece of thigh slipped from the side of the bed and to the floor as the knife jagged all the way down her leg, slicing through skin and grating off bone like fingers down a blood-soaked blackboard.

The blade struck her ankle, the serrations digging deep into the bone, biting, holding, sticking for a moment or two before being forcibly pulled free. It rose in front of her and she watched, compelled. Blood and muscle dripped from the sharp edge, the light from the fire dancing across the reddish-black muck that was once part of her.

It came back to her breast, wavered in front of her eyes for a few seconds more—searching for inspiration—before the blade slashed down, slicing her nipple in two.

It splayed open, and she was struck by the beauty of the white skin and the pink muscle inside. Not much blood, this time.

And while she watched, she felt the knife below the cut nipple, slicing upwards quickly, forcefully. Then the whole nipple was gone, thrown clear across the room, landing on the bare floorboards; one half by a piece of her ear, the other falling into shadow.

The knife traced down her chest, the unblemished hand holding the handle tight, as the teeth of the blade caught on her exposed ribs, filling the room with a biting *rasp, rasp, rasp.* Then it cut further down, rending straight across her hips, lower, slashing, cutting deeper, opening her most private areas, cutting through them, tearing wider, gaping holes.

She wondered then about childbirth, whether it would hurt, whether it would damage her this much. She'd heard that sometimes when births went wrong, it tore women in two. She'd always been scared of childbirth.

It was only a fleeting thought, gone in the instant it took

for the knife to slice deeper, cutting further inside her velvet folds.

Nothing mattered anymore.

No one.

Her head fell back against the bed-head, the iron rails hard against her skull. Her left hand tried in vain to cover up her gaping womanhood—she didn't want to be found this way—but she didn't have enough energy.

The knife was deep inside her now. She could see only the handle as it cut deeper, faster. Slicing at her, tearing into her, spreading her insides wide and deep.

She turned her face away, not wanting to see the damage as it happened, and she rested her head on the wet, sticky pillow.

Her eyes tried hard to focus on the window. But night had fallen, all she could see through the glass was darkness.

The courtyard lanterns weren't lit.

She hoped Joseph would return, but after their argument, there was little chance of that. He'd left her, and probably for good.

Would he be the one who found her?

She was alone now.

She'd always thought the worst thing that could happen was to end up on the street. But here, now, in her room, there was blood and death.

The knife sliced through the air and struck hard at her face. She blinked away the blow, felt the air stinging at the hole where her nose used to be. Felt the blood ooze and trickle down her lips and across her tongue.

The blood from her nose mingled with that of the knife—blood from between her legs.

She wanted to spit it out, but couldn't. She tried to turn, tried to say something.

But before she could, the knife drew across her throat, cutting deep into her larynx, slicing skin and muscle and bone, and her words were taken from her.

Then her breath stopped. The air was just...gone and the room grew hot. She looked at the fireplace to see if the flames were burning higher, but the fire had weakened. She could barely see.

Don't take my eyes.

What was left of her chest rose and fell, trying desperately to suck in the hot air of the room. All she could taste was blood, all she could swallow was herself.

She thought of her mother, and a sudden calm flooded through her. It washed over her like the blood washing down her legs, across her cheek, and down her throat.

How can I have any blood left? she wondered. *Shouldn't it be gone, like my breath?*

She didn't know if the figure stood or knelt, just that they were above her, staring down, smiling. Maybe they were even lying across her, covering her body. But she couldn't feel the weight.

Her eyes focussed on the face, only inches away. Beautiful, really. She felt no breath from them, just as they felt no breath from her.

The face above her smiled.

"Almost there." A whisper.

Then the smile moved away.

The figure held out a hand and offered it towards her.

She needed that touch.

The fingers of her left hand moved slightly, hopefully enough to show she agreed.

The hand slipped underneath hers, held hers, tightened around hers.

She took it. Gripped hard.

And finally slipped away...

Burning The Letters

"I've got to get this off."

"Listen—"

"Fuck. No. Don't. Don't *ever* touch me!" Zachary stood in the centre of the stream, scrubbing frantically. He didn't look up.

The clear water ran with colour. Athan could just make it out in the glow of the moon. Not full. He had to be grateful for that.

Athan winced, his head hurting with the volume of Zachary's voice. Blood caked one side of his forehead and his drying skin grew tight around the wound.

The rain had ceased miles ago, allowing them to see, to slow their pace, but not by much.

Athan was impatient and urged his friend on. There was no time to rest, not then and not now.

They ran until they reached this rushing creek. Zachary stopped again, right in the middle of the stream. And there he stayed, scrubbing at his clothes.

Athan paced. They couldn't risk being seen here. He raised cold fingers to his head and touched the graze. His skin came away slightly red and his stomach rolled once more in lazy nausea.

He couldn't even remember her face.

He had no idea how long they'd run. It seemed like an eternity, like they'd never done anything else. Like their lives before this were non-existent.

They had run through the scrub of the farmland until it became field, then forest. They heard the baying of the dogs, the distant voices and shouts bouncing off hills, the sound of gunshots fired by over-eager hands.

Athan's head pounded in time with his feet on the hard turf, every step bringing pain. Zachary followed doggedly, slower, running more from necessity than from their pursuers.

Athan tilted his head and held his breath, trying hard to listen to the forest around him. He couldn't hear the dogs, but with the stream rushing fast over the earth, he couldn't hear a damn thing besides Zachary's breathing and his own pounding headache.

The farmer shot me.

The bastard.

He sighed and looked back to the creek, then wished he hadn't. Zachary's red hair faded in comparison to the red that washed from his soaked pants into the water.

So much blood.

Athan bounced on the balls of his feet, ready to move, still listening.

There was no way to tell who was nearby, or who could see them. They could be right over the next rise. Dogs and guns. A bloody lynch mob.

"Zach."

No response.

"Zach, hurry!"

"I'm not done."

"Yes, you are." But he didn't drag Zachary from the creek.

Athan had no blood on him other than that drying on his forehead. He was clean. Zachary's fingers were crimson with cold and with blood; his hands shook as he scrubbed hard. Athan didn't want to risk pushing him further. If Zachary broke, they stopped for good.

He waited for another five minutes. It was all they could afford, but it seemed to stretch for hours.

"Zachary—"

"No."

"For the love of Mike, we *have* to go."

"I don't *have* to do anything. Leave me alone."

Athan picked his way down the muddy embankment, placing his feet carefully until he stood at the edge.

"Zach, I understa—"

"You don't." Zachary stood and stared straight at him for the first time since they stopped running. "You weren't the one looking right into her fucking eyes."

Athan, frankly shocked at his friend's language, just stood as Zachary walked towards him, the water sloshing around his legs, bubbling up around him. He stopped right in front of Athan and held up a blood streaked hand in front of Athan's face, the cold palm touching his nose for a second.

"I was this close to her," Zachary said, his eyes hollow in the gloom "So don't tell me you understand. You weren't there." He let his hand drop to his side.

"I was there. I was right nex—"

"You *weren't* there!" Zachary shoved Athan with his left hand, flat palm hard on a trembling chest. Athan went sprawling, landing on his back without having time to catch himself.

"You weren't," Zachary repeated as he strode up the bank.

Athan heard Zachary's steps as he sprinted, now leading their flight. Zachary had always been the faster one.

Athan ran a hand through his hair, then wiped at his nose, making sure there was no blood. He looked down at his shirt to where the faint, wet imprint of Zachary's palm darkened the material with water and...

Damn.

Slowly, he clambered to his feet and followed Zachary at a safe distance.

At least they were moving again.

Zachary didn't feel safe to stop until well into the night; until they were well into the trees.

Under the canopy, he couldn't see the stains on his knees. He hadn't scrubbed long enough to get it all out and he wondered now if it would *ever* come out.

A few hours after dark, they found themselves in a twisted gully, deep and dark and meandering down the valley. The trees stretched out overhead, their branches and limbs reaching to the night sky.

They stopped near an overhang that was relatively dry and sheltered from the biting wind.

Athan began to gather any twigs, sticks and leaves that weren't soaked through.

"We should light a fire," he said, even though he had found no dry tinder.

"No, they'll see." Zachary's voice shuddered and he hated it. He didn't know why he was still shaking; he no longer felt cold.

"No one's going to see, not here," Athan said. "Besides, you'll catch your death. Look at you."

"With what?"

"Eh?"

"What are we going to light it with?"

Athan gestured for Zachary's bag. Zachary just stared at

16

him, so Athan walked over and took the bag from his shoulder. He watched Athan rummage for a few moments, then draw forth a packet of letters tied with string. Zachary blinked. He remembered taking them from the postmaster and promising to deliver them.

"We are not burning the letters," he said.

"We need to start a fire. The leaves are damp." Athan scrubbed a hand through his fair hair.

"They're hers."

"She won't be needing them anymore." Athan didn't look at Zachary as he opened a letter, breaking the wafer and unfolding the paper. He lit a match and Zachary watched as his eyes squinted in the light of the small flame. Scanning back and forth.

"Don't *read* them. If you're going to burn them, the least you can do is not read them."

"Why not?"

"They're private."

"*Were* private."

Athan leaned forward and blew out the match. Zachary couldn't see his face, now, just the ghost of the flame imprinted on his eyes.

Athan started a fire using three of the letters and some dry twigs from under the overhang. Everything else was soaked.

Once it was burning convincingly, Zachary huddled close to the flames feeling his clothes dry and his body warm.

They didn't talk. They just stared and listened to the night, to the wind in the trees and the sounds of night animals in the undergrowth.

When he was no longer shivering, Zachary retreated to lean against a tree, pulling his knees to his chest and wrapping his arms around them tight.

From the other side of the fire, Athan just watched. He said

17

nothing.

Minutes passed and the dark night stretched on.

"Warmer?"

"A bit."

Zachary uncurled his fingers and placed his hands over his stinging eyes, obscuring the view of the flames and his friend.

He abruptly let them fall, and his eyes stared down at his open hands. Nestled in his right palm was a copper coin. He stared at it, uncomprehending.

He picked it up, peeling it from his skin, seeing the sharp imprint in his flesh where he had gripped so hard.

He wondered how long he'd been holding it that way.

Scraping his nail back and forth along the surface, he removed the brown crust from the relief, digging into the grooves, trying to make it clean.

After a while, he stopped and nodded. He remembered now.

"What?" Athan asked from across the fire.

"Nothing." He put the coin in his pocket and closed his eyes.

"What is it?" Athan asked, insistent.

"It's hers."

They emerged from the gully in early morning. A cold, crisp day, the fog was heavy and the air damp. They saw no men, heard no dogs. Everything around them was silent, except for their breathing and the sound of their footsteps in the undergrowth.

They walked until midday, barely uttering a word. They were hungry, but they dared not stop. They had no food, anyway. Their only solace was the water they drank from the rushing streams.

Eventually, they ran on. Even though the forest was silent, they couldn't shake the fear that they were still being hunted.

They didn't speak until they reached a sharp incline.

Scaling it on all fours, using their hands to grip the wild grass, they pulled themselves up and discovered a large curving expanse of train line. The rails stretched in both directions, cutting through the forest and bending out of sight. The frosted metal was bright and slick with dew.

They looked at each other, unsure.

"What do we do?" Athan asked.

"Follow it."

"Why?"

"It leads somewhere," Zachary replied.

Athan nodded; that fact was self-evident. "Which way?"

Zachary fumbled around in his pocket and took out the coin. He flipped it into the air quickly, without calling it.

Athan was about to call heads, but Zachary caught the coin and looked down into his palm, just like he did the night before.

He nodded and put it back in his pocket before Athan could see it.

"North."

HER CALLING

From a distance, the two men watched the coffin of Sacha Turgenev being lowered into the ground. One of them shook his head while the other dabbed at the sweat on his forehead.

"People should only be buried in misery. Rain and black umbrellas—isn't that what a funeral should look like?"

"Not today."

They looked at the crisp blue sky through the leaves above, at the headstones that littered the ground near them, at the ground itself. Anything but watch her descend, un-avenged, into the freezing dirt.

The ground swallowed the cheap coffin as two family members watched dispassionately. The muted sounds of the preacher's voice reached their ears, but they couldn't hear what was being said. They didn't want to know.

They both knew that deep in the earth, out of sight, was the best place for Sacha now. For everybody. Even when it hurt to watch it.

Edward and Douglas stood out of sight. No one was looking in their direction anyway, but they whispered just in case, out of habit more than anything.

"She hasn't been the same since," Edward said.

"It was her first," Douglas replied, scratching his nose. "And don't forget, that woman was *butchered*. I've never seen anything like it."

"What *this* one?"

"No, the girl in the court. That was worse than this one."

"Really?" There was a hint of chiding in his voice. "Your worst then?"

"You saw me. You saw how it affected me."

Edward nodded. "Yeah. You took it hard. Why was she different do you think? Than the ones before—than this one here." He lifted his chin from his scarf towards the most recent victim. The tidier victim.

"Damned if I know."

The funeral ended and the procession moved off slowly, heads bowed and in silence. Douglas and Edward waited for the mourners to walk down the path and climb into the carriages.

The old gravedigger who waited behind respectfully, puffing on a cigarette, now took the last few drags before flicking the butt down into the hole.

"*That* was nice."

"He's just doing his job."

"He could show more respect to the recently deceased."

"Like we do?"

The men looked at each other, but the conversation ended.

They turned back and watched as the old man shovelled fresh brown earth down on top of the coffin.

Douglas turned away, averted his eyes. He shoved his hands deep into his pockets, shuffled on his feet to keep his toes warm.

The headstone nearest them was a new one, like most in the section where they stood.

Jack Cuthbertson: Died Age 36
William Cuthbertson: Died aged 17
Jessie MacKenzie: Died aged 78.

Beloved mother of William.

"Looks like she lasted a while after the other two. Good for her." Douglas noted, nodding towards the stone. He looked away and forgot about it almost immediately.

"How'd that happen?" Edward followed his nod. "Why is she buried with her husband and son?"

"What do you mean?" Douglas replied, not really listening, his eyes focussed back on the gravedigger.

"Look at the date. He died when he was thirty-six. She died when she was seventy-eight. That leaves...dozens of years without him. Look at her last name. She remarried," Edward said.

"So? It doesn't matter."

"Think about it," Edward continued. "He was thirty-six. Say she loved him dearly and loved her son and couldn't bear to be without them. They live a happy life and nothing could be better. Her son goes off to find his fortune, and then *bang!* Her husband, Jack, the love of her life, dies. He...I don't know, he falls under a carriage and breaks his neck. She's devastated. She grieves. She beats the walls with her fists and all that.

"Then *bang!* Ten months later, her baby boy William gets consumption or the pox and he's gone too. Again, she's devastated. So she grieves for a while because these were the dearest people in the world to her. But people keep saying, 'Move on. You have to move on.' So she does.

"She meets...Larry MacKenzie. And Larry is everything that Jack was."

"Jack?" Douglas was peering into the trees now, his eyes searching, his mind on other things.

"Cuthbertson." Edward pointed to the headstone. "Jack Cuthbertson. Pay attention, alright? She loves Larry. She grows to adore him as much as her Jack who died so young.

23

They have a son. I'm figuring she was younger than Jack so she can still have a child with Larry. And they're all set to live happily ever after.

"Then *bang!* Larry cashes in his chips. It's quick, it's neat, but he's dead and Jessie grieves like she did for Jack, another true love lost. Some time later, *bang!* Little..." Edward started clicking his fingers in the air, trying to conjure up a name.

"Antony?" Douglas suggested.

"Yeah, that'll do. Little Antony—who you've gotta figure is nearly a man by now—let's say seventeen and make it poetic—gets hit by lightning on a stormy day because he was daft enough to go walking by the fiords."

"Why is that daft?"

"It doesn't matter. The point is he's dead too, and Jessie hangs on for another...I don't know...many years. She's seventy-eight, she's ailing. Someone asks her 'Jess, luv, where do you wanna be laid to rest?' What does she do? The lass really has to think about this. Two husbands, two sons. She spent roughly the same amount of time with each. She loved each equally. Where does she get buried? Why did she choose Jack and not Larry?"

"Perhaps she didn't remarry. Jack might've been an unkind husband and beat her."

"That's not my point," Edward sighed. "What do you do if you move on with your life and then have to choose where to lay your hat at the end of it all? I mean is Larry walking past old St Peter and saying, 'Hey Jess, why are you lying next to this bastard? What about me and Antony?'"

"And is Antony there? What does she do then? Both Jack and Larry are waiting at the Pearly Gates like two gents at a crowded port for their Jessie. What happens then? What if her children are waiting for her?"

"The evils of the drink again, Ed?"

"It's just too much aggravation."

"Yes. It certainly is," Douglas agreed.

The digger swung his shovel over his shoulder and walked off toward the cemetery gates, lighting up another cigarette and puffing on it furiously. Sacha's grave was now a mound of fresh soil.

"Who does she choose? It's a daunting decision."

"It makes no difference, now."

"It does to Jack and Larry."

Douglas nodded towards the gravesite, at the woman who had stepped out of the trees and was now approaching them. Her silhouette was familiar, foreboding. Douglas shivered and then looked at his companion.

"No, no. I mean, it *really* makes no difference."

"Oh," Edward's eyes narrowed. "I didn't see her there."

He knelt and reached toward the base of Jessie's final repose. He gripped the wooden handle of the nearest shovel and stood, just as the woman reached them.

"Here you are then, luv," he said, holding the shovel out to her.

She eyed them both, her head tilting slightly, her long curly dark hair brushing across her face in the breeze. She took the shovel without a word, turned and walked toward Sacha's grave.

"Good luck!" Edward called after her, ignoring the look Douglas gave him.

"Shouldn't we help?"

"Don't want to get in her way, now."

The woman reached the gravesite and looked around her quickly, making sure she was unobserved. After a few seconds, she bent her back and forced the shovel into the dirt with an unpractised foot. Slowly, she began to dig.

"There's an awful lot of dirt. Could take her a while." Edward smiled, a wicked glint in his eye. "It's her calling, not ours."

"Digging is her calling?"

Edward sighed. "No, not the digging. You know what I mean."

They both nodded.

And watched.

Out of the Madness

They ran with their heads down, watching their footing. Their steps jarred with heavy and tired legs, the ground blurred as it had day after day after day.

Broken laces had been re-tied into knots, worn soles replaced with newspaper.

The sound of their steps echoed around the fading dull green hills. Dusk began to settle even as the weak sun blinded their eyes.

Both cursed the light between deep, belaboured breaths, and hoped it would sink quicker behind the mountains.

The cold air was biting.

Still, they ran on.

Occasionally each would stop, doubled over, hands on knees, fingers gripping faded trousers as their chests billowed. Sweat suspended in droplets at the ends of their fringes, down their noses, pooled at their backs. Silver clouds of breath frosted the air.

Their fingers were dirty, their nails broken. Once their breathing calmed, one would slap the other on the back and they'd be off again. They could run for miles before finally having to stop and rest.

They'd had practice.

The trees grew thicker and greener. The lush gullies more frequent. The railway was a life-line, a steel-wood path that would lead them out of the forest. Out of the madness.

The air was thick with mist. The forest seemed to hold the chill within its very canopy.

They stopped to take food out of one pack; half a loaf of stale bread. Their dirty fingers tore into the crust and they ate, feeling it adhere to the roof of their mouths, sucking up all moisture. It was an effort to swallow a single mouthful.

As they were eating, Zachary sniffed. He cocked his head and stopped chewing. Athan inhaled, smelled it too. Their eyes met.

Carefully, Zachary put down his bread and slowly made his way down the gravel embankment to look.

He turned back. Athan nodded, so he continued.

At the bottom of the embankment was a fox's head, staring up at the sky with hollow eye sockets; eaten out. Two disturbed crows lifted with cawing shrieks before settling again. Zachary immediately scrambled backwards and vomited. Only the bread was purged, his first meal in hours. He'd seen dozens of dead foxes before. It was the blood that did it. He never wanted to see blood again.

He started to shake and he stumbled as he made his way back up to the rail line. Athan stood and walked towards him, reached down to hold him, support him, his arm around his shoulder.

Eventually, the shaking passed.

"Thanks." Zachary shook from his grip.

Athan nodded.

When they were ready, they continued on in silence.

They ran further, then slowed to a walk, kicking pieces of freshly hewn ballast across into the underbrush. The rocks disappeared with a hollow, satisfying *thump*, bouncing and jagging into the darkness.

They spoke little. Everything had already been said between

them. They had screamed at each other, argued, threatened, cried and blamed. They had lived a lifetime in a few short weeks.

They walked a while longer, sharing a water-bottle.

"You tired?" Athan asked.

"Today, yes. I was all right yesterday though. You?"

"It feels like it's right in my bones."

"My toes hurt."

"It's the rocks. Walk on the sleepers."

"I would, but I'd either have to stretch like a giant or walk like a dwarf. See?" Zachary demonstrated. He was shorter than Athan.

"I see."

"I can only hit the wood when I run."

"Yeah."

"We'll walk a bit longer, then. Get our breath back, have something to eat. Then I'll sprint you over that next rise, al-right?"

"Uh huh."

They walked on. The sun finally disappeared behind the hills.

Twilight fell.

Soon, they ran again.

The rhythmic pounding echoing around them endlessly.

Their knees ached with each impact. Their packs, filled with near-empty bottles, fishing gear, tea and one extra shirt each, slammed hard against their lower backs.

They made it up the gradient where the steel rails curved over; smooth, as if painted by a calligrapher's brush. They raced each other, hands scrabbling the stones when they stumbled, shoes pounding the wooden sleepers.

They skidded to a stop.

Zachary almost fell, so abrupt was their sudden standstill.

He grabbed the other man's arm to steady himself, clutching at his shirt, grabbing hold of the worn fabric. He was surprised his hand wasn't shaken off.

Like last time.

Neither moved. They just stood there, breathing heavily, looking.

Their feet were caked with the mud of the freshly dug ground where the rails had yet to be laid. It congealed on their shoes where they had skidded to a stop.

Newly-felled trees, their pulp gleaming in bright orange circles and jagged shards, lay on each side of a huge swath of mud. The smell of raw wood and wet sawdust was heavy in the air, making it hard for the men to breathe without gagging. Equipment and materials covered the area, abandoned for the day in mid-dig, mid-lift.

The plate-layers had gone for the evening. The light had fled them, just as it had fled the two men.

The line just stopped. Right in front of them.

Beyond the disarray and across the clearing lay a town at the base of the mountain. The street lamps glowed in the darkening twilight.

It was the first town they'd seen in a week.

Both men whispered at once.

"Oh no," said Athan.

"Thank God," said Zachary.

UP TO HER ELBOWS

The hallway was long, dark and cluttered with wall hangings and decorations; thin tables were obscured by trinkets, ornaments, pieces of clay. A hand here, a leg there. A huge mirror with an ornate frame hung at the base of the stairs; she could tell it was ornate because the cloth that covered it rippled due to the protrusions. Another hung over the top landing. Both were covered with large pieces of heavy material. A smaller mirror near her head was covered with a shawl.

Rose smelled the familiar dankness of the house as she closed the door on the fresh afternoon air behind her. The odour was not unpleasant, just heavy. Dust-filled, tightly woven rugs lay on the floor. The whole place seemed cold, even in this dreadful weather. Two lit oil lamps hung on iron brackets, producing the only warmth. It would be warmer upstairs, probably, but Rose had never been allowed up there.

She looked up at the nearest lamp. A spider sat perfectly still in the shadow of a hanging screw, its cobweb stretching the length of the lamp, curving from the outermost side and back to the wall.

"Mrs. Belle!" she called.

No answer.

She began to walk towards the kitchen at the end of the hallway. As she passed the base of the stairs, she paused.

To her left there was a figure, a man in shadow, recessed under the stairs that led up to the second floor. He was huge, imposing; a sentry standing guard at the base of the first floor.

Rose stared at him. He was taller than most; she guessed 6 foot or more. He was also naked. His skin was a burnished cream colour, darker at the extremities, brown at the hollows of his eyes. His features flickered with the light, both sharp and indistinct, the shadows dancing across his figure and making him look as if he were alive.

He wasn't there this morning, was he?

Rose wondered how he got there or, worse still, how she could have missed him.

At the back of her mind was an irrational fear that any second now he would reach out and grab her. The metal tray in her hands grew hotter, but she found herself holding it tighter, just in case. She'd discarded the basket outside the door before coming; now she wished she hadn't.

She took a step forward, almost a tip-toe. Then she heard a creak from above her.

She glanced up quickly to see Bronwyn walking down the stairs, graceful, almost lazy in her movements. Her black skirt brushed the risers, the old wooden boards squeaking with every step.

She'd told Bronwyn on many occasions that Sawyer could replace the squeaking boards, but Bronwyn had always turned down the offer. "I won't let him in," she'd always say. "He's not coming inside here."

Bronwyn wore a charcoal corset with a black shawl. Her braided hair didn't have a strand out of place. It was as impeccable as always, blending into the shadows, cascading across her shoulders. It suited the solemn nature of her place.

Rose unconsciously looked down at her own blue dress. The

material made her look like a splash of colour on a dark winter's night. She liked that; she liked bringing light to darkness.

The tray was still too hot. She placed a part of her long shawl between her gloved hands and the metal.

"Mrs. Belle," she said.

"I've told you to call me Bronwyn."

"Of course."

Bronwyn smiled without warmth and walked past Rose, wafting perfume and cobwebs as she did. The older woman stopped in front of the man. She ran her hand, smudged with dry clay, lovingly down the face of her newest creation, her skin rasping the unglazed surface.

"Is he your latest effort?" Rose asked, her voice swallowed by the stillness.

"Yes," Bronwyn answered absently. While her cheek was smudged with white clay, her dress was immaculately clean. She reached out to the nearest table and took a pre-rolled cigarette from a metal case. She lit it with a long match. It flared briefly.

Rose wrinkled her nose in distaste at the older woman's habit. She didn't know any other women who smoked—at least not in front of other people.

She placed the tray on the corner of the same table with some relief. Then she stepped up, hesitated a second before taking the man's cold, clay hand in hers.

"He's...unsettling," she whispered, looking up at his blank, pupil-less eyes.

"You think so?" Bronwyn stifled a laugh.

Rose released the hand, stepping back from both the clay man and the smoky breath.

"Yes." She tilted her head to the side, seeing the roughness of the figure. It was unrefined and raw, yet strangely almost complete. Like most of Bronwyn's statues, he simply appeared one day; in the house or in the garden. Rose never saw a work in progress, never heard about a new project or sudden inspiration and never asked.

"If you find it so unsettling, stop looking," Bronwyn said.

"It's hard not to. They are macabre, but...fascinating." Rose picked up the tray of food once more. "I don't know how you work with them."

She made a flippant gesture with her hand and drew hard on the cigarette once more, blowing the smoke into the air.

Rose held her breath until the smoke cleared, then she let it out.

"He reminds me of someone," she said, using the tips of her fingers to take the brunt of the heat from the tray.

"He should," Bronwyn smirked and turned away. She flicked the ash on the floorboards and rug without a second thought. That was nothing new.

"I can't place the face."

"It's Josiah."

"Oh." Rose bit her lower lip, feeling her cheeks flush a little at her own stupidity. "I, ah..."

"That's alright," Bronwyn offered. She patted the cheek of the man once more, then walked towards the kitchen. Rose followed, edging slightly away from the likeness of the deceased man.

"I...I should have realized," she called after the retreating figure.

"Rose, it's fine."

They reached the kitchen. It was a small, cramped space, with little room for anything more than a tiny bench and two chairs. The room was as cluttered as the rest of the house, and just as cold. The only streak of colour came from the back garden, which could be seen out the window. The stove was old and rusted, and the pots lining the shelves were dust-covered. They'd always been like that, for as long as Rose had known her.

It's not as if she'd ever use them anyway.

As far as Rose knew, Bronwyn only entered the kitchen when she visited her to drop off her food tray, once in the morning and once at night.

The woman had never stepped outside her front door once her husband had died, according to the stories she heard at the Three Belles. Before then, Bronwyn was an accomplished artist in sculpture, but the sudden loss of Josiah had caused her to withdraw from life completely.

Rose could understand the way she felt. But now, as a recluse, Bronwyn relied on Rose to bring her food and other supplies, for which she paid handsomely.

Rose put the tray down and lifted the two bowls, placing them on the bench. She retrieved the empty bowl from breakfast that morning and placed it on the tray.

She leaned against the bench. "How long has it been? A year?"

"Almost, yes." Bronwyn stabbed out the cigarette in a nearby cup and tossed the end into the pile of discards heaped in the cold fireplace in the corner. The fire hadn't been lit since Rose started coming with meals.

Rose played with the ends of her shawl, rolling the fringe in her fingers. She looked outside, seeing the white, still figures half-hidden in the foliage and covered in the darkening night. She'd never counted them, but she guessed there were about 20 statues in the garden. Now that she looked, they *could* be Josiah. It was hard to tell from in here.

There were more upstairs, she'd been told.

Bronwyn was more talkative tonight. She hadn't been that morning when Rose delivered her breakfast. That was fine.

Rose was used to the other woman's moods. They could change quickly, and for no apparent reason. Rose preferred it when Bronwyn was happy. Although that didn't happen too often these days.

Bronwyn was chatting absently about her craft while Rose eyed the steaming bowls.

"Your food will get cold," Rose said.

"I know."

Yes, you do. But it never makes a difference.

"You should eat more," Rose offered, trying not to annoy her, but wanting to get her point across. She peeled off her right glove and sucked the red tip of her index finger.

"I know," Bronwyn repeated.

"It's not healthy."

"I understand."

"Bron—"

"I get by, you know that. I've gotten by before and I'll get by now," Bronwyn replied.

Rose nodded, knowing it was time to drop the subject. She sat at the kitchen bench and traced her finger along the wooden edge, gathering dust on her skin, covering the burn mark. Once she circled the edge of the bench, she wiped away the dust, dragging her finger across her skirt.

"How is Three Belles?" Bronwyn changed the subject.

"Very well."

"You still enjoying your work there?"

"Yes, it's very rewarding," Rose lied. She didn't want Bronwyn to think she was ungrateful. "The people are splendid. I've really got to know them now."

"And Sawyer?"

"He's still there."

"I see," Bronwyn nodded, sitting down on the other chair, directly across the bench from her.

"There's not much work for him now, not in these parts." Rose really didn't want to talk about him.

"He should move on."

"He's trying, I think. There's some work in the next county. He sometimes goes there and comes back. He might find more work, soon."

"Good."

Rose needed to change the subject. "Pea soup," she said, pointing into the closest bowl. "Fresh made."

Bronwyn leaned forward and looked into the bowl. "It looks nice."

"It *is* nice."

She pushed the bowl away from her. "I'm not hungry. Not now."

There was a pause between them.

Rose wanted to say something, to start a conversation, but the words just wouldn't come. Bronwyn was the only other woman in the town that Rose had grown to know, but that didn't make it any easier to talk to her. Rose wasn't sure if it was the house, the coldness in the air and the stuffiness in the rooms, or just the way Bronwyn related to her, but sometimes it was very hard to talk with her.

She wanted to confide in her. She knew Bronwyn would never break that trust, but it was still hard to do.

So the silence continued, until Bronwyn broke it.

"They keeping my kitchen clean and tidy?" she asked.

Rose knew she didn't mean the one they were sitting in.

"Yes," Rose replied. "Just as you'd expect."

"Good. I don't want that place going to ruin. What would Josiah think?"

Rose's eyes dropped down to stare at her hands in her lap.

I should've recognised his face.

"He'd be proud of how they've carried on without him."

37

"Good," Bronwyn nodded. "I hope so."

They talked until the sun went down and Bronwyn lit the three oil lamps in the kitchen.

"You should go, love," she said then. "You've got quite a way to walk home and with all the strangers in town..."

"I'm alright. It's not that far," Rose replied.

"I'm surprised Sawyer hasn't accompanied you here at night."

"Why would he?" Rose asked, confused by her statement.

"No reason." Bronwyn shrugged as she stood and walked Rose out of the kitchen.

They continued along the long hallway to the foyer and past the Josiah clay creation. Bronwyn opened the door for Rose and she stepped out into the warm night air.

"I'll see you in the morning, Bronwyn."

"Yes, you will," she replied with a crooked smile as she closed the door.

"You should go eat!" Rose called as the door was shutting.

"I know," was the muffled reply.

As she opened the door to the Three Belles, Rose noticed Sawyer hanging off the bar, talking with four men she didn't recognise.

Automatically, her eyes lowered and she looked at the tray she was carrying in front of her.

The men were probably railway workers. Since the laying of the train line, the town was full of men she didn't know, strangers who made her feel uneasy. Burly men with stubby, bruised fingers and shoulders that looked like barrels.

They stood between her and the kitchen. She paused. To stop and retreat now would only call more attention to herself.

As she approached them, she could almost hear what they were talking about, but as she neared, their voices dropped in volume, before stopping altogether.

All eyes turned to look at her and she felt a faint flush creep up her cheeks.

"There she is," Sawyer said in a loud voice. "I told you she wouldn't be long."

Rose looked up to stare at him.

Sawyer smiled at her. He took a step forward, bringing his body between her and the nearest of the rail workers. He was a little taller than the men there and didn't have the same workman's slouch.

Sawyer had brown eyes, black hair; the casual lean of a gentlemen, not a stair-maker. His hands were calloused, not swollen. His body was lithe and his face was kind.

She welcomed the familiarity of him as she squared her shoulders, nodded at him in greeting. She did not look at the other men.

"I'm just going to wash these," she said, hefting the bowl-laden tray.

"No worries, Rose," Sawyer said. "Take your time."

Without giving them a second glance, she marched past them and through into the kitchen.

The door swung shut behind her, the sound of the latch clicking home flooding her with relief. She let her breath out, surprised she was holding it.

Strangers made her uneasy, always had.

She eyed the wash barrel and knew she should wash out the bowls before leaving, but the kitchen staff had all left for the night. That was what she wanted to do, as well. Feeling only a little guilty, she placed the tray and bowls on the closest shelf and turned to leave.

Her hand reached out to the door, but something stopped her from opening it. Instead, she leaned forward and put her ear to the door, listening to the muffled conversation that had started once more at the bar.

"...in this direction?"

"Yes. Well, that's what the papers say, at least."

"It's bloody horrible."

"I have a brother who was in the town where the second girl got it—St Leonard's. He said he saw the body—"

"You're pulling my leg, mate. He didn't see no body."

"He did! He said the girl was butchered. Torn apart. I almost lost my lunch just hearing about it."

"Shhhhhh! Keep your voice down!"

Rose pulled away from the door, she didn't want to hear what they were talking about, but something compelled her. Slowly, she leaned forward again.

"What else did he say?"

"Who?"

"Your brother."

"Oh. Well, the coppers first thought she was wearing dark gloves, but *no*."

He paused. There was no sound from the bar for a few long seconds.

"She was up to her elbows in blood! Her elbows! And they weren't even sure if she was...ah...how can I put it?"

"Cut up?"

Sawyer.

It was the first time he'd spoken while she'd been listening.

"Yeah, but more. She wasn't cut up so much as...just...cut. Ripped."

"You've been reading the papers again. You'll give yourself nightmares, you will."

"Awful." Sawyer again. His voice so quiet she almost missed

40

his reply.

"Any way is awful, mate, but your right; this is downright gruesome. And to do that to a woman living by herself..."

Silence again. Rose could almost picture them all shaking their heads slowly while they finished off the last round of their beers.

"So they're on the move? These killers?" someone eventually asked.

"Yes, I said north. Right this way!"

"Why do you say that?"

"You follow the rails, you've got nowhere to go but Oak Ridge—not until the line meets up with that of Long Gully—and that won't be for months. This *is* the next town on their route. Remember, the first one was in London proper and the second was in St Leonard's. That means—"

"Yeah, *alright*, I see what you mean."

"It means we be careful. You lock the basement entrance?" Sawyer asked someone. His voice was quiet, but determined.

"I think so."

There was the sound of a chair scraping against the wooden floor. "I should check it anyway."

"Good idea. You fellas should get back to your tents before you drink us out of whiskey."

The cold night chilled Rose.

Even though she hadn't heard all the conversation, she'd heard enough to scare her. All she could think about was the nameless woman.

The girl was butchered, that's what they'd said. She was the second in a month.

Even though she knew it was just her mind playing with

41

her, she felt more alone in the night. It seemed darker than ever before. She didn't chide herself for walking quicker than usual.

The darkness between each street lamp was a void in which anyone could hide, laying in wait.

She kept up a steady pace, making sure there was no one around her, making sure she could flee if needed. Her boots clipped sharply on the stone street, a confident sound in the silence.

She lived alone.

Like me.

She probably had an ordinary job, cleaning other people's things, looking after other people's well being.

Like me.

She thought about whether the dead woman had worked that day, the final day of her life. Had she cleaned or cooked? Did she make her way, eyes closed, to her kitchen and, instead of turning on the oil lamps and finding her warm and safe place, she found her killer?

A life snuffed out quicker than a flame. One minute burning, the next gone.

Thank God I'm almost home.

Almost—not quite. The street lamps from town had yet to run out; they were only built for the main roads, not for the trail up to her house or the farmland beyond the valley. Rose carried with her a small lantern with a fat candle in the centre for when she reached the dark road that led, winding through the trees and the hills, to her home.

It made her acutely aware of how far from town she lived.

It was then she saw the figures.

Two of them. Half-walking, half-slipping down the embankment near the railway. The two railway lamps illuminated their descent, probably more than they realised. They were skidding down the slight hill, hands behind them to keep them steady. They reached the bottom, stood quickly and slapped their hands on their thighs a couple of times. They looked around for only a moment before they moved off, leaving the lights of the railway behind them.

Within seconds, they appeared out of the darkness again, both stepping quickly into the warm glow of a nearby street lamp. Then, almost as quickly, the darkness swallowed them once more.

Rose stopped in her tracks and waited, wanting to make sure she had really seen them and that it wasn't her mind playing tricks.

She focussed on the next street lamp. Started counting in her head.

One...two...three...four...

And then they appeared, both walking strong, one taller than the other, one slightly out of step with the other.

She could see them only for a split second before the light left them again.

Plate-layers, she told herself. Probably plate-layers.

She wondered why they had been up there. What they were doing there this time of night.

Why weren't they at the pub?

She didn't care. Not right now. She didn't want to spend any more time out on the streets than she had to.

I must get home.

She threw off her fears and suppressed her suspicion; she told herself she was being silly, acting on the thoughts and images placed in her head by a group of soused rail workers at the Three Belles.

They're probably just bragging anyway, she told herself, as she neared her house.

She walked quicker, glancing all around her. With stumbling fingers, she unlatched the front door and slammed it behind her, pushing her back hard against it.

Even when she lit every lamp and burned every candle in the house until it shone like a squat lighthouse, there were still dark corners for nightmares to crouch ready to pounce.

Take Whatever You Want

The next morning, Rose found him in her kitchen, kneeling in a spread of broken glass from the once-intact kitchen door.

She stopped in the doorway and drew in a deep breath, the tune she'd been humming, cut off in mid-chorus.

The man turned to look at her, his eyes fearful and wide.

He had fairish hair that was longer than most men's. He wore a stained white shirt, a shabby coat and blue trousers. He was slim and looked tall, even though he was kneeling.

His fear surprised her. She thought he'd look angry or insane. Not afraid.

He held her porcelain sugar bowl in his hands—the one Sawyer brought back from a trip to the city months ago.

Sawyer had said she needed something new in a house full of old, dead things. It was the kind of backhanded compliment he always gave.

Rose and the man just stared at each other.

The silence was heavy as they both waited for the other to make the first move.

His body jerked up from its half-crouch and then he froze. A lock of dirty hair fell across his right eye, near a still-healing scar. The hair made his eyes blink and twitch.

His right eye started to water. She just saw the twitching.

"Oh Lord!" she whispered diving for the wooden table and

grabbing the first thing she could see.

The fruit bowl. Heavy and solid.

The plan was to throw it at him, to scare him into running. But her hands didn't follow what her brain was telling them. They fumbled and shook, and the fruit bowl went twirling across the table, spilling its contents of wrinkled apples and lemons. It tumbled off the edge of the table and clattered to the ground.

They both jumped at the sound.

Rose grabbed whatever was left, the closest yellow apple.

She didn't stop to aim or to think, she just threw it straight at him.

The apple arced gracefully in the air.

It hit the man hard in the side of the head. Hard enough to make him think twice about attacking her, hard enough to hopefully make him turn and run.

Instead, he jerked back with pain and surprise. His head flung backwards, and he caught his temple on the corner of a protruding shelf, the jars shimmying and rocking violently. He went down fast and hard, sliding against the wall and hitting the ground, the sugar bowl falling from his hand and shattering on the floor.

"Oh my..." she whispered.

He didn't move.

Rose could only hear the sound of her own breathing, harsh and dry.

Slowly, she knelt and tilted her head, but she couldn't see if the man was bleeding. His face was relaxed and peaceful and his right hand was curled up near his cheek. He wore a copper bracelet around his wrist. Once, it may have fit snug, but now it hung loose near the base of his palm.

She took a wary step closer. She was unsure if he was really unconscious or playing a game to get her closer. Her eyes slipped down to his chest. It rose and fell, steady and sure.

At least he's still alive, she thought. *I haven't killed him.*

Then she suddenly started to cry. Stopped herself, just as quick. Swallowed those premature sobs before they could cripple her.

Keep your head, girl. Don't lose it now.

She wanted to move, to act, but she couldn't do anything but crouch. Her ankles grew heavy and hot, her hands shook with a cold tingly feeling.

He just lay there in the glass and the spilled sugar and Rose stared at him until she had to force her eyes to blink. He was unconscious, taken down by an apple thrown from her very own arm.

She leaned forward, her shaking arm reaching out towards the man's shoulder.

And then she heard the footsteps from outside, running fast, getting closer.

Her arm darted back to her side and she straightened up quickly, her head turning to look through the broken glass door and out into the morning light.

A young red-haired man ran inside. His eyes met hers, and his face changed from an expression of determination to one of shock. He pulled up quickly, his boots skidding in the sugar, his hand grabbing the doorjamb to steady himself.

Rose reached down onto the table and grabbed another apple. She looked at him, trying to intimidate. Steely-eyed. But her shoulder burned, her hands shook.

In two seconds, her mind flashed through all the ways she could be killed or tortured.

All because of a bowl of sugar.

It didn't seem right. It didn't seem fair.

But then her resolve returned.

I'll be damned if this happens over a bowl of sugar.

47

"Take it," she said.

She pointed down to the man on the floor, but then she remembered the bowl was smashed and the sugar was spilled all over the floor.

"Take whatever you want," she whispered.

He looked down at the man, sprawled unconscious at their feet, lying in shards of pottery and glass.

Slowly, he walked forward and knelt, his eyes darting between them both. He reached out and felt the other man's neck then looked up, not smiling, not glaring, just blank. "You?"

She nodded. All hope of speech was gone, her mouth dry and her tongue dumb.

They stared at each other for a few more seconds.

And then he began to laugh.

It sounded loud and strong in the silence.

He sat down with his back against the door and reached out to ruffle the blond man's hair. He laughed more, but the sound of it changed. The happiness slipped into hopelessness.

He slowed and took deep breaths, the laughter eventually fading to nothing.

"Are you going for the police, miss?" he asked her, but his eyes stayed on his companion.

She shook her head, but then realised he wouldn't see it.

"No," her voice croaked, like she hadn't spoken for a thousand years. It sounded strange.

She wanted to call for help, to get the police, but she didn't know what would happen if she tried. She had no idea what the men were capable of. They'd broken into her house, tried to steal her sugar; they were stronger than her.

"You can take the sugar, if you want. Or tea," she offered, hoping that was all they needed.

"No," the man replied, turning his head to look at her. "We

have tea, but Ay here, he hates it plain. He likes to just about kill everything with sugar. So I said to him, 'Athan, if you're so desperate for sugar, why don't you just go steal some 'cause I haven't got the money and neither have you.'"

He pronounced it like 'Nathan,' but without the first N. He smiled and ruffled his friend's hair once more. "And I guess he tried. I didn't really mean for him to do that, but he was gone before I knew it. It's been a bad coupla weeks."

She watched as the smile slipped from the man's face. Darkness grew across his forehead and his lips turned down in sadness.

The door to the kitchen was still wide open. The cold morning air leeched in, making her shiver. Athan lay still. The other man lifted a hand and ran it over his own face like he was trying to erase his fatigue.

Rose realised then his hand was not shaking.

Hers were.

"He has a wife who thinks he's a... Well she thinks he's a bad person, miss," the man continued. "And that's been hard for him."

Rose knew he was going to say something other than 'bad person,' but he stopped himself just in time.

The man turned to stare up at her again. A smile spread back across his face. "He's harmless. He wouldn't have hurt you. Neither of us would. I'll just wait here 'til he wakes up if that's alright with you, of course. Then we'll be on our way."

She nodded. She didn't believe she had much choice.

"What is your name?" she crouched down about four feet away, her hand reaching out to the floor to steady herself, and also to be within easy reach of the fruit bowl under the table. She was ready to grab at it and leap back to defend herself, just in case he was some sort of lying, murdering thief.

"Zachary Vaughn, miss," he replied. His eyes never leaving

hers. "And this is Athan Stowall."

"Rose," she replied, feeling that telling them her first name was telling them nothing. Her last, however, she'd keep for herself. "He's your friend, then?" she asked. They didn't look like brothers.

"Yes, miss," Zachary nodded. "My best friend in the world."

"You're..." she didn't know how to say it. She just went with her gut instinct. "...in trouble?"

"A little."

She nodded. Bronwyn would've boxed her ears if she knew Rose was talking with two strange men who had broken into her house.

"This a nice town?" he asked.

She blinked. "I beg your pardon?"

"Here. Do you like it here?"

"Yes, it's nice. Quiet. It's small, but we have the mine to keep us all busy. A new railway is being built as well."

He nodded. "We followed the line." Then his eyes slipped from her to the ground. "Bad idea, I suppose," he said, almost to himself.

Athan groaned then. His leg jolted, spasmed like a slumbering dog.

Rose flinched, bracing herself on the tiles and ready to spring backwards. Her eyes darted across to the fruit bowl, but she stopped herself from diving towards it.

"I'll get a cool towel for his head," she said as calmly as possible as she slowly straightened, feeling her feet go hot again with the sudden circulation.

Zachary nodded at her as she turned and walked from the room.

His gaze followed her. The cream dress swirled around her as she spun to leave, and her brown hair swung from side to side across her shoulders as she strode deliberately down the hallway.

She had a nice face. A nice smile.

He thought about following her to make sure she was doing as she said, but he couldn't leave Athan. He tilted his head, trying hard to hear her moving inside the rest of the house, trying to work out exactly where she was and what she was doing.

As the seconds stretched, the silence grew. Zachary started to worry. Taking one last look at Athan, he slowly got to his feet and quietly walked over towards the kitchen doorway. He leaned against the doorjamb and peered into the rest of the house.

Parlour, hall, sewing room...but he couldn't see her anywhere. It was a large house for one lady.

Athan moaned again.

"M'head," he mumbled.

Zachary turned and dashed back to his friend, kneeling beside him and placing a hand on his shoulder.

"Ay?" he whispered. "Ay, can you hear me?"

Athan shook his head as his right hand reached up to feel the back.

"Ouch," he muttered, but he still hadn't opened his eyes.

Zachary concentrated hard, almost willing Athan to come back to reality as soon as possible, so they could get out of there.

"Come on," he whispered. But it wasn't working. Athan was still groggy.

Looking around the kitchen one last time to make sure the woman hadn't returned, Zachary slipped his hands under Athan's arms and lifted him. It took three attempts, but finally he had Athan resting against him, and he was able to drag his friend through the doorway and out into the garden.

"Mate, can you walk?" he asked as he leaned Athan against the back wall of the house.

"Hit my head," Athan replied. He looked up and squinted at his surroundings. "We need to get out of here."

Zachary's eyes darted back into the house. Still no sign of her.

What is she doing?

"It's alright. She's alright."

"No, we have to run. We'll be caught..."

"She's already seen us, Ay." He shook his friend a little.

It was the mention of the woman that caused Athan's eyes to open. A look of fear crossed his face as he turned to look at Zachary.

"What?" he asked. "We have to run if she's seen us."

"Run?"

"Yes!" Athan rubbed his head.

"I can't."

"Yes, you can. You have to." Athan was suddenly awake.

Zachary reached out and grabbed Athan's arm, pulling him away from the wall and walking down the path with him, just to get him moving, to make sure he was recovering. Athan pushed away after the first few steps, shaking off the grip on his arm.

Zachary stopped in his tracks and looked at his friend. "We're staying."

Athan was shaking his head. "No, no, no," he whispered as he started pacing up and down, his mind sharp once more.

And then the argument began.

As they talked, neither heard Rose walk back towards the kitchen.

Rose carried a cloth for the lump on Athan's head.

She heard them talking as she reached the base of the stairs. Padding carefully across the floor and avoiding the ˈeaky floorboards, she listened.

ʸ, calm down."

She peered around the edge of the door. Apart from that initial soothing comment, it was Athan who talked. Zachary just listened.

Zachary had deep red hair and a few freckles, but not too many. Right now, his face was waxen as Athan paced unsteadily up and down in front of him along a winding path that took him out of her sight and back again.

Zachary's light blue shirt was open at the first two buttons. She could see that his belt was almost double around his waist and the smudges of dirt on his neck and the backs of his hands had been there longer than a day or two. It was too cold for clothes like that.

His head was down and he shook it slowly at each of Athan's statements, not because he didn't agree, but because he didn't want to hear.

Athan had long legs and they carried him in an unbalanced gait due to the knock on the head. He was quite tall, and every time he paced near Zachary, he used that height to emphasize his point.

"We can't stay here," Athan was saying. "We've already committed a crime."

Zachary raised his head and the look in his eyes was clear.

"Alright, alright. *Me.* I did it. Me and the sugar bowl. Still... We have to move."

Athan swept agitated hands through his hair as his boots kicked up clumps of wet dirt in front of Zachary.

"She'll get help, get the police." He pointed in the direction of the house, as he stopped pacing. "She could've already done something like that. Gone out the back way. Who knows how long I was out for?"

"You weren't out for long, mate."

"Even if it was just a few minutes, there's no telling what she might've done. And, *yes*, maybe they'll take ten or fifteen minutes to ride out here, but they'll come and she'll describe what we look like and we'll be history! I'm just not ready for that."

He spun on his heel, walking the longer trail that took him just out of her sight again before he made the return trip.

Back and forth, back and forth.

"I'm just not ready," he repeated. "I didn't do anything and neither did you. We can keep running until they forget about us. They will, I know they will. But here...it's not even far enough away for—"

"We haven't been here a day, Athan. Not more than twelve hours. How can you tell so much about this place? How? We have to stop sometime." Zachary shook his head and sighed deeply. "And, anyway, if you *had* done it, I'da turned you in myself."

"Thanks." Athan sounded hurt.

Zachary continued. "You know I would've. You can drag us all over this bloody county if you want and, yes, that'll get us away from this whole mess, but you have to stop one day. This place is as good a place as any."

"Not here. Not now. We have to get as far away from her as we can," Athan replied.

"It's not *her* that's chasing us, Athan." Zachary's voice went quiet. "She's dead," he whispered.

There was a silence between them that stretched for some time.

Athan made an annoyed sound in his throat and resumed his pacing. His footsteps were steadier, now. "I know that! But you understand what I'm saying. You do or you wouldn't be standing there like a simpleton."

"Oh? Is that what I'm doing?"

"Please, Zach?" Athan pleaded. He stopped, his voice catching.

Rose had never heard a man beg like that before and his words sent pity rushing through her.

"We've stuck to the rails pretty good, so far," he continued. "Let's just keep going."

"For how long?" Zachary shot back, stepping closer to his friend, his arms out wide. "The rails have run out, now. We have to stop, Athan. I need to stop."

Zachary hung his head and folded his arms across his chest. He reminded her of an exhausted animal. Like a horse that can no longer go on, no matter how much the bridle is tugged. Rose had seen horses get their mouths torn up before they moved an inch. They'd rather die than move.

Zachary wasn't going to move right now, she could tell. Zachary wasn't going to move until he felt safe.

She watched as Athan walked over to him and placed one arm around his shoulder and rested his chin on that red hair. Like family.

Like brothers.

She wondered then what the boys at Three Belles would think. She stepped over the broken glass of her kitchen door and into the weak light toward these two strangers.

Athan turned his head slightly, hearing her feet crunching the gravel. He just looked at her and she felt like she was small-town and this was big. She hated that feeling. Once again, she felt uneasy.

"You want something to drink? A pot of tea?" she asked,

trying to sound relaxed and at home in her own house. "With sugar?"

Athan's arm slipped from Zachary's shoulders and she saw Zachary's cheeks were wet with tears.

Exhaustion?

Or something else?

It wasn't grief. She knew grief.

No, he was struggling to contain whatever was tearing at him.

The silence was broken when Athan spoke. "Are you—"

"I'm not going to get anyone," she countered.

Rose wanted to get Zachary into the house, sit him down, and let him rest. He'd feel better once he felt safe and her house was as good as any.

It was obvious they needed someone to help them, and she felt guilty for knocking Athan out. If they needed time, they could have it.

Athan nodded and almost smiled. "I'm sorry about your window, miss."

"Me, too," she replied without thinking, then kicked herself for being so rude.

She walked inside and over to the counter, soaking the cloth with water from the pitcher. She beckoned them into the lounge room and they followed.

Zachary sat down and looked around the room, his eyes not really focusing, more absorbing everything in a blur. His shoulders relaxed, his thighs splayed in loose trousers on the chair. His hands rested slackly on the wooden arms.

"Do you mind if we stay here? Not for the night, or anything, but just for an hour or so? Just to sit?" he asked.

The two men exchanged a look, but no words.

"No. I mean, no, I don't mind." Rose's voice was steady, but her hands twisted like bed sheets in a wash-barrel. Two strange men in her house, sitting in her chairs, dirty, tired...

Thieves, no less.

Athan sat on the floor, his back to the wall, one hand holding up the cold towel to his head, the other resting palm-up in his lap. "If you have anything you need doing around here, we can help with that. We're a little short on money to tell you the truth. We're a little short on everything."

"What happened?" Rose couldn't resist. She had to try and find out, more for the sake of her own safety than for anything else. "I mean, why are you running?"

She bit her lip, held her breath.

Zachary turned his head slowly towards her, like he didn't want to look, but had to.

Rose swallowed, sorry she'd asked the question. Fear welled inside her.

"We didn't do anything," Zachary said. "But..." He shrugged.

"But what?" she asked.

"People think we did. But we didn't. I can't *begin* to tell you how much we didn't."

"Right." She nodded quickly, but her mind was heading back to the conversation they had not ten minutes before.

"It's not her that's chasing us, Athan. She's dead."

"Right," she repeated, still nodding. She tried so hard to appear normal that she didn't blink. Her eyes stung with the dryness of the air. She could hear her own deep breathing, and she knew the men could as well.

"Oh, Christ..." Zachary said quietly. He sat up in the chair and leaned forward, continuing to speak in a soft voice. "It's not alright, is it, Rose?"

She didn't reply. She turned her back on them to look out the window over the garden.

Zachary continued, "I understand you must be scared. But whatever you may hear or whatever you may read in the papers—"

"Where are you from?" she asked, her eyes closed now, her breath held.

Please say another country. Please say from the north.

"Oh, a long way away from here."

She pictured them behind her, looking her way. She remembered the sight of Zachary's hands. Strong and sinewy.

Inescapable.

"300 miles away?" Her voice dropped to a whisper at the end, her courage running out like it had run those miles as well.

Zachary's voice was steady. "At least."

There was a creak. One of them had stood. She heard the footsteps behind her, straining the boards.

"Zach, she knows," Athan said. He was close.

Rose bolted.

58

A Woman's Last Happiness

December 27, 1888

Emma dismounted, holding her horse steady with a palm on its broad neck. They'd followed the trail for weeks at a steady pace, and couldn't risk wearing out the horses, nor risk biding their time. They had followed these rails for the last week, as summer bled into autumn and the mornings grew colder like this one.

They were close. She knew it.

She wiped her hair from her face, flicked it over her shoulder and out of the way.

Edward and Douglas, her shadows, followed a good distance behind. Not once during their journey together had they ridden at her side or in front. She glanced back and saw they had stopped their mounts behind her. More than twenty feet away. Far enough to be respectful, though she doubted there was any real respect there, but close enough to be at her side if anything happened.

She often wondered how they would do it—and who. Edward, probably. He was the more practical of the two. Edward had the harder face, the salt and pepper hair, the moustache and the butcher's hands.

Douglas was younger, had black hair and clear eyes. But as much as he followed Edward's lead, he occasionally spoke to her as a person, not just a means to their end.

Emma turned from them and looked up, breathing deep

and smelling the raw wood from recent cuttings. She glanced around, left to right, but could see no evidence of logging.

She walked toward the rise, coaxing her horse forward, careful to step on the sleepers and not the rails.

The fingers of her left hand constantly played with the gold band around her finger. She found its presence both a vast comfort and an ineffable sadness. She didn't know how many miles were between them now. It seemed some nights all she did was ride further away. She thought about him waking up alone, getting breakfast, dressing their child and telling her that mother would be home soon.

How many miles to go before this is done?

At least he was safe in London. He had much of Scotland Yard helping him with his case; trained inspectors, constables and dogs.

The sounds of Edward and Douglas following her snapped her out of her reverie, brought her crashing back to the present. She hated them sometimes and sometimes that hate was sharp and bitter and made her want to scream—or run.

Yet she needed them.

She quickened her pace, pulling on the hard leather bridle and climbing the small hill. The morning was still and cold, the air thick with mist, heavy with the scent of wood and wet earth. She loved early morning when everything was fresh and new. Daylight was all about new beginnings, stark realities.

The night, at least, hid some of the horrors of the day.

But not all.

Her horse was uncertain of the ground under his leather-shod feet. She pulled him further forward as she walked, not giving him an inch.

She took a steadying breath and crested the hill which revealed a ravaged landscape. The line stopped. Steel rails lay in stacks along the side where large trees had been hewn to the ground and dragged aside.

A massive wound in the earth, orange teeth and steel fingers.

It was exactly as she saw in the dead woman's palm.

She looked behind her. The track upon which they had been travelling was well established but this was new, recent. She stood watching the wreckage of the forest, aware of the impatient presence behind her.

The trees had been ripped apart by saws and men.

Everywhere I go, something is torn apart.

She looked away from the sight of those ruined trunks.

Beyond the trees, beyond the abandoned piles of plates, track, carriage wheels and muddy furrows, were soft gas lights. And beyond them, a line of street lamps barely visible, rooftops and wisps of chimney smoke from a town beginning to wake to the morning.

Her feet grew cold inside her boots. She wanted to go home, but knew she couldn't.

"Ummm... Ma'am? Mrs. Godley?" It was Douglas.

"Yes?"

"Well, are we going forward? Is this the place, then?"

"Hope so. I'm bloody starving." That was Edward.

"This is the place," she nodded slowly, but didn't move. They wouldn't ride to meet or pass her. It was the only power she had.

She watched the dawn brighten into full day, felt the light struggle behind grey clouds to burn away the mist that surrounded them. She enjoyed the pause as well as their discomfort.

Her horse nuzzled her, butted her head with its nose. She reached up to stroke the soft hair near the nostrils.

"Come on, boy," she finally said, in a soft voice.

As she started down the rise, avoiding the rails, the plates, the bolts and the staples, Emma heard the distant voices of the workmen. They sounded like a large group, maybe fifteen men, and their voices were getting louder.

They would most likely follow the lamps, come up the main street and branch off to the train line.

She guided her horse behind the work area and into the thinned-out forest.

Quietly, her shadows followed.

"Keep the change, good sir," Douglas said, his voice brash and booming.

Emma watched him snatch his hand back from the porter who was about to hand him a few, loose pennies. The publican smiled at Douglas, quickly pocketing the extra pennies he had received. He looked as if he'd been up all night; dirty apron, tired eyes and a sluggish hand. Well past his shift.

They, too, had been up all night, which was why Douglas and Edward had no qualms about continuing to imbibe at such a rate.

Douglas returned to the corner table next to the fire where Emma sat hunched over, arms folded and shoulders high.

They were the only patrons in the bar, having deliberately missed any lunch crowd. It was quiet and Douglas' footsteps, like his voice, carried.

Emma's brown curls obscured most of her face, which is the way she liked it, particularly now. She pulled a loose thread from the cuff of her lace glove, twirling it between thumb and forefinger as the questions continued.

"Come on, you've been tight-lipped about what you saw ever since we left the cemetery," Edward was saying. "That's just over a month ago. You've been in a right mood since then, my dear."

"Maybe it was the digging," she said softly, with delicate sarcasm.

"Listen, you—" He took a breath. His ability to calm himself was the only thing she admired about the man. "Tell us what you saw. You promised that once we got here— You must know *something* or we wouldn't be here! If we have a chance to catch—"

"I saw a woman," Emma interrupted him. She closed her eyes and opened them almost immediately as the intense flashes of blood and white hands played against her eyelids. Constant, devastating images.

Edward, his lager in one hand, his fob watch in the other, didn't understand. Neither of them did. She couldn't provide a time, she didn't know the place. You couldn't anticipate death with the ticking of a watch.

"A woman? Brilliant, luv," Edward said. "Utterly brilliant and when—"

"Leave off," Douglas said. "We've been through this."

Emma saw them exchange a glance. It was Douglas' turn. His try. A stone fist, an iron glove. Each as bad as the other.

"All right, you saw a woman, and...?" he began, a smile breaking on his face to try and make her feel at ease.

"What did she look like?" Edward persisted. "Her hair? Her height? Her dress? Give us something!"

Emma blinked slowly.

Blood. White hands. Men and a single woman. Full skirt. Broad smile. Nice laugh.

"She was happy. She was surrounded by men. There were... smudges on her dress."

"And?"

"And nothing else," she replied.

"That's it? That's your big revelation?" Edward's large hand

clenched around the ceramic handle of his mug, his anger leashed for now in that pressure.

"That's what I saw."

Emma wasn't scared of him, not in here at least. She didn't tell him that the woman had a nice laugh. Edward didn't deserve to know about a woman's happiness—her *last* happiness. She didn't tell him about the white hands. She would keep that to herself for now.

A little more power, and maybe something that could just save her life.

Besides, she was in a mood to hate him right now.

"I need a drink," he said.

"You've already got one," Douglas pointed out.

"We've been up all night, creeping around like beggars all morning. I need a real drink. Lager's not going to cut it, not with this shite." Edward didn't look at her, but stood instead, his chair scraping against the stone floor with a noise that made her teeth ache. He mumbled something under his breath, turned and marched to the bar.

Douglas just shrugged and followed him.

Emma was left in the corner, alone for the first time in weeks. She had a cup of tea and a small jug of fresh milk at her elbow. She pushed them aside, took a deep breath and let it out slow. Then she folded her arms on the lacquered tabletop and rested her head.

She was so tired. She wanted to sleep, but every time her eyes closed, the images would flash back into her mind. The blood. The white hands.

Instead, she gazed into the flames of the hearth and thought of home.

"It's not her fault that she doesn't know. Keep the change, mate." Douglas nodded to the bartender who smiled broadly at this second donation. They took the bottle and two glasses to the table at the very back of the bar, furthest from the door. It was positioned in the corner, both walls coming to a point right behind them.

Two walls behind meant no sudden surprises.

From there they had a direct line of sight on Emma in the dining area. If she moved, they'd know about it. Right now, it looked as if she was sleeping.

The hotel looked old and uncared for, especially inside, although the bar itself—with its heavy mahogany top and brass rails—looked polished and new. Probably had something to do with the barman's incessant need to polish whatever part of the bar he was standing at.

Details. Always the details.

Douglas was getting heartily sick of noticing details. Details like travel made Edward irritable. Rooms cost them money. Night-time made Emma sad, but he couldn't care about that. Not much, anyway. He couldn't afford to.

"We have to stop it, Douglas. It's our job and—" Edward stopped and looked pointedly at the bottle. "You going to pour that or—"

"It's coming. Hold your horses," Douglas replied.

"I have no problem with her. It's not personal, you understand? But if she lets us down, in any way—"

"I know." Douglas poured the whiskey hurriedly, some of the liquid spilling onto the table.

Edward took his glass and shook his head at the loss of such fine alcohol. Then he leaned back in his chair. "No one lets me finish a sentence. No one. You notice that lately?"

"No, I hadn't." Douglas replied, putting the bottle down and grabbing his glass. "And I'm not going soft, I just think that there's a...way to handle her."

"Handle her?" Edward's tone was dangerous. "What is she? An animal to be trained? A horse to be broken? I'm not *handling* anyone."

"No. What I mean is she's got more to tell."

"Oh, you reckon?" Edward's voice echoed around the bar and was harsh with sarcasm.

But Douglas spelled it out, anyway. "You know that look. She's got more to tell than she's letting on, but she's...fragile. That first one hit her hard. As it would anyone. I've known grown men who couldn't stomach something like that, let alone the fairer sex. *I* didn't stomach it!"

"It's her bloody job!" Edward threw back his whiskey and held out the glass for another.

"And it's our job to use her. We're just not using her properly. That's all I'm saying." Douglas eyed his companion and drank his whiskey down quick so he didn't taste it. He'd never liked the taste, but it wasn't worth the argument or the inevitable character assassination, so he drank. At least he and Edward could have drinking in common, for now.

"Fine." Edward sighed. "You do the handling, then." He drank once more, wiped his finger under his moustache, left then right, smoothing the whiskers.

"That's not what I'm saying."

"I don't care anymore. You think you can do better? Go right ahead."

"No, my point is—"

"Try your hardest," Edward poured himself another drink. "You won't get any further."

Silence fell between them while Edward downed the whiskey. Douglas decided it was better to let the subject drop. He didn't need to get on the wrong side of Edward *or* Emma right now.

"One thing, though," Edward leaned forward. "You think she's holding back deliberately?"

"You mean do I think she'll try and hide it from us on purpose? Try to stop us from doing our job?"

Edward nodded slowly. "Yeah. Or hers."

"No. I think she's shaken, is all. She'll come good."

"She'd better. I'm not going to be the one to lose this trail."

"She knows more. I can feel it." Douglas turned to look in her direction. Emma's head was still resting on the table; she hadn't moved an inch.

"Yes she does. And she knows what will happen if this goes bad." Edward reached down to pat the stock of his rifle. It was custom made with hard woods and bone. No metal exposed. The way it had always been.

Douglas nodded. He poured himself another drink.

"Cheer up," Edward beamed then. "We're in this picturesque town. We're looking for a woman... It's all tidy. What can possibly go wrong?" They both laughed, Edward's a genuine guffaw, Douglas' a polite rejoinder.

The bar doors opened and two men entered wearing wool caps and heavy work coats. They were mud-splattered and smiling. A woman followed them, her light laugh carrying all the way across the bar to the corner table.

Douglas sat up a little and took notice. She was not beautiful, but in this rundown bar with its heavy labourer stench, she was more than striking, with her honey-coloured hair and full lips; more than acceptable for someone who had been riding non-stop for months. He tried not to be obvious in his scrutiny.

A third man entered the bar. He wasn't smiling like the others. He held her bonnet in his hands and his eyes were on her. He never stopped watching her; the way she interacted with the other two. His eyes told his story.

Details.

She stopped just inside the door and finished laughing. Leaning forward, she tried in vain to remove the smudges of dirt from her skirts.

"I really must clean myself up before I begin work," she said.

The first two men stood on either side of her, looking at her, their backs to the rest of the bar. The third man was behind her, staring over her shoulder, his eyes only leaving her for a few furtive seconds to roam around the bar and the other men's faces.

"We're sorry we kept you out so long," the man to her right said.

She leaned towards him and smiled, "It's alright. The bar is never busy at this time anyway."

"But I don't want to get you in trouble."

"She's more than able to look after herself," the man behind her replied.

The two men in front exchanged a glance and an uneasy silence enveloped them all.

"Well, I really should get to work," the woman replied, smiling and turning to take her hat from the man behind her.

She walked behind the bar and the three men watched her go.

Douglas looked at Edward. They both grinned.

"Cheers, mate."

Douglas' eyes darted across to Emma.

Her head was still down on the table. She was still asleep.

She hadn't seen a thing.

DANGEROUS TIMES

"It sounds like you had a wonderful time," Bronwyn said.

"Oh, I did," Rose smiled. "It was probably the best day I've had for a long while, despite the cold." She led the way down the dark, long corridor towards Bronwyn's kitchen, her smile hidden from Bronwyn.

"It was perfect in a whole lot of ways," she continued. "Even the rain clouds were perfect. Time seemed to slow." She stretched her shoulders and smiled. "You know how that is? When you just want to keep everything the same?"

"I'm surprised you even have the time to stop by."

There was something in Bronwyn's voice that made Rose stop walking. She turned to face her in the dim light.

"Pardon?"

"Nothing." Bronwyn didn't look her in the eye.

Rose stood for a few seconds, unsure. She'd not spent as much time with Mrs—. With *Bronwyn* in the past few weeks as she'd have liked.

It's not that easy. Life is busier now.

Rose felt guilty, wanted to make it up to her. She didn't know how.

"I'm sorry," she said, as she turned and continued walking to the kitchen.

Rose placed the meals tray on the bench. She lifted the lid and steam rose from the dinner filling the room with the smell of potatoes and gravy.

"You should eat this before it gets cold," Rose said, noticing the untouched breakfast tray from that morning.

But Rose was alone.

I shouldn't've told her. Shouldn't've been so happy.

Rose backtracked down the hall to the study. The door was ajar and she pushed it open. Bronwyn was at the far end of the room, in her work corner, running her hands over a half-finished head and torso. It was a malformed, lumpy mess; as if it had melted from being placed too close to a fire.

Rose walked closer, coming up behind her friend and watching over her shoulder.

Far from being incomplete, the statue looked as if it had been fully finished at some stage, but was now raked with deep, long gouges. The surface of the face and chest had been ploughed, violently scored from top to bottom.

It scared her. It made her think of death.

"What happened?" she asked.

Bronwyn shook her head but didn't turn around. "Some-times things don't work out how you'd hope they would," she murmured.

"Oh."

"And there's nothing you can do about that."

Rose took two more steps to stand next to Bronwyn; reached out her hand and felt the destroyed face. It was clammy to the touch.

"Can you fix it?" she asked.

Bronwyn moved her hand across to Rose's and pulled it away from the statue. Then she leaned forward and picked up a long sheet draping it over the head, hiding it from view.

She turned to Rose. "There's nothing to fix. Tell me more about today," she said, slipping around her and into the kitchen. A waft of perfume and cigarette smoke marked her passing.

"Not much more to tell, really." Rose followed her to the kitchen, determined to downplay her afternoon. "I took the men their lunch as usual, but they invited me to stay this time. We ate and drank everything I took out."

"In that dress?"

"Yes, I know. It's one of my best. I just hope I can get the dirt out of it with a few washes."

"Sawyer had no trouble retrieving your bonnet?"

"No, it was blown a long way, but he insisted on running after it. We let him. He wasn't gone too long."

She was suddenly conscious of using "we" and wondered if Bronwyn had noticed.

"I see." Bronwyn sat down by the bench, pushing the meals tray away from her.

"Potatoes and beef."

"Yes. Thank you."

"You should eat."

"With all the rail workers in town and your work at the Three Belles, I'm surprised you had time to go on a picnic," Bronwyn said.

That comment hurt; a thinly veiled slap.

"It was a special occasion," Rose replied defensively, her hands fidgeting with her hair. A pin came loose and she struggled to push it back.

"Still, to disregard your duties at the Three Belles..." Bronwyn said, sounding like an aunt or a mother, not a friend.

"Everything was fine," Rose said, with a little more force than she intended.

"Really?" Bronwyn looked back at her now.

"Yes."

"How? It's just you and Sawyer and—"

"I've had...help," she regretted it as soon as she said it.

71

"What sort of help?"

"My cousin," she replied, quickly.

"Your cousin?"

"Yes. And his friend."

"You didn't tell me your relatives were visiting you."

"Oh, didn't I? It just slipped my mind."

"In fact, I seem to recall you telling me your relatives had all died."

"He's a distant cousin."

"You seem very reluctant to talk about him," Bronwyn leaned a little closer. "And his friend."

"It's just..."

"You never talked about him. Isn't that the reason you came to live out here? No family. No ties."

"Yes, but—"

"You told me there was nothing left for you, so you came out here to start again."

Rose sighed and sat down on the chair opposite Bronwyn, pushing the meals tray back towards her.

"I promised..." she began.

"You don't have to tell me," Bronwyn replied. But she didn't break her stare.

Rose swallowed. "No, I...I probably should. I mean, I'd feel better...I'd like to... But you have to promise not to say *anything* to anyone."

"Why?" Bronwyn's eyes, always a little vague, always a little too uncaring, narrowed and Rose saw a shrewdness in them she'd never noticed.

"Please, promise me." It was important to hear the promise out loud.

Bronwyn leaned further forward and smiled for the first time during this visit. "Rose, who am I going to tell?"

That would have to do.

Rose fled from them on that first day, when she had found them in her kitchen. At the time, she'd thought running was her only chance.

She'd made it to the front yard before Athan caught up with her easily. He grabbed her shoulders.

"Ma'am! Please, come back, come back."

"Get away!" she screamed, hearing more footsteps behind them.

He turned her, his fingers bruising, twisting her off balance as she fought him.

"You're hurting me!"

At her words, Athan abruptly let go and she fell.

Tumbling to the ground, her hands reached out finding nothing but air—and rose thorns.

Their tiny cuts weren't deep. They didn't even bleed.

They hurt all the same.

She sat amid her skirts with her back against the stone wall.

Zachary ran up to them, skidding in the dirt, fear in his face as his mouth formed an almost perfect 'O.'

"Athan, get away from her!" he yelled as he dragged Athan back. "Are you *mad?*"

Zachary reached down to Rose, offering her his hand and helping her to her feet.

It was a nice gesture, but Rose shook his hand off as soon as she was steady.

"Get away!" Her voice bounced off the hillsides, fading quickly.

They were wanted killers and she was alone, far away from help, and their strength and speed proved to her that there was no real way she could stop them doing whatever they wanted to do. She felt dizzy.

"Keep back, or I'll scream again," she threatened, knowing full well screaming wouldn't help her.

By the time any help arrived, if anyone was fortunate enough to hear her, Athan and Zachary could have had their way with her and fled.

I'm going to die.

Zachary took a step towards her again, his hands held open and out for her to see, like he was trying to calm an animal.

"Rose, *please.*"

"I'm warning you," she replied. Her hands shook, her knees were weak like their centres had turned to liquid.

Athan stood to the side of the path, his head bowed.

"It's no use," he muttered.

Rose didn't know if he was talking to her or Zachary.

"I won't let you kill me," she replied, bracing herself.

"Rose..." Zachary tried to smile, but it slipped. "Just listen. Please. She was already dead."

"I don't—" She stopped in mid-sentence.

I don't care. I don't understand. I don't want you here.

"It's the truth." Another step forward. "She was already dead when we got there."

"Rose, you're right. We are the men they're talking about. We've seen the papers. We know what you know. The whole story is there, but they've got it wrong."

Zachary's voice had taken a pleading tone, almost desperate. He sounded as scared as she was. His eyes were clear, despite the tears he had cried before. They weren't the eyes of a madman, a killer. He wasn't hiding anything...not from her, anyway.

She wished she could cry like that.

"It's a waste of time," Athan said.

Zachary ignored him.

"We *are* running from the police. But we did *not* kill her. We didn't kill Sacha. We *found* her, that's the truth, but we didn't kill her."

"Zach, let's just *go*."

Zachary broke his gaze with Rose to turn back to Athan. "No. I'm sick of all this. Someone else has to know the truth."

"She won't believe us."

"She might."

"We can't let her tell the police."

"Yes, we can. If we did that in the first place, none of this would've happened. She can tell them for all I care. I won't run. I just won't. We didn't *do* anything, Athan. Let the law decide. I'm tired. I can't do this anymore."

"We have to."

"We can't. How long can we keep running? *Forever?* I can't. I don't want to run until I die. I'd rather be in gaol for something I didn't do than be running every night, every day, until I drop."

Athan said nothing. He turned away from them and walked back towards the house, shaking his head as he did so.

Zachary faced Rose, the fear was still in his eyes, but so was the truth.

Surely killers don't argue with each other like that.

"You're not going to tell anyone, are you?" he asked. His voice small, shaking. "We *are* innocent."

The sun warmed her arms and shoulders.

They stared at each other for a long time.

It was long enough for Rose to think about what they said.

And decide.

Bronwyn pursed her lips and poured the tea. She hadn't said anything while Rose spoke. She didn't say anything now.

Rose sat staring at her, having told her more than intended. She felt better telling someone the truth. It was hard living a lie, hiding things from the people around you.

Suddenly she knew how Athan and Zachary must have felt before they confided in her.

Bronwyn sipped at her tea and looked down at the table. She arched an eyebrow.

Rose raised her cup to her mouth and noticed that her hands were shaking. Quickly, she placed the cup down. It clattered against the saucer, making her flinch.

Rose swallowed. It sounded loud in the silence.

"That explains why you've been so distracted in the last few weeks," Bronwyn finally said. "You've taken a big risk, don't you think?"

Rose undid the top collar button of her dress.

"I don't know if I'd have done the same," Bronwyn continued, her fingers grasped tight around the cup.

"It wasn't an easy choice."

"The important choices never are."

"But you can see why I did it, can't you?" She didn't know why, but she needed the older woman's approval.

"I can see why *you* would do it, yes." Bronwyn pushed the chair backwards and stood up. "I have work to do," she said. "Thank you for the food. I'll see you tomorrow morning."

She took her cup and walked out of the kitchen and into the lounge.

Rose watched her go.

I shouldn't have said anything.

She waited a few seconds longer, hoping Bronwyn would return, but knowing she wouldn't. She heard the creak of floorboards above her head. She never went upstairs. It wasn't that Bronwyn didn't let her, it just...wasn't done.

Carefully, she picked up the breakfast tray and rose from

76

her seat, turning around and walking to the front door as quietly as possible.

As she passed the lounge room doorway, she glanced through and caught a quick glance of the covered statue. The sheet had slipped to reveal the statue's warped face.

"Goodnight," Rose said as she opened the door and walked out into the night.

There was no reply from upstairs.

She stepped down the front steps into the gloom of dusk. The crisp air refreshed her.

For the first time she'd felt uneasy and unsure of herself in Bronwyn's house. Especially as she'd been caught lying about her 'cousin.'

She wouldn't tell, would she?

But Bronwyn was right. Who was she going to tell? Rose was her only visitor. No one came up this end of town—there was nothing here except this house.

Rose slowly walked down the garden path, avoiding the puddles.

She was halfway to the gate when she heard the noise. It sounded like a footfall. Heavy. Just one. Near the house.

An animal, perhaps.

She stopped, looked over her shoulder towards the house, peering into the shadows. Her fingers tightened around the tray. Tilting her head, she listened.

Nothing.

It wasn't Bronwyn. The last time Bronwyn had tried to leave the house, she'd fainted on the porch steps.

Rose shivered. She thought of what the boys at Three Belles had said about the woman who died, about her killers, and about all that blood.

She wanted to go home, lock herself in like Bronwyn and be safe.

77

As she turned to continue down the path, a figure stepped out in front of her. Startled, she dropped the tray and it fell to the gravel path with a heavy clatter; spilling its burden of congealed porridge, stale bread and a pot of orange preserve.

Sawyer.

"What are you doing here?" she asked, suddenly short of breath.

"I could ask you the same question." His cheeks flushed and he cast a furtive glance in the direction of the house.

"You *know* what I'm doing here," she said, folding her arms across her chest. "Were you spying on me? Answer me. Why are you here?"

"No, I was just checking on something."

"Checking what?"

"It doesn't matter."

"It matters to me." Rose quickly looked around them. The street was empty. "You scared me half to death. You don't simply..." She held up a hand and waved it, unable to find the right words.

"I was on my way home," he said, looking over her shoulder back towards Bronwyn's house.

"Home?" Rose scoffed, getting her breath and strength back. "You live on the other side of town."

"I like to walk."

"Do you?" She didn't believe a word.

"Rose? Are you alright?" It was Bronwyn's voice.

Rose took a few more steps away from Sawyer until she could see the house. One of the windows on the ground floor was open by only a few inches. A few inches were a chasm for a woman who nailed blankets to the shutters to keep out the daylight.

"I'm fine, Bronwyn!" Rose called to her. "It's just Sawyer. I'll see you tomorrow!"

Rose couldn't see Bronwyn's face, but after a few seconds, the window closed, the curtain fell across the glass.

"You didn't have to tell her that," Sawyer said. He sounded angry.

"She asked. I couldn't lie."

Again.

He sighed and shoved his hands into his pockets.

"I really wish you hadn't."

Rose didn't want to stand there defending herself. It was none of his business what she did or didn't tell Bronwyn. Nothing she did was his business.

"You shouldn't be out here this late, Rose," he added.

She ignored his familiarity. "I was giving Bronwyn her meal, like I do every night. You know I do."

"These are dangerous times, you know. There are dangerous people around." He took a step towards her, but she stepped away again.

"I can look after myself," she replied.

"Can you?" He smirked. "I very much doubt that."

"What is *that* supposed to mean?"

"Let me walk you home." He held out his hand to her.

She shook her head. "You don't have to."

"I insist."

"And I insist you *don't*."

He sighed, his head shaking slightly as he withdrew his hand.

"I'm going away again," he muttered.

She said nothing.

"I thought you should know," he continued. "I won't be here to welcome in the New Year with you."

"Very well."

He looked at her once more. "Will you be alright? I don't have to go."

"I think I'll be fine."

Zach will be here.

They both stood in uneasy darkness. Rose ran her hands up and down her sleeves, the cold night air no longer quite so refreshing.

"You look cold."

"I'm fine."

Another pause. Rose took a further step back. She was almost five feet from him now. She could feel the fast hammer of her heart.

"When do you leave?" she asked.

"Tomorrow."

She nodded, relieved at the answer. "Fine."

"I'm back in a few days," he added.

"Fine."

She turned to leave, willing herself to remain calm.

"You don't want me to walk you back?" He sounded defeated now.

"No," she replied. Leaving him by the side of the road, she walked away, heading in the direction of the Three Belles.

She wanted to walk faster, to run, but she controlled herself and travelled at her usual pace. She didn't want to give him a reason to follow.

She counted slowly with each footstep.

One...two...three...four...five...

Only when she reached one hundred did she turn around and look over her shoulder.

Sawyer had gone.

And so she ran.

Bubbles of Safety

There were no shadows on the walls.

Four large oil lamps lit every corner, clearing the small room of potential voids of blackness. They burned all night. Every morning Zachary would get more oil, top up the reservoir so it wouldn't run out. He needn't have bothered. Oil burned slow.

Athan had pilfered the three extra lamps from unused rooms on the second floor. Neither of them wanted to see shadows. Shadows held death. They held Sacha who was already present in their nightmares.

Athan had the bed this night, while Zachary took the bed roll on the floor near the wall. Both lay looking at the ceiling, arms above their heads, a ritual they had begun three weeks ago, since their first night under this roof. It was almost home to them.

Both men were tired but could not sleep.

Their weight had almost returned to normal, they worked hard, kept their heads down and occasionally, they relaxed.

Even smiled.

Each night they climbed out of their clothes and crawled into bed or bedroll. And they lay there, silent for hours.

Zachary waited patiently for fatigue to drag him down—because he would not go willingly.

Athan chose the bottle.

"Haven't you had enough?" Zachary asked, hearing the clink of bottleneck on glass for the fifth time in half an hour.

"Not nearly." Athan's words weren't even slurred. "Not enough to sleep, anyway."

Zachary didn't comment. Athan didn't mean sleep. He meant 'dreamless' sleep.

The cold earth had been tilled, the wood cut, the fires stoked, the vegetable patches cleared for spring planting, and the curing house mended. They'd eaten their dinner of crackling pork, roast pumpkin, potatoes and broad beans smothered in buttery gravy. Pleasantries were exchanged with Rose, with the rail workers, with Sawyer, or maybe not with Sawyer. After each day, they came to this room and lit it up, banishing the dark with flame and wick.

Athan couldn't face sleep even with two pints of lager and a warm bed. Zachary couldn't either.

He watched Athan stare at the glass in his hand.

It was empty. Athan tilted the whiskey bottle once more; a loose, liberal pour. He wristed the glass and downed the mouthful. No enjoyment, no savouring the taste, just resolute numbness by degrees.

Athan sighed. He put glass and bottle on the night-table.

Zachary rolled over to prop himself up on one elbow. "Penny for 'em."

"Nothing. It's nothing."

"A sigh like that doesn't come from nothing."

"How long are we going to stay here?"

It was Zachary's turn to sigh.

The question had been asked so many different ways these last weeks.

"How long are we staying?" "When are we leaving?" "Is it time to move on, yet?" "We should go."

"It's good here. I like it here," said Zachary, as he'd said

82

each time Athan had broached the subject.

"Yeah, I like it, too, but we can't stay."

"Why not?"

"You know why. People are still looking."

"They're not looking *here*. We've been here for three weeks. It's been...over a month since Sacha. No one is gonna find us."

"I wanna move on. I wanna..." Athan trailed off, waved a hand like he was trying to conjure the perfect words that would finally convince Zachary.

"What? Visit Sweet Moll?"

Silence from the bed. Zachary nibbled at his lower lip, pulling at the skin until he tasted blood. He sucked on it a while as the silence stretched between them like elastic about to snap.

He shouldn't have mentioned Athan's wife. Bad enough they were on the run, but Zachary had no ties. Athan, however...

He was about to ask for a glass of the scotch when Athan spoke.

"She doesn't want to see me." He made a grab for the bottle again.

"You don't know that."

"I'll only bring this trouble to her."

"You don't know that either."

"I don't want to see her. She thinks—"

"You don't know *what* she thinks, you haven't seen her. You haven't even written her a letter."

"Leave it."

"She's probably worried sick or worse. She might think you don't care."

"Leave it, Zach. Or so help me, I'll belt you." Athan tipped the bottle to his lips and drank. His eyes were half-way to being angry, but not even the alcohol had brought him that far.

If anything, he'd descended into lethargy.

"No, you won't. You've never hit me, Ay. You won't start now." Zachary sat up and leaned against the pale yellow wall. Athan didn't reply. Zachary dabbed at his lip with his knuckles, saw blood spots and licked them.

Athan stared at the ceiling.

"You want to stay for *her*," he said after a long while.

"What do you mean?" Zachary felt a warm flush begin at his jaw and crawl up to his cheeks. He was glad of the orange lamps. Pink oil, burnished glass; the musty light hid the giveaway in his face.

"Rose," Athan snorted and the sound was filled with derision. Tainted by the alcohol, it was an ugly and honest sound. "You, 'like this place,' ha! You like *her*."

Athan said it like Rose was plagued. It took three attempts for him to place the bottle on the night-table. He kept his hand there for a few seconds until he was sure the bottle would stay.

Zachary wanted to deflect the conversation, while at the same time, wanting to finally have it, get it all out and come to blows if needs be.

But Athan would never hit him.

"Don't you like her? Isn't she a nice lass?"

"You know what I mean. How long do you think it's going to take for her to doubt us? It's all adventure and whimsy right now. Hiding two men on the run, playing house and having picnics." Athan's hand made what he thought were whimsical patterns in the air. "But what happens when the whimsy wears off? When you get attached and she starts to doubt? Sawyer already has us pegged."

"He doesn't."

"Yes, he *does*."

"*She* won't."

"She will. *I* would. Look at us!" He rolled onto his side, the springs shifting and grating. "We *look* guilty." Athan half smiled, but it was all whiskey. It was guilt about Molly and had nothing to do with Rose. "We *were* there. I mean, we *told* her we were there. Sooner or later... Your little bubble of safety is going to burst, mate. It's going to damn well explode."

"Just because you'd doubt us, doesn't mean she will."

"Right, because everyone is nice here and this town is perfect." Athan fell back down to lie on his back. He pinched the bridge of his nose like a man desperate to control a thought or sober up. "The line stopped, Zach. Doesn't mean we have to."

A thousand retorts to those words knee-jerked their way into Zachary's brain. He softened them.

"You wanted to get away from Sacha. We've done that. Why can't we stay?"

Athan let his hand drop to his side.

"There's no getting away from her. She's there every time I close my fucking eyes."

SACHA

"Ay, slow down."

They walked along a low river made black by the rapidly disappearing sun, each flinging stones into the deeper parts and pushing each other into the more shallow wades.

For both, work had finished for the day. Zachary had waited for Athan on a nearby hill, under a tree and, as always, he looked like he'd been waiting a while.

They hurried through the paddocks, leaping over low, stone walls and wooden fences. They walked along the meandering creek they had played in as boys.

"We should check on our shirts," Zachary said.

"You reckon?" Athan replied over his shoulder. "They probably won't be ready yet."

"They might be."

"She hasn't been too quick lately."

Athan slowed, waiting for Zachary to catch up. "Anyway, your pants are soaked."

"Yeah, well, you should see yours." Zachary drew level and smiled. "Sweet Moll's going to kill you when she sees those boots."

Zachary leaped back, avoiding Athan's inexpertly thrown rock, which sent up a brief fountain of water as it splashed beside him.

He always called Molly "Sweet Moll" and Athan hated the term.

"You think Sacha's gonna talk today?" Zachary asked. They were rounding the bend, to the path that led to her house. Sooner or later, one of them had to ask the question, mention her name. It took longer and longer each time.

Shots sounded nearby, over the next hill. Probably a farmer shooting at crows or foxes.

"I hope not," Athan whispered.

"Yeah, I know what you mean. I don't know what to say to her, anymore. She looks awful."

"Molly made her some carrot cake and some pumpkin soup, before she left last time for Long Gully but she didn't even see her when she dropped it off."

"How is Molly?" Zachary asked.

"She's tired," Athan threw another stone. "The travelling is getting to her."

"How much longer do you think she'll be away?"

"It's hard to say. Her mother is very ill. I understand why she goes to visit her, but I don't like being apart from her for so long. A week was too long last time."

Zachary nodded. "It's hard on both of you. When does she go back again?"

"End of the week."

They walked on in the stream, only the sound of their legs wading through the water. As they drew closer to Sacha's house, it was Zachary who again broke the silence.

"When's the last time you talked to her? Sacha."

Athan shrugged. "I dunno. Um... 'Bout...two months ago? When you were there and she told us about Richard."

"Yeah."

"Remember how sad she was and how she thought he'd come back like he promised?"

88

Zachary nodded. "She told it like we weren't even there."

"I know. It gave me the chills just listening. I wouldn't be surprised if she's taking something. I saw poppy seeds and needles on her window sill last time."

"Bastard." Zachary ran a hand through his hair.

"I just meant—"

"Not you," Zachary interrupted. "Him. Richard. He's a bastard."

"Yeah. He was her bloody husband; the least he could have done was told her he wasn't coming back. He should've told her right then instead of making her wait and hope. It's not right. Husbands shouldn't do that. I'd never do that to Molly. It's just a coward's way out." He sighed tightly. "A man shouldn't do that."

"She knows, though," Zachary said, turning to look at his friend. "You can see that. She knows he's not coming back."

"What a waste."

"This from the married man."

They walked on in silence, both lost in their own thoughts. It was only when they rounded the bend and saw the candle-light on in her front window that they stopped to look at each other.

"She's home," Athan said as he placed one foot on a large rock, the other on the bank of the creek. He sighed and took out a tin of cigarettes from his trouser pocket. He opened it and took one out, clamping his lips over it.

"Sure looks like she is."

"God, I don't wanna do this," Athan added, lighting the smoke with a match from a new box.

"We've got to get our shirts," Zachary replied. "I'll be all out in a day or two. And we can't just sneak in and rob her."

"You know, I could work naked. Even in this freezing cold. I'd rather do that than see her again." Athan inhaled deeply, then blew a breath of grey smoke.

Zachary gave him a worried glance. "I'd rather you didn't. There'd be talk." He smirked and turned back to peer at the house, a dark silhouette against the darker trees, only the light from the candle shining out towards them. It was almost a quarter to five.

Zachary slumped back against the embankment, against the wet grass. He looked up at the sky and Athan followed his gaze. Dark clouds. Low and full of rain.

The house looked quiet, as always. Even Sacha's dog no longer barked. It had become as listless as she. People said dogs inherited traits from their owners, and Athan figured it stood to reason.

Zachary shook his head and sighed deeply. "I don't wanna do it, either, but we've got to get our shirts. If not today, then tomorrow. And it may as well be today. We're here."

"We don't have to."

"Well...maybe we should deliver her mail. That gives us another reason to be here. I hate just picking up my washing from her. It makes me feel guilty getting her to clean for me when she's all...I dunno, dead inside."

"Oh, good idea," Athan replied, his voice heavy with sarcasm. "We'll just run back to town and go to the postmaster and—" but he stopped as Zachary pulled a modest bundle of letters and leaflets from his satchel.

"You already went?"

"Guilty." Zachary tried to look chagrined, but he failed. "She had about three months worth of mail."

"I can't believe you did that."

Zachary added quietly, "One's from Richard."

"Oh," Athan sighed. He knew when he was beaten.

Zachary peered over towards the house once more. "Won't take long. We get our washing and get out and that's it."

"Right you are." Athan almost groaned it out, hoping Zachary would change his mind.

Zachary didn't answer.

Instead, he walked resolutely toward the small house.

I should be walking towards Molly, Athan thought.

She'd watch him eat while talking about her trip, her mother's illness, her own tiredness. Then he'd curl up with her on the couch and try to coax her to bed early so they could make love before falling asleep, dreaming of a better house, children, more money, a better life.

But that wasn't going to happen, he knew. With Zachary striding so purposefully towards the house, the bundle of letters under one elbow, Athan knew that his peaceful night would have to wait.

If he knew he'd be waiting forever, he would've turned around.

He jogged a little to catch up to his friend. Together they passed the road and through the gate, up the small, cobbled path with rose bushes growing wild on both sides. Zachary knocked on the door of Sacha's house.

"She's not here," Athan said before Zachary had even finished knocking.

"You reckon?" Zachary smiled a quirky smile. "She's always here."

They waited a little longer, their breathing the only sound. Further away, crickets clattered their nocturnal song and the deep, long rumble of a goods train rattling along the rails could be heard.

"I don't think she is," Athan said again.

"Maybe you're right. But I don't want to be the one who didn't check on her, just in case. What if she ground up those seeds like you said? Made Laudanum or something. What if she's fallen asleep with the gas and a cigar—"

91

"She doesn't smoke, Zach," Athan replied, trying to keep calm. "Can't we just go?"

Before Athan could stop him, Zachary was turning the handle of the door, pushing forward, letting the door swing inwards.

The hall was illuminated by a dim yellow light from the hallway oil lamp. Inside, the air was like a tomb, Athan thought. Still, heavy; oppressive.

The shadows danced along the walls, brought to life by the night breeze flickering the lamp's flame.

Zachary stepped inside and, without a word or any thoughts of stopping him, Athan followed right behind.

He had the strange feeling that every step they took into the hall, across the worn strip of maroon and blue carpet, was taking them further into some kind of weird dream, to somewhere they had never been.

They had never ventured further than the porch before. They'd never had the opportunity.

Usually, Zachary would knock and they would both wait to see the curtain to the side of the door flutter against the window as Sacha looked out to see who was there. Then she would open the door, hold out their shirts in one hand, while taking their coins in the other. Sometimes she would say thank you. Sometimes her sad smile would slip off her face as she turned to close the door.

"We're making her carpet dirty," Athan finally whispered.

"Shhhh," Zachary replied, then he called. "Miss Turgenev? Sacha?"

No answer.

Athan followed Zachary, followed his red hair like a beacon as his friend walked steadily along, peering into the empty parlour, glancing into the empty sitting room, and then heading down the corridor without stopping.

"We should go," Athan added. Starting to feel uneasy.

Zachary shook his head and kept on walking, reaching the kitchen door and slowly pushing it open, groping for the jamb to steady himself.

The wall felt wet, clammy, but he figured it was just cold.

The light from the porch was weak at this end of the hallway, and didn't illuminate anything other than solid blocks. Over his friend's shoulder, Athan could see the kitchen table, the bench, the windows. Everything else was shrouded in darkness.

"Matches," Zachary hissed as he stepped into that darkness, disappeared into it.

Athan pulled them from his pocket and obediently passed them to his friend, their hands fumbling in the dark for the exchange of the box. He heard Zachary drag the match across a surface and the large kitchen table briefly illuminated in the match's flare. There was the smell of sulphur.

Athan listened to Zachary drag something closer to him. He stood on tiptoe and saw an oil lamp on the table. Zachary lit the wick, then blew out the match.

The wick caught and the slow illumination pushed back the dark like a tide.

And revealed a picture of pure, bloody hell.

Athan wanted to stop the light, snuff it out and wipe the images from his mind, but it was too late. The wick reached its zenith, leaving everything stark and real. The naked orange flame did nothing to soften the scene.

It lit everything.

Blood lay in bright splashes on the floor, the bench, and their neatly-folded and ironed clothes. It smeared on the door jamb in long streaks, where Zachary had slid his fingers. It dripped from the ceiling, and pooled on the kitchen counters, slick and starting to congeal.

The crockery was lined up neatly along the shelves; one glass sat upside-down on a towel near the sink, dry from washing, but splattered with droplets of blood that had slid down its clean, curved side.

A row of porcelain dogs seemed to be the only things untouched by what had happened here. Bloodless and clean, their faces were half in shadow. The flame from the lamp made their eyes look as if they were darting from side to side, and their mouths as if they were laughing.

So much blood.

Athan wasn't thinking straight. His world had flipped over. He looked at those dogs, stared at them for long seconds.

He should've been thinking about what had happened here, or where all the blood came from.

How crass, he thought instead. *I didn't expect her to have trinkets like that.*

He felt like a shell of himself, looking around the blood-soaked kitchen in silence, not crying, not screaming—not even panicking. Just watching it from behind his eyes as if he was a thousand miles away, looking through a telescope.

The blood pooled in the grooves of the stone floor. It pooled down there, because that was where she lay. Both men looked down to her at the same time.

In the few seconds that passed since Zachary lit the lamp, they knew every corner of the room. It had been etched into their minds forever, as if the blood had made its own unique brand, as if they'd been looking at the splash-patterns for a lifetime.

Then, slowly, everything started to move again.

As Zachary leapt back, instinctively trying to get away from the body, his foot slipped. He grabbed at the wall, his face white; his mouth open like a string had been cut in the top of his head.

Athan shut his eyes, but knew that the image would be with him until he died.

She lay in a large dark pool, her face red and torn, her eyes closed. He could tell because her eyelids were the only part of her face free of blood.

The sight of her almost stopped his heart. At least, that's what it felt like.

On every exposed area of skin, were great tears, fissures of skin, clefts, gaps, absences of flesh. As if some frenzied beast had torn into her, mauled her, but had not fed. Or like someone had tried to turn her inside out, but had failed. He saw intermittent glimmers of bone along her legs and arms, and a deep gash in the side of her forehead.

Near her left hand lay a pile of scattered coins. The glass from the coin jar lay shattered nearby, its tin lid resting near her leg.

She used to give us change from that jar...

The blood ran rivulets around the coins and glass. Face up, the coins were clean.

Athan's stomach grew heavy and tight.

She had been taken apart. It was frenzied, it was—

Zachary was gasping beside him, like a man who just couldn't get any air, like he was drowning in that thick, tomb air. Old death. New.

"Damn it, oh damn. Bloody hell. *Sweet Jesus Christ.*"

Athan took a further step forward, towards her. He didn't know why. Captivation, repulsion; either of those bloody magnets pulled him closer to where her ruined body lay, even as the sour saliva of nausea flooded his mouth. He didn't want to throw up, didn't want to mix his vomit with that blood.

The cuts and tears to the skin on her face made it look as if she was smiling. A big, toothy, bloody grin.

Athan felt himself abruptly jerk to a stop, his dream-walk

ending as Zachary's clawed fingers dug into his arm with a strength that made Athan's breath draw, hissing, into his lungs. It made the sickness pass for a few seconds.

"No! Are you mad?" Zachary said between bellowing breaths. "She's dead. Are you going to check her pulse or something? Look at her arms. Leave her."

Athan turned to face Zachary. They stared at each other for a long moment before he turned again and tried to step closer.

"No, Ay. Don't! The coppers will do that. Don't touch her. Please don't touch her." Zachary's voice shuddered.

Zachary's mention of coppers thudded him back into reality. He really didn't want to go near her. He didn't want to smell this room any more. He didn't like her colour, or the rips in her skin. She looked more abhorrent, more destroyed to him now than even just a few seconds before. He couldn't go closer, he wouldn't.

Zachary was looking wildly around the kitchen. It was as if he expected her killer to leap out from the pantry or the cupboard; or to spy him in the darkest corner of the room, like he'd been standing there all along and they'd just missed him because of all the blood.

Zachary ran a hand over his forehead leaving a dark smear across the skin.

"Sacha?"

A female voice called from behind them, from the open front doorway where the night air crept in.

Zachary pulled at Athan, trying to jerk him back. But as he did so, his boot slid again across the wet floor. His shoulder and back slid down the wall, his balance failing him. Athan grabbed his hand, held tight, but Zachary reeled, slid down further.

Athan almost followed him. But the sight of Sacha's body

terrified him so much that his fingers gripped the table with a strength that hurt the bones at the tip. The lamp wobbled on the table, its flame flickering and dancing, sending the shadows into a wild frenzy.

I will not fall. I will not fall near her.

He ripped his arm free of Zachary's desperate grip, letting him go, watching him fall into the blood.

Zachary stretched out both hands to cushion the fall, as he fell hard; his knees hitting the floor with a dull slap, his trousers soaking up the blood. They both watched it leech into the cotton, darkening the fabric in an increasing circle.

Zachary stared at his knees like he was trapped by that growing stain. He seemed so far away down there.

Athan remembered later that he'd never let Zachary fall before. Never in their childhood, not while they were working, not even when he married Moll and Zachary was left behind.

Never.

But he let him fall now and didn't know why.

Zachary's breath grew rapid, his shoulders shuddered. He was staring at the coins. Then, he reached out and picked one up.

Athan saw a flash in the lamplight—one side shiny, one side red—before Zachary's right hand closed in a tight fist around it.

"Sacha!" The woman called again. Closer now.

"Whoever you are!" Zachary's shout shattered the silence in the kitchen. He didn't look up, just yelled from the floor where he was staring at his trousers, then at Sacha's face close-up, "Get out! Don't come in here!"

Athan turned to look at the doorway.

A young woman, no older than Sacha, walked through the door. She was wary, tense, ready to flee.

She didn't look around the kitchen. She didn't even look at

the men.

She saw Sacha, the red dress, the strips of skin.

Horror flooded her face.

Zachary reached out with his left hand, his bloody fingers splayed as a warning to her.

Just like a killer, Athan thought and stepped back even further from Zachary.

They could hear the woman's breath as it puffed out in little gasps.

She was backlit with the weak flame from the porch lamp. She wore a woollen shawl over a heavy cotton dress. Her hands fisted in a spasmodic grip.

"Don't scream," Zachary pleaded.

Athan heard her suck in a breath. He couldn't move towards her, he couldn't leave the safety of the table and the darkness. So he carefully put his hands over his ears and pressed down hard.

Behind his hands, he heard her scream. It was muted, but it was still high-pitched and primal.

She screamed and screamed again, backing away slowly, her eyes wide and spilling sudden tears that stained the front of her dress. Her blond hair came out from its clip as she threw herself backwards and ran.

Both men watched her sprint from the kitchen, her boots loud on the floor. She reached the doorway and turned back to look over her shoulder. Fear was still etched on her face. As she turned, her foot caught the edge of the hall rug and she went flying, arms out and body arched, down onto the porch. They watched her, neither of them moving to go after her. Zachary stuck to the floor with red glue, Athan immobilized by the solidity of the table.

They watched her come crashing down, her bare knees slamming down onto the hard wood with an impact that must have split the skin to the cap.

It didn't even make them wince.

All the pain a woman could feel was on the floor between them. A pair of bleeding knees didn't even register.

The soles of her buttoned-up boots flashed briefly from beneath her skirts, then she was up and running once more, down the steps and into the darkness of the yard.

The world outside looked clean and safe.

Safer than in here with...her, Athan thought.

"We have to go, Athan," Zachary whispered.

Athan looked down at the red hair of his friend, not the red blood, not the red stains, but the red hair.

"*What?*" He was going to be sick, but still couldn't bring himself to do it in here. Not where she had bled.

And I'll be dammed if that isn't everywhere *in here.*

"Whoever did this has gone," Zachary continued. "We have to go follow that girl. Tell the police. They can catch him."

Athan nodded but didn't say anything. He watched as Zachary turned his head to face him.

"Okay? Athan?" he asked. "So we're going to go now." Zachary nodded like those words made sense.

Murder. Police. That's right. Get the constables.

Zachary stood slowly, swallowing heavily as his trousers stuck to his knees briefly before the material slid past his skin. Carefully, he made sure he wouldn't fall again. He took two long steps and walked out of the kitchen, not once looking back.

Athan followed him out, still feeling sick and suddenly feeling the vomit spasm through his stomach and shoot up past his teeth. He managed to push past Zachary, stumble forward and make it to the porch before throwing up over the side. He closed his eyes against it, not watching the splatter patterns on the earth, trying not to smell it.

But with his eyes closed, all he saw was red.

He felt Zachary's hand on his shoulder and nodded a couple of times as if to say he was all right. But he wasn't. There would never be an all right again.

Quickly, they managed to navigate the stairs, watching their booted feet, the tops of which were wet from the clear creek water, the bottoms stained reddish brown with Sacha's blood.

Rain fell, a light shower. But soon the water soaked their hair, and cleared their minds.

They heard the soft whickering of a nearby horse and the tinny jangle of a Gig harness, the sound of a woman crying through the rain.

But none of that registered, not until the first shot was fired.

It exploded from the darkness at the end of Sacha's yard. Athan heard three distinct sounds; a strange whooshing, then a loud bang from behind them as the bullet collided with one of the solid beams that held up the porch roof.

Then the shot, last.

Zachary spun around, following the bullet, seeing the damage but not believing it.

"Bloody hell," he whispered. He turned back to the road and held his hands up. "Wait! Please, wait!"

Athan turned to his friend. In the darkness, in the rain, Zachary looked crazed, pale, blood on his hands, his knees, his shoes. He *looked* like a killer, a monster.

Another shot came from the end of the yard. They couldn't see who was firing, it was too dark, but they saw the muzzle flash and light up the darkness. They were in farm country; every farmer had a rifle.

It wasn't the woman that was for sure. They could hear her, hysterical, screaming about killers, murderers and blood.

Athan grabbed Zachary's arm. "Let's ge—"

He heard the rifle again and then his body was dropping, falling to the ground like a sack of wheat toppling over. He couldn't help it. He saw Zachary's stained knees as a dark shape rushed towards him. Then he realized the darkness was just his eyes closing.

Pain in a million colours and shapes exploded between his temples like firecrackers, constant and blooming every few seconds.

Zachary's hand was on his arm again, holding him steady.

The rain fell heavier now. In sheets. Blades.

Two more shots were well wide of the mark. The shooter's view and aim obscured by the rain.

Athan felt Zachary lift him up and drag him back towards the creek. He tried to stand, but his legs and arms were almost useless to him right then. The best he could do was stagger.

The creek ran along the edge of the town toward the railways and more farmland, wilderness. A narrow path worn flat and hard by years of local children and labourers, wound along the top of the embankment. Zachary dragged his friend along it, and Athan let him, not thinking anymore, just running from the rifle and the sight of her body.

Young oak branches slapped their faces and the hard path hurt the balls of their feet.

Athan didn't know how long they ran. He tried not to slow Zachary down, tried to place his feet where there were no twigs or holes. He saw the rain hit his boots so hard, it backsplashed onto the hem of his trousers.

They ran.

For weeks, they ran.

PRISONERS

"If you want to go, go," Zachary said after a long silence. He was surprised by the offer he just made; he was glad of the light that was bright, yet hazy and hid the lump in his throat he couldn't swallow.

He'd allowed Sacha to become a memory, a feeling, pain; people forgot pain. It was easy to do if you concentrated on other things, like running or gardening or Rose.

Clearly Athan hadn't forgotten.

"No. We started this together," Athan said. His words were slurring now, whether from tiredness or from the alcohol or from the event they had just remembered in detail. Zachary didn't know. It didn't matter.

"I want to stay here. But you..."

"Don't." Athan sat up and fixed his gaze on some point on the opposite wall, his fingers absently playing with the copper bracelet; a present for Molly which he'd never had the chance to give. "We wake up every morning in this place. Oh yes, it has clean air, sunshine, the smell of bacon and birds singing in the *fucking* trees. But it's not...safe." He afforded Zachary a fleeting look, then stared at the wall again.

"No. I don't want to stay. Who knows, maybe I will leave, but not today or tomorrow. If—"

A swift tapping on the door made Athan pause. He looked at Zachary, who shrugged and slowly rose from the bed roll.

"Who is it?" he called, softly.

"Rose," her voice, quiet at best, was muffled behind the heavy oak door.

Athan groaned and fell back against the pillow. Zachary glared at him and went to the door.

"Are...are you decent?" she asked.

Zachary smiled, but wondered why a young lady would be knocking on the door of two men she didn't *really* know.

"Nothing is decent anymore," Athan murmured from the bed.

"Yes, we are." Zachary opened the door a crack. She stood in the hallway, her cheeks flushed and her eyes wide.

"Can I..."

"Of course," Zachary said and opened the door, moving aside for her to enter. He took a robe from the back of the chair and slung it around his shoulders, tying it closed as she stopped a few feet from the bed. Athan gave her a lazy wave as he, too, grabbed for his robe and stood, staggering slightly.

Zachary sat on the edge of the bed and smiled. "What can we do for you?"

"I..." Now she was in here, she looked uncertain. Some of her hair had come loose from the intricate lattice of pins and rolled across her shoulders. The curls shone in the lamp-light.

She looked like she'd been running. It was cold out, but her shawl hung from her left arm, wrapped once so it didn't drag on the ground. Her hands shook as she flipped one of the curls from her neck. Zachary stood.

"Rose, what is it? What's happened?"

"It's nothing." She shook her head quickly and pressed her lips together. Her flushed face turned pale at his question and even Athan looked concerned.

"Here. Sit down," Athan said, gesturing to the only chair,

his arm hovering near her elbow. She sat and Zachary crouched in front of her.

"What happened"

"I just had a fright, that's all. I'm all right, now, though. I should probably go." She laughed a little.

Athan stood and walked to the door. He gave a pointed glance at Zachary. "I'll get a brandy, warm you up."

She nodded and Athan left, closing the door behind him. Zachary almost smiled.

Athan was all talk.

He let her compose herself for a few moments, watched her look around the room at the lamps, the bed, the near-empty whiskey bottle. He wanted to tell her it wasn't his.

Instead, he smiled encouragingly. "Tell me," Zachary said.

"Really, it's nothing. I was up at Bronwyn's and— I got startled."

She fisted her dress and Zachary placed his hand over the top. He could feel the tremors. She couldn't avoid his eyes from where he knelt.

"Startled?"

"Scared," she admitted. The door opened and she broke the gaze. Zachary removed his hands from hers, but not before Athan saw. The other man smirked, a cold tug of his lips as he entered with a small bottle and a glass.

Athan poured a couple of fingers and handed it to her. He kept the bottle in his hand.

"Scared of what?" Zachary asked.

"Scared of *who*," Athan corrected as she took a sip. "Isn't that right?"

"Yes, but it was a mistake. He didn't mean it."

"Sawyer," Zachary cursed. He smiled at her to soften the tone.

"Well, I wanted to hit *someone*," Athan murmured under his

breath.

"And give him an excuse to turn us in?" Zachary's voice felt bitter in his mouth. He hated it. He wondered when that bitterness would go away. He suddenly saw that Athan was right. He hated that, too. Sure, they could stay here and be safe, but if they made a wrong move, rocked the boat even a little, then it could all fall apart.

We're still running. Still prisoners in this room.

Athan sat on the bed behind Zachary, out of sight. Zachary was glad of it—he didn't want to see Athan right now.

Rose was watching them, her eyes flitting back and forth between them. She settled for looking at Zachary and he asked, "You see Bronwyn every day, don't you?"

"Morning and night. For her food. She doesn't leave her house," Rose replied. Then she bit her lip. "I forgot the tray."

"Pardon?"

"It doesn't matter. Morning and night. Why?"

"I'm going with you tomorrow."

"There's no need. Sawyer's leaving tomorrow. For work. He does that often. Goes here and there for work. Always comes back. He's going to Long Gully again."

"Long Gully?" Athan blurted it out. A sudden shriek of springs as he stood.

"Yes." Rose looked understandably puzzled.

Zachary cleared his throat before he spoke. "How far is that from here?"

"Twelve miles."

"Only twelve? That's not far, is it?" Zachary said. He wasn't talking to Rose now, and she knew it. Zachary watched her eyes move to Athan behind him.

"Not far enough." Athan's voice was expressionless, but Zachary didn't need to turn to know that his friend was glaring at him. That his hands were clenched and his eyes were cold.

The hissing of the gas light on the wall and the steady glow of the oil lamps marked the minutes of awkward silence. Zachary heard the fast ticking of the pocket watch they had borrowed from Rose. Her brother's.

Rose stood from her chair, smoothed her skirts with hands that no longer trembled and said, "I should go…"

"Yes, you should." Athan said.

"You can't *ignore* this, Athan," Zachary said softly.

"You should take her home." Athan walked up to Zachary, a familiar look in his eyes. He used his height to emphasise his unspoken point.

Leave it.

Zachary nodded. He didn't want Rose to see or hear any of this. It was their last secret—Athan's secret—and Zachary had no right to divulge it. "Rose, let me get dressed. I'll be out in a minute."

Rose nodded and left the room. She closed the door without a sound, delicate.

"You could go see her," Zachary said, pulling on a pair of trousers.

"She might not even be there."

"Twelve miles, Athan."

"Get your coat and get out." Athan turned his back and walked two steps to the side-table. The hollow release of a cork.

Zachary watched the shoulders rise and fall, two deep breaths before Athan tossed the scotch back. He didn't use the glass, nor did he turn around.

Zachary pulled on his boots and walked out. His footsteps were loud and the door closed on the whiskey-soaked room with an audible *bang.*

Rose stood in the gaslight, small, quiet and patient.

THE STAIRMAKER

December 31, 1888

He watched her lying on the lounge, her fingers combing through the long black strands of her hair.

From where Sawyer stood, he could see her whole body. He could see the outline of her long legs, her full hips and the strong, round mounds of her breasts beneath her dress.

He wiped the dust from his forehead and rested against the door jamb. She was, as usual, unaware of his observation.

Except for her hair, she looks like Rose, he thought, but immediately wished he hadn't.

He was four days away from going home.

Each time, it became harder and harder to stay away—to keep himself from doing or saying something he'd regret.

Mrs. Knight turned on her side, and for a moment, Sawyer thought he'd been seen. But her eyes were shut, and she was smiling. He silently backed away and picked up the sandpaper from the floor at the base of the stairs.

He had work to do.

Sawyer sanded the grain of the stairs, working away at the rough surface. The sandpaper was harsh under his fingers, catching at his skin as it smoothed over the fine splinters of wood. His arms ached with the effort, his back pulled from the strain, his breath timed to the rhythm.

He inched forward, moved up to the next stair. He was halfway up the main staircase. Halfway down.

A drop of sweat fell from his forehead onto the unfinished surface, staining it a darker colour, like rain on dirt, blood on skin.

"It must be horrible."

His hand slipped from the paper, a fingernail bending on the unfinished wood. He bit his tongue on a curse and looked over his shoulder. Mrs. Knight stood at the bottom of the stairs.

Again.

She was leaning against the newel post, newspaper in her manicured fingers. The last time she'd brought him fresh water, the time before that was a bread and cheese.

"You knew her?"

He shook his head. "No, I said I heard *of* her."

She smirked, as if she didn't believe him.

"We get the papers in Oak Ridge too, just like you," he continued.

She nodded, her teeth biting at her bottom lip while a finger played with her hair once more, spiralling and twisting. A woman trying to cast a spell.

"Does it scare you?" she asked.

"I beg your pardon?"

"Travelling like you do, between towns, all alone. Does it scare you?"

"No."

"It sounds dangerous. I hope you have a fast horse."

"I can take care of myself." He placed the sandpaper on the stair and turned around, sitting and wiping away at the sweat on his forehead. "What about you? You live by yourself most

110

of the time. Now *that* would be frightening. Don't you think?"

He stared at her, his head cocked, willing her to leave. Most women would feel confronted with a stare like that.

"I try not to think about it," she said, her eyes dropping to the stairs between them.

"You're a long way out from town. Your husband has the buggy, you have a long way to run, should trouble strike."

"I can take care of myself." She repeated his words, but without conviction.

Silence stretched between them.

"You try not to think about it," she continued.

"Indeed."

"Awful times."

"Yes, they are."

"And to think, those poor women butchered in such a way."

He nodded, not offering anything else.

A sly look came into her eye, a smile at the corner of her mouth. "Still, it's very exciting, don't you think?"

"Exciting?"

"Yes, living in these troubled times with danger all around us. I can't understand how frightening it is. How horrible it would be for someone to have total dominion over you." She unbuttoned the collar of her dress.

"It would be," Sawyer agreed.

"Are you hungry?" She changed the subject, biting at her bottom lip once more. "You don't have to work so hard all day."

"No." He had no time for her prattling. "I'm fine."

"I can get you anything."

"I'm sure you can."

"Awfully warm, don't you think?" she tried again.

"Mrs. Knight, it's winter. I really should continue with these stairs," he replied, trying not to smirk. "I have to be finished in four days."

She nodded, a shadow passing across her face. "I understand."

No, I don't think you do, he thought as he turned back to his work.

He picked up the sandpaper, trying hard to cast the image of Mrs. Knight from his mind knowing full well she was still behind him, staring at his back, watching it move beneath his shirt as he worked.

"It's a pity," she muttered.

He didn't answer.

"Lost opportunities..." was all she said.

He thought of Rose, tried to picture her. He thought of her every second of every day, but try as he might, he couldn't clearly see her face right now. It had been replaced with the pouting lips and smudged rouge of Mrs. Knight. Now that he looked at her she was nothing like Rose.

He cursed under his breath, trying to keep his anger in check.

Bitch.

He pushed with the sandpaper, pushed hard, forcefully. Taking his anger and frustrations out on the wood below him.

He finished the next three stairs before glancing behind him.

Mrs. Knight had gone. He assumed she had retreated to her bedroom.

Right where he wanted her.

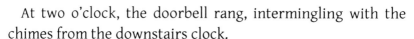

At two o'clock, the doorbell rang, intermingling with the chimes from the downstairs clock.

"Be a dear, and get that for me!" Mrs. Knight's voice wafted from the bedroom.

Sawyer placed the hammer on the floor and walked to the door, thinking of ways he could better use the tool, while also knowing that if he refused, Mrs. Knight would come and strike up a conversation with him again.

He didn't need that right now.

He was more worried about Rose and the strangers she'd taken in. What they were doing. What *she* was doing.

They'd appeared out of nowhere and she'd just let them stay. Believed whatever story they told her and gave them free reign of the town, the bar...

...of her.

He reached the front door and opened it wide.

"Hello?"

Two men stood on the porch. One was wearing a deer-stalker cap and glasses; his brown moustache was finely bar-bered. Better than most. The other man had curly golden hair and a fake smile. He was older and confident.

"Good afternoon, sir," the man with the smile, said. "My name is Inspector Foster and this," he pointed to his compan-ion, "is Sergeant Collins. Are you the owner of this property?"

"Ah," Sawyer's eyes darted between both of them. "No, sir."

"I see," Collins replied, nodding slowly. Sawyer smiled, but didn't mean it.

"Is the owner home?" Foster said, looking over Sawyer's shoulder and into the house.

"Yes, she is," Sawyer turned to look for Mrs. Knight.

She was draped over the newel post.

Again.

"Hello there," she smiled avidly. "Invite the nice gentlemen in, Mr. Sawyer."

He did as he was commanded.

She led the men into the lounge room without a word, gliding across the floor as if she walked on air.

"And what can I do for you both?" she asked as they took seats.

"We're in town inquiring about the recent spate of murders in these parts."

Mrs. Knight nodded. "Oh dear, yes, I've heard about them," she said, looking worried. "Sawyer has been telling me all about them. Tea?"

Sawyer, the only one still standing, looked towards the two inspectors, suddenly feeling out of place.

"Has he now?" Inspector Foster turned to look at him. All three men ignored the invitation of tea.

"Just what I read in the newspapers," Sawyer countered, his voice suddenly raspy and dry, like the un-sanded stairs.

"If you ask me, a good too many people hold what they read too highly," Foster said. "Half-truths and suppositions do not make a solid case."

"I'm sure with bright, handsome men like you on the case," Mrs. Knight interrupted, "we have nothing to worry about."

"We hope to clear this up as soon as possible, madam," Collins nodded.

Mrs. Knight smiled and leaned closer towards him. "I'm more than happy to have you protect me," she smiled.

Collins sat back in his chair and Foster cleared his throat. "We're looking for two men. Two strangers in town, who may have been acting suspiciously in the past couple of weeks. Have you seen anyone who would fit this description?"

Mrs. Knight's forehead furrowed and she thought hard. Slowly she shook her head back and forth, her eyes squinting, searching, but coming up blank.

"No, I'm sorry, Inspector," she conceded. "No one comes to mind."

"I see," Inspector Foster sighed. "Well, if anything *does*

come to mind..." He started to stand.

"But Sawyer might know," Mrs. Knight nodded in his direction.

The two inspectors turned to face him.

"Well?" Foster asked.

Sawyer shook his head and looked vacantly back at them.

Then it all fell into place.

He looked at Inspector Foster and smiled.

CURSES AND INTERVENTIONS

January 1, 1889

It was their fourth round today.

The first two arguments had been in the street where Emma had set up a small cloth-covered table under a Chinese elm. There, she read palms for coins she wouldn't touch.

"Just place them in the hat, thank-you."

Life lines, heart lines and fate lines. In them, she saw possible births and crop failures, mine collapses and derailments. She told of love and luck and 'challenging times.' As each person moved away, smiling and grateful, Edward whispered in her ear. "Well?"

"Nothing."

He would sigh or curse, or kick the stones that lined the path. Douglas watched from the other side of the street. Edward acted like her father, her keeper. He brought people in, smiling with an ingenuousness Douglas didn't know he possessed. She was a novelty in this tired and inconsequential town. The New Year brought with it hope and dreams and promises. People wanted to know.

The third argument occurred when they were packing up. Edward demanded why there was no sign, no clue.

"Do you even *know* what you're doing?"

Emma threw the hat at Edward's feet; money spilled around his shoes. Douglas felt no small amount of pleasure as the larger man leapt back from the scattered coins, fear in his eyes, biting his tongue on an insult not fit for the daylight.

both followed Emma into the Three Belles.

Edward remained silent until they got inside. They soon spied Emma in the meals area; 'decent' women were not seen in the bar.

Rose was certainly there—out the back, helping clean the kitchen ready for meal time tonight. They knew this because they knew almost everything about her by now. A simple woman.

Such a shame.

Emma ordered tea, which arrived as a set of six items that the serving girl placed carefully in front of her. He waited until the girl had gone, then asked Emma again, the same question.

"What do we do, now? You must have seen something; what?"

Emma said nothing.

It was there Edward pronounced the ineptness of Emma's abilities; her lack of compassion, her general deficiency in both her scruples and her concern. He took out his own frustrations on her and Emma didn't want to hear it. She didn't look at him; didn't even acknowledge him. Her eyes stared at a point just in front of her. She was seeing something else; she *was* somewhere else.

Home probably.

In the face of her prolonged and continuing silence, Edward stalked off to the bar. Douglas was left there, not wanting to follow like a lap-dog, but not wanting to stay at the stony-quiet table; a man on the outside.

Emma blinked, coming back, and looked resolutely at her empty cup. The tea brewed in its silver-plated pot next to the small jug of milk and the bowl of raw sugar. She tapped a fingernail against the metal pot and Douglas flinched.

"Should you be *doing* that?"

She looked at him, her expression vacant, uncaring. She tapped it again, daring him to say something. He frowned, twisted in his chair to look at the bar. Edward hadn't seen anything.

"At least put some gloves on, girl."

She shrugged and turned the ceramic jug around to grip the handle. She poured milk into the cup and sighed; a small sigh, all her own. She pulled her gloves over her hands and placed the strainer over her cup, picked up the pot and poured.

Douglas relaxed a little.

"Any more about her?"

"Her *name* is Rose," she said.

"Oh, she speaks!" Edward's voice was just loud enough to carry across the room. Douglas watched Emma's shoulders hunch a little further, her fingers grip the cup tight.

He twisted in his chair again to see Edward, a sarcastic smile on his lips. His eyes were hard and cruel. Douglas had never noticed that before. Then again, he'd always been on the other side. Following Edward. Doing what Edward said.

"So," Edward continued. He placed two pints on the table top and flipped his chair around, straddling it and leaning his elbows on the table. "Rose, yes. Christ, even *we* managed to find that out."

"Must you always take the Lord's name in vain? If you know it all, why don't *you* go and read the palms and I'll sit around the pub and drink the ale?" Emma smiled sweetly at him over her cup. Douglas noticed the circles under her eyes when her face creased like that; he hadn't noticed them before. He thought back to when they met her and, for the first time, regretted his actions on that night—and the night after.

Especially that second night.

Edward gripped his pint, his fingers squat and suddenly brutish. "Listen here, Missy. We don't have much time."

"Yes, I'm well aware of your agenda."

"My— You hearing this, Doug? My *agenda*. No, Mrs. Godley. It's not my agenda. It's yours, it's his," he pointed to Douglas, "and it's hers; whichever poor unfortunate lass is the next to end up a butchered wreck on the floor of her own house!" His voice started sharp and loud, but ended up in a harsh whisper, an avalanche, petering out.

She stared him down, watching, as Douglas did, the glistening saliva that flecked his chin.

Edward took a long swallow of his beer and shook his head.

"Not an agenda, girl. A job. *Your* job."

"I'm doing the best I can. I keep telling you that. I can't tell you any more. I don't know what else you expect me to do."

"Really? Nothing out there? Nothing at all?"

"What possible reason would I have to keep anything from you?"

"Oh I dunno." He shifted back in his chair a little. "You might just be fixin' to get home sooner. Back to that nice husband of yours. Your little girl?"

"Don't you talk about them. Ever!" She put down her cup and for a moment, Douglas thought she would reach across and strike him. Wouldn't be the first time for Edward. He had trouble relating to women like Emma. In their years together, Douglas had seen Edward slapped more than a few times. Kicked as well.

Once, he was even cursed. Didn't take, though.

Tea spilled over the delicate rim of the cup onto the table top.

Douglas drank from his own pint mug even though he'd never felt less like beer in his life. His stomach was one big, hard knot that wouldn't shift. He hadn't said a word since Edward sat down and wasn't going to. Edward was stubborn and dedicated.

Emma, they were finding out, was equally stubborn and dedicated in a way they hadn't foreseen.

"Well, my apologies, *Mrs.* Godley. If he loves you, he'll wait. But I wouldn't hold my breath." Edward winked, a dirty, sly wink that made Emma feel physically ill. She stood, her thighs rocking the table as she did. Douglas lifted his pint mug to avoid spilling his beer.

"How *dare* you!" Her words were strangled.

Yep. A slap for sure.

"Excuse me, Miss?"

As one, Douglas, Edward and Emma turned to face the intruding voice.

Two men stood near their table. One clutched a deerstalker cap, the other ran his fingers through his curly hair. The latter smiled; wide and insincere.

"I'm Inspector Foster, this is Sergeant Collins."

Emma looked at Edward, her eyes no longer stunned, but calculating. Douglas saw the other man flush slightly. Edward's eyes narrowed and his mouth curled, ready to utter another threat.

"Are these men bothering you, Miss?"

"It's *Mrs.*, Inspector and—" Emma stepped back from the table, taking her nearer to Collins. The Inspector straightened slightly, setting his shoulders as duty called.

"Yes," Emma said. "Yes they are."

Secrets and Lines

"**W**e've been tracking you through four towns. We know what you've done," Inspector Foster said as he grasped the cell door, the metal slick with moisture. The whole place was damp; the concrete walls, the glistening floor.

"We haven't done anything," Edward repeated.

"No? You're lucky I don't call the local lynch mob. You're lucky I don't let the locals here have a go. You haven't done anything? *Right.*"

"We haven't."

"That's for us to decide."

"No, it's for you to prove, my lad," Edward said. "You've got nothing on us."

The Inspector's eyes narrowed slightly at the blatant lack of respect. Edward's manner was not endearing him to the pair.

"You were harassing that lady," Foster said, tightly. "I'm sure her story will be different than yours."

"That *lady*, as you call her, happens to be our charge. *Ours.* Separating us from her is—" Edward stopped as Douglas placed a hand on his arm. "Unwise," he finished.

"Exactly what are you inferring?"

"He's not inferring anything, Inspector," Douglas calmly interjected. "He's merely trying to apprise you of the situation in which we find ourselves."

"You have a *situation?* With this woman?"

"No, we just want to get out of here. That's all."

"You'll leave when we're good and ready. When we're satisfied with the facts."

Foster turned his back on them and closed the door with a solid *clang.* They heard the key turn in the lock and both men winced as metal scraped on metal.

"That lying shilling whore," Edward spat onto the damp ground. "I didn't even get to finish my pint."

"She'll come and get us."

"*Will* she." It wasn't a question. Not really.

"Of course." Douglas' voice left no room for doubt.

"She'd better."

"She's doing this because of *you*. You pushed her too far. I *told* you..."

"Shut it, Doug."

"You've got to be careful with her, remember? You've got to handle her. It's not an easy job she's doing."

"Oh, *I'll* handle her. When we get out of here, I'll handle her good and proper."

"No you won't. It's your 'handling' that's got us into this *metal* cell."

"What are you saying?"

Douglas sighed and closed his eyes briefly. "Ed, just be thankful he didn't put us in cuffs."

There was a pause between them.

"Jesus Christ," Edward mumbled to himself. "That's *all* we'd need."

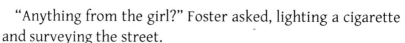

"Anything from the girl?" Foster asked, lighting a cigarette and surveying the street.

"She recanted," Collins replied, stopping by his side, looking back up the road toward the Three Belles.

"Recanted?"

"Yes. She's...requested they be held overnight—just so they can cool off. She knows 'em and doesn't like 'em seems to me, but she says they've been travelling together for a coupla months. A good, solid alibi for 'em all."

Foster nodded. "I might've known. Doesn't help us, though, does it? So, are we going to let them out?"

"Nah. She's going to come and collect 'em in the morning." Collins shook his head in disappointment.

"Serves them right," Foster ground his cigarette into the dirt. "So we're back to where we started."

"Seems that way. With the railway going through and the number of strangers in this town, this job is bloody impossible."

"They're here, Collins. We'll find them. I can feel them. They're here, I just know it."

Emma stared at the delicate china cup in her hands; tiny blue flowers on white; a pale gold trim. It contrasted against the pale skin of her fingers.

Delicate hands for delicate china.

Douglas and Edward's pint mugs sat on the table, half-finished. Stout mugs which suited their hands; unrefined, crudely shaped. Edward's chair was still flipped around, away from the table.

Almost as if he had only stepped away for a second.

She sipped at her fresh tea, enjoying its solace and warmth. For the first time in weeks she was alone. No questions, no fear, no blame. She was free of them for the moment. Instead of enjoying it, she wondered what the repercussions of her actions would be.

"We'd like a word with you, gents," Inspector Foster had said. "Come with us."

"Inspector, we're *with* her," Douglas replied, pointing in her direction.

"Tell 'em," Edward demanded of her.

She smiled, remembering the look on his face; the utter fury in his eyes.

"They were interrupting my tea," she'd said after a few seconds, managing to look both wounded and a little frightened. Douglas' jaw had dropped.

"Emma. You tell them. *Now!*"

No 'Mrs.' or 'Ma'am' or manners of any kind gilded Edward's words. He had forgotten he was in public and his attitude cost him.

Foster squeezed Edward's arm, tugged it. "There is a *lady* present, sir. Come this way. We don't want a fuss now."

Edward resisted for a second, but a look passed between him and the policeman, and suddenly he gave in, letting the inspector guide them towards the door.

Emma watched them leave. Inspector Foster between them both, one hand on Douglas' shoulder, and the other wrapped around Edward's elbow.

Inspector Collins didn't follow. Instead, he sat down next to her, ordering the fresh tea she now drank and a pint for himself.

His initial questions were subtle. To begin with, she didn't know what story she would tell him. She didn't have time to create one.

His was the first genuine face she had seen in the last few weeks. Because of that, she found herself telling him the truth. She didn't even try to hide it. What was the point? It would only cause her more pain in the long run.

His smile told her he understood. He nodded slowly and bought another beer.

"I just need some time," she'd said, unable to convey the absolute weariness she felt in her words. Having them out of the room was enough to lift her burden a little.

"Then leave 'em overnight. Teach 'em a lesson."

Emma looked quizzically at the Inspector.

"We can do that for you," he said.

She nodded. They sat in comfortable silence for a while.

After finishing his beer, he bid her farewell and left quietly.

As a gentleman should.

Once Collins had gone, Emma let her mind wander and let the tension drain from her shoulders. The lethargy was wonderful. She looked around the Three Belles for the first time seeing it as a normal patron would; polished tables, the smell of burning pine, food smells from the kitchen. It was warm and cosy in here and she took in a breath that was mostly free of worry.

Mostly. One thing nagged at her.

Home.

Edward and Douglas were in the lock-up overnight. She was free and clear to leave, take her horse and ride as fast as she could back to her husband.

Then what?

Edward and Douglas knew where she lived, they had come to her house late that terrible night and ordered her to come with them. She had, of course. Her duty bade her. The family tradition.

If she hid, they would find her.

If she moved house they would find her.

Edward would kill her, she was sure.

More than that, he'd kill George. No, George can handle himself.

But Lucy.

Then there were the deaths. They would continue unless she tried to stop them. Could she live with that?

Her shoulders tensed once more. She tilted her head to rest her cheek on her hand and looked about the room.

Rose was standing at the bar.

Emma straightened.

The girl who Douglas and Edward were fixated on, rightly or wrongly.

Now's my chance.

She waited until the girl came from the serving entrance, caught her eye and gestured to the cluttered table. Rose walked over eagerly with eyes that spoke of intrigue, gossip.

"Can I take your dishes ma'am?" she asked politely.

"Yes, thank-you." Emma watched as the girl hooked her fingers through abandoned flagons, picking up the lot in one scoop.

Emma smiled at her, and Rose smiled nervously in return.

"Begging your pardon, ma'am," she ventured. "But your gentlemen friends seemed to make a hasty exit."

"You noticed?" Emma raised an eyebrow.

"It was hard to miss." Rose looked over her shoulder before leaning forward, her voice dark. "Was there any trouble?"

"No. Just a slight...misunderstanding."

"Oh, right." Her face fell, as if she was expecting something more.

Rose started to move away. Emma knew her opportunity was fleeing.

"Is it possible to take a meal in my room?" Her voice sounded rushed, unsure.

"Of course, ma'am," Rose replied. "Is there anything you need?"

"Yes," she replied.

You.

"I don't understand what you mean."

"There is a faint casual line across your travelling line. It tells me you've travelled in the past and that journey was a bad time for you—or you journeyed because of a bad time. That causal line will be gone, soon," Emma said, leaning over the table. Her eyes concentrated on Rose's palm, which was stretched out before her under the dim lamplight. "You're a long way from home."

Rose nodded. "I am. Or I was." She didn't give anything more—she didn't even know why she was here.

Emma's fingers traced along the thin creases of her palm.

"I see...mystery," she continued. "Someone close to you is dark, a shadow across them. Hiding something, perhaps? Or hiding from someone?"

Her eyes rose and looked deep into Rose's.

"No. Not that I know of," Rose said, softly.

She can tell I'm lying.

"I see men." Emma pushed further. "Men reaching out. There is danger for the one surrounded by men."

Rose leaned closer, her eyes searching the skin, but seeing nothing other than the lines and veins and the chapped skin from her work. "What sort of danger?"

"That I cannot see."

Rose hadn't taken the woman seriously at first. When she'd entered the room with the food tray and placed it on the bed, the woman had kept her distance. Like an apparition in the corner, she lingered. That alone unsettled Rose.

The woman had held out the money for the meal in her gloved hand. As Rose reached forward to take it, the woman's hand grasped hers and tilted her wrist.

"You'll have twins," she murmured, studying the creases of skin at the base of Rose's curled fingers.

"Excuse me?" Rose replied.

"You'll have twins. If you have children, that is. They'll be twins." Emma's expression turned a little sad at that.

"How do you—?" Rose started, then realized how stupid the question was. The woman *knew* things, she'd seen her doing it outside the Three Belles for days. Much to the perturbation of other guests and the locals.

"It's written in your hand."

"Oh." Rose didn't know what to say to that, she just stared back at the woman.

"Would you like to have me read your palm?" she'd then asked. "Glimpse your future?"

Rose withdrew her hand from the soft grasp of the other woman. She wiped it on her skirt, cleaning off sweat and kitchen grime.

She'd agreed. Part of her wanted to know, part of her didn't.

And here she was, hearing it all now.

Secrets.

Men.

Emma must have seen her frown.

"It's probably not as bad as all that," she said. "Do you know anyone hiding something? Anyone with a secret?"

Rose's mind clambered for an answer.

Someone hiding a secret.

Her thoughts led her immediately to Athan and Zachary and she felt her forehead prickle with fearful sweat.

What else can she see in my hand?

She had the sudden urge to snatch her hand back, but doing that would give credence to the woman's allusions. Emma would know.

It would break Zachary's confidence, break her promise to him.

The pause between was long and noticeable.

"Ummm..." she stammered. "You, you must mean my friend, Bron..."

"*Who?*" Emma's eyes narrowed.

"Mrs. Belle," Rose continued. "She's a friend of mine who lives on the other side of town. She's a recluse. I take food to her every day."

Rose knew she was talking too fast, but she was trying everything to steer the conversation away from the possible mention of Zachary and Athan.

"I see." The woman didn't sound convinced. "And she is hiding a secret?"

Rose shrugged. "I guess so. I mean, I don't really know. Maybe. I wouldn't know one way or the other really."

"The other side of town?"

"Yes, out by the—outside of town."

"I see." Emma nodded, letting Rose's palm slip from her hands.

Silence again stretched between them.

Emma nodded, staring down at the bed, almost as if she was disappointed. Her curls fell across her face. Lovely burnished curls. Rose thought of her own hair, always up, always tangled or smeared with something from her duties in the hotel.

"I really should be going." Rose stood and backed towards the door.

"Thanks for...everything."

There was no reply.

BEYOND THE SEA OF MEN

The gate opened soundlessly with one push of her hand.

Emma looked at the house in front of her. She paused for a moment as she watched the windows, making sure all the curtains were shut, before she took a step sideways, abandoning the path to walk through the garden, heading for the side of the house.

As quickly as she dared, she approached the windows on the side wall. Light from within seeped from beneath the curtains and into the night. She carefully checked if there were any gaps between them, or to the side, where she could peer through.

There were none.

She stopped and held her breath, listening for any movement from inside, hoping it would give her an idea as to the location of the widow Belle. But there were no sounds either.

She continued along the side of the house, stopping occasionally to listen for sounds, or to check behind her for any movement. She ran her knuckles along the peeling, damp boards until she came to a large stone wall. The wall intersected with the side of the house, halting her progress.

The iron fence was twice her height and covered with ivy. The thick branches made it virtually impossible to see between each of the iron rods.

Emma took a step backwards, eyeing the fence from ground

to sky. She noticed the sharp spikes against the night sky. A chill settled on her shoulders.

I must be careful.

Turning once more to ensure she wasn't being watched, Emma moved left along the wall until she came to a small gate. The wooden lintels bowed with the weight of an ancient ivy plant growing above it. Its many gnarled trunks twisted upwards, along the wall, and up the side of the house to the roof.

The gate was waist high and had a simple iron latch on the left side. Emma placed her hands on the wood and leaned over to peer into the garden.

She saw a sea of men.

They stood at various angles, in various poses and each and every one looked toward the house, up to the windows or where Emma presumed the back door to be. Some were crouching and clothed, others exultant and hunched.

Men everywhere.

Emma took a step back, trying not to breathe. Her heart was beating fast as she sank into the shadow of the ivy-laden gate, tiny leaves tickling her neck.

She waited.

The first thing she noticed was there was no sound. No breathing, no talking, no movement of bodies. Those men closest to her had made no move towards her. They were perfectly still.

Pale skin glowed in the moonlight, dew remained undisturbed on shoulders, cheeks, lips.

Then she finally realised it.

Statues.

The whole garden was filled with statues.

Slowly, Emma crept back to the gate, leaning in further, concentrating on those closest to her.

134

A thin smile curled her lips. She didn't know whether to laugh or kick herself for panicking. She let her breath out with a soft *whoosh*.

She unlatched the gate and slowly opened it. This gate *did* squeak and she froze, waited, her eyes dancing from statue to statue.

Nothing. No movement.

Taking a step forward, she turned to the right. Light shone from the windows along the back wall. The curtains were open and the light spilled down the back stairs, out into the garden and across the faces of the statues nearest the house.

Slowly, she crept forward, concentrating on the window and the room beyond. She tried hard to block out the dozens of men she slipped past to reach the window. Tried to concentrate on the job she had to do, not the deathly white-pupil stares behind her.

They're only statues, she said to herself over and over.

As she reached the window, she squatted down and peered inside, waiting for her eyes to adjust to the light. She didn't know how long she could afford to stay there. The outstretched hands and imposing bodies waited just a few feet behind her.

It was a test of her nerve, her mettle.

She didn't take long to see what she'd come for.

THE DEMONS BEHIND HER FINGERS

January 2, 1889

Foster unlocked the cell door and opened it. Emma took a step forward into the cell and smiled first at the crumpled pile of Douglas on the cot, before sweeping her gaze towards Edward.

He nodded leaning against the back of the cell.

"Morning, gentlemen," Emma said.

"M'sses Godley," Douglas slurred as he rolled over, his bulk making the springs creak.

Edward made no move. He watched her and suddenly saw her as a different woman. She had something now. Confidence, maybe. Something to hold over them. Frankly, he was surprised she was even here, and hadn't run back to that family of hers to hide in the attic like any other sane woman would.

"Do you *want* to stay here?" she asked. "Come on, get up. We don't have all day."

Edward made a concerted effort not to reply. Doug was right. He didn't handle her well.

Douglas sat up on the bed. He nodded as he scratched his hair slowly.

"Right," she said. "Then let's get you out of there and see about a more *equal* partnership, shall we?"

She stood away from the door, giving them ample room to pass through.

Edward left Douglas struggling to climb from the cot and stalked past her with a tight, "Thank you." He couldn't say any more. He was furious, tired and hungry. More than that, he knew she had changed.

That annoyed him more than anything.

"I'm hungry," Edward mumbled as they walked from the gaol. With a flick of his cap and a slight bow, he was off down the street, striding ahead of them towards the Three Belles.

Douglas wavered, unsure whether to follow his friend, or to walk beside her.

Emma's mind was on Rose, on her palm, her lines, her brush with violence in the near future. Rose with blood on her cheek. Everything she'd hidden from the poor girl.

Her entire life was about hiding things from people, but in some cases, it was a blessing.

If Douglas expected a conversation, he was sorely disappointed. They walked without talking.

"Maybe we'll see you later?" he asked as she climbed the stairs in the Three Belles.

She didn't reply.

Once in her room, Emma leaned back in the hard chair by the window. Outside it was overcast and cold; the dead of a mild winter.

She thought about George and Lucy. The way he smiled, the way his moustache curled up at each end as he did so. The sincerity in his eyes and the strength of his hands as they cupped her face.

138

And Lucy, her long hair in plaits, the way she would curl up by the fire to listen to her father read to her before bed each night.

For weeks she'd been travelling away from them. Bloody weeks.

She rested her head in her gloved hands and sighed. Everything else disappeared until all that remained were the demons living behind her fingers; all the thoughts and deeds of the past. Not just in her lifetime, but hundreds of years separating her and the events that mapped out this present.

"Mrs. Godley?"

Emma swept her hands down her face and wiped the misery with them. She smiled at Douglas because she wouldn't give him the satisfaction of letting him see her sorrow. He stood in her doorway, leaning against the jamb. She hadn't bothered to close it. She didn't hear him approach.

"Yes?"

"I just want to say..." he swiftly removed his cap, his stubby fingers drawing at the rim, round and round. "Well, I just wanted to see if you were alright. I mean...after..."

"Edward and his outburst yesterday?" Emma looked at the window.

His reflection was a dark smear in the glass, a man-shape whose white fingers stood out as they fidgeted in front of him. She shuddered and turned to face him. She'd seen enough blurs and shapes lately.

Taking her shawl from her shoulders, Emma laid it on the table and began folding it. It gave her the illusion of nonchalance; it gave Douglas a couple of seconds to think about that question.

He needed those seconds, she figured.

"How are you? I mean, how are you doing?"

She wondered how accustomed Douglas was to talking to

139

women on a personal level. He wore no ring and never spoke of a girl close to his heart. She found herself studying his hands, the creases as his fingers tightened, slipping the cap around in circles.

Round and round, roundroundround.

The hands of a loner.

He probably doesn't even have a sister.

She swallowed, realizing she was identifying with him, feeling for him. She didn't want to. He wasn't her friend nor ever would be.

"I'm fine," she said without conviction.

"Good." He nodded a confirmation or acknowledgement, she didn't know which. "Well, I suppose this will all be over, soon," he added. "For you, at least."

She could tell he didn't mean it like it sounded. It had slipped out.

"Yes," she muttered, her fingers playing with the shawl.

He took two brave steps into the room, as if eager to put them both at ease with his conviviality, but also needing to find out more. "What did you see?"

"I'm not sure."

"I understand," he replied quickly. Another two steps brought him to the table. "It's not easy. It never is. We've never talked about your first time. I was there, remember? Outside. I *know*. I'm here if you want to talk about it. And I'm sorry you have this terrible task."

"Douglas!" Edward's voice snapped from the corridor like a whip. They both flinched.

Douglas looked Emma in the eye for the first time. He sighed and almost smiled at her.

"Coming!" he yelled over his shoulder. Then softly, "He means well. We both do."

Emma was about to smile back, but she stopped herself. She

didn't want him to think she was alright. A few coddling words for the 'little lady' and 'she'd be right.' No. It wasn't alright. They took her from her home and they made her...

She abruptly reached forward and gripped his wrist. The fact that she couldn't feel his skin gave her a sense of detachment; power.

Douglas started like he'd been bitten, tried to pull away, but she held on tight.

"You can *never* possibly understand what it was like. *You* put me there. You and *him!*" she hissed. "You *locked* me in there with that..." She saw the fear in his eyes.

Fear of me? Or all women?

She let him go.

"You can *never* understand," she whispered.

"I know." He took a quick step back to a safe distance, out of reach. "Honestly, believe me, I know. We shouldn't have."

"No." She watched him settle the cap back on his head and turn away, fear still evident in his hasty steps that carried him out and away from her. She wondered if there was now any respect there at all.

George respected her. She knew that for certain; he'd let her go on this journey with only her words to persuade him. Now he was miles away with Lucy. He had no idea where she was or if she would be coming back. Did he weep at night like she did? Was he burying himself in his work?

She'd read the papers. He was right in the thick of it where he was; murder most appalling. Was he glad of her absence—if only to spare her the horror of his work? Would he be surprised when she came home and told him that she could equal his experiences body for body?

Stripping off her gloves, Emma looked hard at her faintly sweated palms. The left, her past, the right, her future; water hand like all her family. Concentrating, she tried to make sense of her own path.

But it didn't work that way.

Never had.

She turned back to look out the window into the street. Life continued for those on the other side. They went about their business without knowing, without even caring. Their lives were normal.

She'd forgotten normal.

What would George think of her?

So many weeks had passed since she had left. How could she ever relate to him how she felt, the terrors she had seen?

Did she even have to? He'd seen his own share.

She knew, given time, the memories would fade; the horror would dim. But on evenings like this, when she closed her eyes, she saw it all again.

The girl. The blood...

The start of it all.

"Give you a pound if you can hit that barrel," Edward smirked.

"You're on," Douglas replied.

They stood at the darkest point between two lamps, looking at the pile of rubbish illuminated near the ally junction. Douglas bent over, picked up a stone and lined up, testing his arm before throwing it at a large tin barrel on the other side of the court. The stone hit the rusted rim and clattered into the interior with a loud *clang*. It echoed for a few moments.

It brought them back to reality; the reason why they were here. It also brought the rumble of windows opening, and mumbles from the dark silhouettes of slumbering citizens at each and every window that faced out on the narrow lane.

Edward looked up and immediately the shutters around them closed, the curtains drew, the windows slammed shut. They were alone once more.

"Nosy parkers and paper-thin walls," Douglas said.

They continued walking down the lane, Douglas running a gloved hand along the brick work and crumbling mortar. The red bricks were wet, as were the cobbles beneath their boots. The gas lights hissed and sputtered as occasional drops of water leaked into the fractured glass cases.

Edward watched and walked slightly behind, mindful of where he placed his boots. He didn't want to fall, not out here with the detritus of society littering the streets; all their pins and tins, broken blades and laces of half-minds and half pennies.

He didn't want to touch any of it.

You could pick up anything.

Then he realized Douglas had said something. "What?" he asked.

Douglas sighed. "The walls around here. With the apartments so close, they'd be paper-thin, wouldn't they?"

"The walls?"

"Yes, the *walls*. Of the apartments." He swept his hand impatiently left to right.

"I suppose," Edward replied. "I've never lived in one."

"Me neither. And I wouldn't want to. Give me clean country air any day."

Douglas stopped his exploration of the wall and joined Edward in the middle of the lane. He angled his head to stare above them, at the windows on the second storeys.

"No one heard her scream," he murmured.

"Figures," Edward replied. "People will run to the window for a loud bang, but not for a struggle." Was there a struggle? Or was it quick? He hoped it was quick.

No reply from Douglas. The cold night air settled around them.

Douglas spun around on his heel and stared past Edward. "She coming?" he asked, walking backwards. His eyes were hidden in the shadow cast by his bowler, but Edward knew he was squinting in the darkness, trying to see.

Bad eyes.

Edward craned his neck to follow his gaze; not squinting, not peering, just searching the darkness for any sign of movement.

There.

144

"Yes, she's coming," he replied.

Douglas nodded, turned and resumed walking forwards. With a few more steps, they were outside the door to the last flat in the row.

Four children ran past them, almost tripping, bumping into them then giving the silhouette of Emma a wide berth.

"Bit late for you to be about!" Edward yelled, checking his pocket-watch once they'd gone.

"You ever think about it?" Douglas asked, ignoring his companion's outburst.

"What?" Edward replied as he stopped by Douglas' shoulder. It was quiet here. The flat looked like every other in the row, but Edward got a sick feeling just looking at the walls.

"What she does. What they do."

"What do you mean? You know I don't." Edward knew exactly what he meant, but he was giving Douglas a chance to end the conversation.

Douglas didn't. "About what she does...in there."

"I try not to," Edward replied. "I'm more concerned about her coming *out* of there. Either we move on to the next one, or..."

Douglas nodded, feeling depressed. "Yeah, I know." Then his eyes lit up. "Head-shot you think? Be quicker."

"Nah," Edward shook his head. "Knees or nothin' mate. We don't want her dead."

"Painful, though. Loud."

"For her, yeah, but not for us. In fact, it's better for us, yeah?" Edward waited for his companion to nod, then he turned back and placed a hand on the old, tattered wooden doorway, his foot on the second of two concrete steps. "We'd better check it, make sure it's clear for her."

"Check for what? We're too late. There's no helping this one, not this time."

"That's not the point," Edward reached down to the handle and grasped it tight. Then he paused, released his grip and took a step backwards. He looked at Douglas expectantly.

"Flip you for it?" Douglas asked. He tried to smile, but it broke half-way.

Edward snorted a cloud of icy breath. "With *what*, genius? We're on the job. Besides, I went last time, so it's your turn."

"All right, all right," Douglas said, his tone taking on that of a begrudging child.

Edward stepped back further, giving Douglas enough room to approach the door. "Locked," he said as the handle refused to budge.

Edward smiled. "Your problem, mate. Not mine."

But Douglas turned his head slightly. He pointed at the window by the door and winked at Edward.

"Some of the glass is broke," he said. He kicked away a small rotting crate that was lying directly under the window and leaned over, reaching a hand in through the glass. He stretched a bit further, his breath fogging the unbroken glass pane in front of his face. After a few seconds, the door opened with a click.

"See? Not so hard."

Slowly, he drew his arm back through the window and stepped inside the room.

Edward plunged his hands into his pockets and rocked on his heels, waiting and listening to the night. The sky broiled above with dark clouds; storms ready to burst. The distant bark of a dog. The low whistle of a steamer. It was quite pleasant. For some.

He leaned back a little to look further down the alley.

There she is. Come on, luv.

"Oh, no, oh my giddy Aunt!"

Edward instinctively took a step forward as Douglas

charged out of the doorway, pale and shaking. His fingers dug feverishly under his silk necktie, tugging it loose in fast, brutal movements.

"Struth!" He gasped in the cold night air, his eyes wide and darting.

Edward moved quickly to his companion's side. He placed an arm around him giving his shoulder a firm squeeze. He'd never seen Douglas like this.

"Calm yourself, Doug," he whispered. "She's coming. We can't afford to scare her, now."

He led him away from the apartment to the largest patch of light he could find.

Douglas finally ripped the tie free and flung it to the wet ground. He looked at Edward, his eyes incredulous, shocked. "*Scare* her? She's—"

"Keep your voice down," Edward continued, keeping his voice low and leaning Douglas up against the lamp post. "This has to be done."

The level, calm voice was enough to snap Douglas out of his panic, at least for a few seconds.

"Yeah, yeah, alright." Douglas nodded as he bent over, placing his hands on his knees, sucking breath deep into his lungs like he couldn't get enough. A thin stream of saliva fell from his lower lip and pooled on the cobbled ground. One shaking hand reached up to remove the bowler hat.

Edward left him there, leaning and dry-retching, walked over to the room and quickly peered inside through the still-open door. His nose adjusted quicker than his eyes and he switched to breathing through his mouth.

Burning. Bad eggs, wet fur.

The smell was almost intolerable, and the heat from inside wafted out, coating him with its oily, hot fingers.

He steeled himself and took a single step inside, careful not to touch the door jamb or the door itself.

What he saw made his hands sweat, his stomach tighten, his balls clench. He swallowed; a quick, dry movement, fighting the urge to vomit.

Sweet Christ.

He genuflected, whispered a perfunctory prayer and stepped quickly back, glad he had the ability to keep his reactions in check. Always had. It made him good for this type of work.

Knowing he had little time left, he pulled the door shut with one finger, making sure the lock didn't catch, but that the door held its position.

He walked back to Douglas whose breathing had not calmed, not even a bit.

"Right, Doug," he said in a softer voice this time. "Sit down. It's her turn."

Another nod. Douglas lifted his head. His eyes were red as they searched Edward's face, then they shifted focus to somewhere behind Edward's shoulder.

Edward turned and watched her approach, all skirts and shawls.

She cut a dainty figure under the lamplight; young, but wise. The shadows grew longer across her face as she walked through the light.

Edward nodded as she walked up, her gloved hands tightly clasped in front of her. She looked pretty enough to go to Sunday Mass. Her footsteps were delicate and careful on the rough-hewn stones. The boots hardly made a sound.

He watched her hesitate as she saw Douglas spitting lightly onto the wet stones, still clearing his throat, still struggling to breathe.

Edward saw fear in her eyes.

"Hope you didn't have a big tea," he said.

She shook her head, her eyes darting back to his. Her jaw clenched, but she said nothing.

"In you go, then." He nodded towards the doorway.

Emma glanced down once more at Douglas before she turned and walked to the door. Edward watched her go; she felt his eyes at her back.

Two concrete steps abutted the door which was open only a crack. She pushed it open with the toe of her boot while digging into her purse for a taper candle and matches. The door swung wide, creating a black hole that terrified her more than anything in her nightmares, her waking visions.

The first thing that hit her was the smell; a waft of hot air that swept her as the door swung in, pushing the air out. Meat. Burned meat. Wet meat. Hair.

Emma took two more tiny steps and stopped in the doorway. A soft, but deliberate cough came from behind her.

Not a threat. Not yet.

She stepped inside.

The cool air from outside dispelled some of the heat, but the air was thick and solid. Her eyes took a long time to adjust. The light from outside was bright enough, for the moment, but she lit a candle and knelt to set it on the floor. The more light, the better.

She held the match flame to the candle's end until the wax pooled and dripped onto the floor. Setting the base in place, she held it firm until the wax set and turned white. The match twisted black in her fingers and died.

She took a breath, stood and looked around the room.

The floor was clear, except for dark smears. The walls were bare except for...

The blood.

And on the bed was a thing.

It lay supine, coiled like it would spring from its bloody mattress and attack. She stared at it, trying to discern features, trying to comprehend what her eyes were showing her. Bits. Bits that didn't seem to go together.

Her breath slowed. She blinked rapidly.

Then the door shut behind her, almost silent except for the *snick* of the latch.

Locked. They'd shut her in with the thing on the bed.

Panic hit her; pure and sharp. Emma's eyes filled with tears of terror, which fell down her face, dripped from her chin onto her lace bodice. She retreated until her back touched the door.

With trembling fingers, she groped for the handle behind her and flinched as her hand touched the wood. She turned and pressed her forehead against the cool surface, trying not to vomit, trying not to faint. Her body shuddered with tremors that hurt her muscles; that would hurt them for days to come.

Her tears blurred the wood grain and she wondered if the thing on the bed had stood, was shuffling over, was *behind* her.

I have to get out!

She needed to go home. She needed to feel safe. She needed to be held and she needed to scream in terror.

But she'd already been warned about making any noise.

She gave the doorknob a quick turn. It moved for a moment, then twisted back against her fingers. She tried again, her gloved hands slipping against it. It didn't move at all this time. Her wrists ached with trying and she cried against the solid surface of the door, deep and painful sobs that threatened to cripple.

"Let me out," she whispered, wanting to scream it, but scared of what would happen if she did.

"*Please* let me out."

"She's brave, I'll give her that," Edward said as he turned to look at Douglas.

Douglas was on his knees now, wiping the bile from his lips, breathing hard and not concentrating on what was happening. "Braver than us."

Edward turned back to face the doorway, his head tilting to make sure no one was watching them from the windows above or to the side. He took a slow step forward, his body leaning forward, trying to hear anything that was happening on the other side of the door.

But the night was quiet. There was no indication. He took another step, then one more.

He reached out and touched the door's rotting, peeling paint and flicked a piece off with his fingernail.

"Don't go *in* there!" The warning came from behind him.

He turned around to see Douglas slowly walking towards him, his hands outstretched.

"Don't worry, Doug," he replied calmly. "I have no intention of doing anything of the sort."

"Good," Douglas replied, nodding, leaning against the alleyway wall. "You don't want to be in there."

"Agreed." Edward smiled as he leaned his back against the door, his right hand grasping the doorknob behind him, and holding it tight. Sure enough, not long after, it twisted once in his hand. He couldn't fault her for that.

"Why doesn't she try to get out?" Douglas asked. His breathing had calmed, his eyes were clearing from his tears.

151

"She's got a job to do. We'll let her do it. Besides," he smiled tightly, "she's trying."

He could hear her, faintly on the other side. Her cries, her whimpers, the soft battering of her fists against the door. Her impotent distress.

He fisted the doorhandle tighter, just in case. People became strong and unpredictable when they were scared.

"How can you be so bloody cold?" Douglas could hear her now, banging the surface, her cries muffled, restrained. He looked ill. "You saw it. I couldn't handle it, either. It's her first. Let her out, mate."

"I'm *not* cold. This is the job and she stays in there until she's done it."

Douglas nodded, miserable, but collecting himself quickly.

Edward continued. "If you get too close to them, you'll just cause yourself grief. She knows. *You* know. I'll do it. You don't have to."

"And if we don't?"

"Then more will die. People like her." He gestured at the door with his head.

"How will we know?"

"Oh, we'll know." Edward was confident about that. He knew their eyes, now. He could spot a lie like blood on white. He'd seen a lot of both. Snow, sheets, walls...

"She'll just *tell* us?"

"Hardly. Would you?" He couldn't—wouldn't—blame them for that.

"Then how?"

"We'll just know, that's all. I'll know."

"And we just do it?"

"Yes."

"There and then?"

"Yep."

"Just like that?"

"Doug, *Jesus.* You have to do this *every* time? You don't even know her."

"I know. Don't blaspheme. I just wondered."

"No time for wonder. Not here in this place. Anything could happen. She could turn on us."

"Really?"

"Wouldn't you?" Edward felt the handle under his fingers finally stop turning. She'd accepted it, at least.

"I guess, yeah."

Emma stopped crying. They wouldn't let her out and she was starting to get light-headed. Her breath hitched a few times and she reached up to wipe her face clear of tears.

Behind her was carnage. Slaughter. Fresh and still dripping from the walls, but not the door. The door was clean and she continued to lean into its comforting solidity.

She thought of her home; her husband and her daughter. She felt oddly relieved that they would never see this; that this would never be a part of their world.

Taking a few deep breaths through her mouth, she turned and faced the room.

I must do this...

She took two steps toward the...body, being careful not to block out the light of the candle. She wanted to see, now. See everything she could. Touch it.

And get out.

Two more steps and she stood next to the side table, the splatters of blood across its surface blending in with the dark whorls of the wood. The lumps of flesh were unidentifiable without the context of a body and she wasn't ready to look at that. Not yet.

Two books stabilized the pronounced lean of the table. Their normality was a good place to start and she bent down to examine them.

As she did, her hip nudged the edge. The table wobbled, tilted and she made a grab with her right hand, steadying it.

Letting out a relieved breath, she knelt, gathering her skirts so they wouldn't touch the floor. The books were unread, their spines free of creases. The table leg had sunk a little way into the cover of the topmost book, leaving a deep mark.

Flecks of blood on the same cover drew her gaze to the floor. She sniffed, wiped her running nose.

Prints.

She looked closer.

Shoe prints on the wood, in the blood.

Not mine.

They were quite small, messy and numerous. A child's prints. Maybe two of them. She could see no other evidence of children living in this room.

Emma wiped her nose again, surprised at the detail she was taking in. Her breath was still watery in her throat from crying, but her hands were steady as she hovered a gloved palm over one of the prints. It barely reached her index finger.

Bigger than her daughter's. Older children. Eleven? Twelve years old?

The prints led to the door and she wondered why they hadn't seen the trail of blood leading out to the alley.

She stood and looked out the broken triangle of window. Outside, the cobbles were wet. She remembered the walk here. The rain would have washed any footprints away.

But why were they in here?

Emma looked around the room in earnest, now having something else to look for.

154

The bed was the only thing she did not look at. Instead, she scanned the interior. She saw the blood first, the disarray second; then the voids. Objects missing. Her brain filled in the blanks according to the room itself. Not expensive. Sparsely furnished. No children.

A ring of blood, the size of a candle-holder...or where a candle-holder used to sit. A pair of shoes near the fireplace... A box open on the mantle, its contents strewn. Buttons and pins were all that were left. Anything else was gone, the street kids taking what they could.

A knife, maybe?

Her fingers dug into the flesh of her arms as she steeled herself to peer at the near-shapeless form on the bed.

It was not a thing, but a person. A woman. All liquid and lumps.

As she took a step closer, her foot slipped suddenly, forcing her to stand still, arms slightly outstretched. Balanced. The adrenalin flooded briefly, a sharp tang in her stomach, along the back of her jaw.

One more step and she was leaning over as far as she dared, holding the tips of her shawl out of the way of the butchery.

Her brain made the picture of the woman, because her eyes could not. She lay on her back, her arms limp by her sides, her legs slightly apart, her head resting against the iron bed-head.

Most apparent to Emma, however, was the amount of blood near the legs and in between. The damage, there. Like an aborted birth with no foetus.

When Emma's daughter was born, she'd been terrified something would go wrong down there. She couldn't see, she could only feel. She could only read the progress by looking at the midwife's eyes. And it hurt so much she thought something *had* gone wrong.

But it was wonderful afterwards. All pain forgotten. Torn skin repaired. Her husband had been waiting outside for the news, or to rush in if she called for him. Knowing that got her through it all.

Not for this woman. No repaired skin. No husband. No child. She'd died all-alone in here with a knife and a killer.

The knife. Look for the knife.

Emma wiped her eyes once more and looked carefully, trying not to see the woman under the offal.

Was a knife used? Yes.

The skin was ripped in places, cut in others. Definitely a knife.

But careful inspection of the room revealed no knife.

The children have it.

Emma slipped off her left glove and removed the gold wedding ring from her finger. She kissed it and held it tight in her right hand.

She ran her fingers along the warm bed-head. It was a simple design; wrought iron and cheap welds.

She smoothed her hand along the iron trim of the side table, avoiding the flesh that hung over the edge. At the fireplace, she touched the pokers, the tattered horse-brass, and the grate, moving quickly as they were still warm.

A single spoon under the wooden cupboard revealed nothing. Her forehead beaded with sweat.

Nothing at all.

She started to laugh, then cry in relief.

Gone.

She was almost finished here.

Lastly, she went to the woman on the bed. She lifted the woman's right hand, so clean on top, despite the blood. She turned it over and looked at the palm.

The lines were streaked with blood, as she expected. She

read quietly, the fate lines, the heart, the forks and the girdles. Then she closed her eyes.

The images came to her like never before.

Flashes, smells, feelings. She saw dogs laughing in a row, heard money falling. There was the smell of paraffin and phosphorous and a gradual spill of light. Casuarina trees in a line leading to a creek. A name called by a woman. "Sacha?"

Emma flinched. It was like the cry had come from inside the room.

Dishes, ironing, a sharp cut. Blood. Someone falling.

Then the sudden report. Like a spike through her head, right to left.

She dropped the hand. It lay limp on the cover, before sliding off, swaying a couple of times before hanging at rest.

Her heart galloped beneath her tight bodice. She wiped her hands on her skirt over and over, but knew only water and salt would remove the stain.

She held tight to the images she'd seen, tried to remember them perfectly.

They'll ask.

It seemed an awfully long way away.

A large part of her didn't want to tell them. She wanted to say she found nothing, saw nothing, so she could simply go home. Home was safe. Home was clean.

But they had guns. If she lied...

Better to start out now and get it over with.

The job was complete. She had no reason to stay in this place any longer. Emma was about to leave when, on impulse, she reached across the body and lifted the left hand, the hand of destiny.

"You done yet? Come on, we need to get out of here!" Edward's voice came from outside. She ignored him.

Curling the slack and ruined fingers into a fist, she squinted

at the creases below the Mercury finger.

"Two," she whispered. Then louder, leaning closer, "You would have had two beautiful children, sweetheart." She laid the hand gently back on the bed, lifted the other and put them together.

She straightened walked those five precious steps to the door. She slipped on her wedding ring, kissed it again and drew her glove over the top.

She knocked, a rapid pattern, soft, but insistent. The door handle clicked as it was released and the cool night air rushed over her, cleansing her skin. Emma almost grinned at the sensation.

"We're too late," she whispered. "The killer is gone."

Edward stepped up—right up—until she was forced to either go back into the room or stand her ground. She stood firm, smelling his warm rosemary-scented breath.

He stared at her and she lowered her eyes under his scrutiny.

"You know where we need to go?" he asked. His fingers came under her chin and forced her head up before she answered.

"I think so."

He held her gaze for what seemed like minutes then nodded, apparently satisfied with the answer. "Good," he said, dropping his hand. "Let's get out of here before *we* get arrested. That is the last thing we'd need."

No Appetite

"I threw up. Remember?"

"I was there, I *know this already.*" Edward rolled a piece of bacon in on itself. His fingers danced over the surface to avoid burning. The bacon was fresh from the pan—not crispy—just how he liked it. Douglas knew the man's habits better than he knew his own sometimes.

Douglas sank down into his chair, his hands deep in his pockets. Right now, he couldn't even remember if he liked bacon. The sight of it, coupled with the current subject of conversation, was making him sick.

He felt ill just thinking of the butchered woman in that room.

Truth be told, he'd felt ill since it happened.

Edward blew air on the tips of his fingers, cooling the skin.

Douglas tried again.

"That's almost two months ago now and I still have night-mares about what we saw."

"So?"

"Do I really have to explain this to you?" Douglas asked.

"Yes, yes I suppose you do," Edward replied. He looked at Douglas from across the small table and raised a thin eye-brow. Douglas couldn't read his expression.

"I'm just saying, Ed, she was— We *trapped* her in there! Man alive..." He ran his hands through his hair and laced his fingers behind his head. "I still don't believe we did that." He was going to say '*you did that,*' but thought twice.

"She woulda run. You *know* she woulda run." Edward looked back at his plate, then added, "*You* did."

Douglas felt like he'd been punched in the gut.

"Yes. I did." His voice was quiet.

Edward didn't seem to hear him, instead he pointed to his last remaining strips of bacon. "This is good nosh."

"She's still unsteady, still head-shy." Douglas figured that if he referred to her like a good horse, Edward could relate.

"It's not from the Three Belles though, it's from the restaurant across the street," Edward continued, picking up his roll of dripping meat.

"I think she has a fair point. You know, about her part in this."

"Bacon. Lovely." Edward pushed the rolled rasher into his mouth with his sturdy fingers, sucked it in. Fat glistened on his chin.

Douglas never wanted to eat again. He leaned forward, looking at the table and not Edward's plate. Edward's eyes, his shoulder, anywhere but the plate.

"Edward, listen to me."

"We've been through all this, Doug, my lad." Edward licked his fingers, one by one. "All I want to know is, did you sort her out?"

"Did I...?"

Sort her out? Mercy.

"I should've ordered more of this."

"We took her away from her family, shoved her in that room, then dragged her all the way to here... She has good reason to be upset, is all I'm saying."

"*Upset?*" Edward's voice rose slightly, the only sign that the man was seething inside. Douglas knew he was.

"Yes!"

"You're not serious," Edward continued. "Who spent the whole night in the clink? *Who?* If anyone's got the right to be bloody upset it's *us*."

At least I got a reaction.

"We *need* her," Douglas replied.

"I know that. But from her behaviour last night...can we trust her?"

"More than you," Douglas murmured. At Edward's puzzled look, he said, louder, "Of course we can trust her. She could have left us."

"Maybe she should have." Edward paused, his stare turning ugly as his mouth curled. "I'm thinking of cutting her loose."

Douglas' mouth dropped as Edward pushed his plate to the middle of the small table and stained the linen napkin with his saliva-coated fingers. He wiped his lips and sat back, one arm draped over the back of his chair.

Douglas took a breath before speaking. "You *don't* mean that."

"No one will ever know."

"Don't be *stupid*. What about her family? Her husband, the *copper?*" He tried to stare the other man down and call his bluff. "You wouldn't."

"It's not stupid, it's sensible. She can't handle it. She can't be trusted. She's a bloody loose cannon!"

There was something in Edward's voice that confused Douglas. He couldn't believe Edward capable of cold-blooded murder. He'd seen him kill in self defence before, but this was different.

He wouldn't kill. So where is this going?

Douglas leaned back too. He wanted some distance while he tried another tack.

"Isn't that exactly what we need, a loose cannon? She's not

you or me, Edward. She's not a hired gun, she's *her*. She's *them*."

"Oh, *very* nice."

"You know what I mean. She can do what we can't."

"She's not the only one, though." Edward smiled. "I'll fix her little white frock."

"You *can't* kill her."

"I know." Edward stared hard at Douglas, then laughed and slapped the table hard with his open palm. "Wasn't planning on it, you *know* that. Just working through my anger. Lighten up, old boy. What *must* you think of me?"

He stood and stretched his arms above his head, the cartilage in his right shoulder crackling as always, sounding like nuts in a bowl.

"That was terrific bacon. I'm going to get some more. Want some?"

"No appetite," Douglas whispered.

Edward snorted. "Didn't think so."

She's in Good Hands

"**Z**ach, slow down."

They walked through the field on the edge of town, their heads bowed, shielding their faces from the bitter wind.

Athan pulled the heads off the long stalks of grass as they walked through them, while Zachary allowed them to brush lightly against his arms and hands.

Work had finished for the day, and they were glad of it.

It felt good to be working, to be doing something that kept their minds busy. Athan didn't want to think about the past; what he'd left behind.

Working in the fields past the edge of town also afforded them the privacy they needed. There were too many people in town during the day, too many strangers.

Too many eyes.

Fixing fences and moving stones at least meant they could hide away. Blend into the background. Be themselves.

He knew it wouldn't replace running. Running to make sure they were never caught. The longer they stayed here, the more chance they had of being found out.

He also knew Zachary wouldn't run. He knew that Zachary, at least for now, was more than content to stay where they were.

Athan was biding his time, waiting for the right moment to

have the argument he knew was coming.

He kept waiting, but the right moment hadn't yet appeared.

The longer it took, the more restless he became; the more nervous.

He lifted his head a little, gauging the time by the pale streak of light on the horizon.

About four.

"I could murder a beer," Zachary mumbled as they walked along.

Athan let the comment slide, choosing not to mention the bad choice of words.

As they approached the stone wall surrounding the field, Athan pulled a tin of cigarettes from his trouser pocket. He took one out and clamped his lips over it, all the while his eyes were scanning up and down the muddy road on the other side of the wall.

No one was in sight, but that didn't stop his uneasy feeling.

"I don't wanna do this," he said, lighting the smoke with a match from a new box. Took him five tries and Zachary's hands shielding the flame against the wind.

"You always say that," Zachary replied.

"And I always mean it." A deep inhalation, a brief cloud of grey smoke.

"They're just people."

"I know. And they're dangerous."

Wearily, they climbed over the wall and headed down the road back to town.

"How much longer do you think it will take?" Zachary asked as they walked.

"Will what take?" Athan replied.

"'Til the work runs out. Until there's nothing more here that we can do."

Athan raised a surprised eyebrow. "Not long. We can only

164

do so much. There's only so much that needs doing."

Zachary nodded. "A few weeks at the most," he said, almost to himself.

"Exactly."

"Probably even less."

"I would think so," Athan replied, dragging on the cigarette. He didn't want to push the conversation, not if he could help it. The last few days he'd hoped Zachary would come to the same conclusion he had done. It was too dangerous here, and they had to move on.

But there was a problem.

Rose.

It was plain to see; the way they acted together, the way they looked at each other.

It complicated things.

They walked further on, nearing the town. Soon they would be seen by those people gathering in the street, and they'd enter the danger zone as far as Athan was concerned.

They had no idea who would be looking at them, who would be watching out for two suspicious and nervous men. Two *killers.*

Just like the newspapers said.

So far, they'd been lucky; too lucky. Their luck wouldn't—couldn't—hold out forever.

We should never have stopped here. We should've kept running.

It was the one thing neither of them would talk about. Athan was sure that if it was playing on his mind, and had been for weeks, then it must've been playing on Zachary's as well.

Both men chose not to broach the subject, but Athan's patience was wearing thin.

They walked in silence, both staring towards the town. Athan dragged on his cigarette until it was almost gone, be-

fore flinging it to the mud.

More people than usual. A crowd.

Dozens of people were spilling out onto the street; some running, some shouting. Others were pushing their way through, trying to see the commotion.

"What the hell?" Athan asked.

They walked on down the main street and towards the middle of the town and the sudden swell of people.

"Something's happened," Zachary replied.

"What if it's us?"

What if someone had drawn a conclusion or two?

A posse? A lynch-mob?

This is it.

His muscles tensed as his eyes scanned the crowd for any sign of trouble directed towards them.

"We have to go," he said, his hand reaching out and touching Zachary's shoulder.

Zachary shrugged it off. "I can't," he replied. "That crowd's outside the Three Belles."

"So?"

"*So?* Rose's in there!"

"I'm sure she's fine." Athan turned to Zachary, but there was fear and worry etched into the face of his friend.

"I have to know."

"Don't go barging in there, Zach. You don't know what might be—"

"I have to."

Before Athan could stop him, Zachary had dropped his tools and was sprinting towards the throng.

Damn it.

Athan had no choice. He dropped his own tools and ran after him.

The scene outside the Three Belles was chaotic. People

pressed tight, trying to look through the windows, while others ran from the doorway. There were sounds of raised voices inside, men yelling, women screaming.

As they reached the crowd and started to push their way through, a tankard of ale crashed through the window to the left of the door, shattering it and spraying those close by with slivers of glass and droplets of beer.

Athan turned away quickly, making sure none of the glass fell on or near his face, but Zachary pushed on, bouncing through the crowd like he would wade through a flooding river.

"Zach!" Athan called to him, but he knew he couldn't be heard over the noise of the crowd. Zachary pushed forward more, his hands quickly grabbing at those people in front of him, pushing and pulling them roughly to the side.

"Let me through!"

Athan heard the voice and at first thought it was Zachary's. But it came from another direction, off to his right, and he turned to look that way.

His gaze met Sawyer's.

It was like the rest of the world dissolved around them as they stared at each other, almost as if the town, the Three Belles, the melee didn't exist.

The same thought ran through both their minds.

You...

And then the crowd surged backwards—elbows and fists and hands—taking Sawyer and Athan with them, forcing them to break the stare just so they could stay on their feet.

As Athan turned back to look at Zachary, he could see his friend struggle to the front door of the Three Belles and force himself inside. It took all of Athan's remaining strength to fight his way through the deafening mass of crowd and make it to the front door as well.

Sawyer arrived at the very same moment.

"What in bloody hell's going on?" Sawyer yelled in his ear.

"I have *no* idea," Athan replied. "But I can guess."

They pushed the doors open and struggled inside.

The bar was a mess.

Gone was the well kept and well ordered bar they were used to. Broken tables and people were strewn throughout the main bar, brawls of fists and kicks and head-buts spilled into the meals area and towards the kitchen. The noise in here, of shouting and yells and breaking glass and screaming women, was even louder than outside.

The main group of men fought in the middle of the bar, while onlookers formed a rough circle around them, shouting them on, pushing those back into the fray who tried desperately to escape. It looked like a crude boxing ring, a slip-shod staging of an informal brawl predictably between the miners and the rail workers, with broken glasses and bottles used instead of fists. Tables were overturned and chairs were scattered everywhere, some broken and some used as weapons. Lamps swung over the bar, the gas pipes straining and bending as the flames sputtered, but held. The large mirror at the bar had been shattered in two places, heavy shards reflecting the scene in a twisted mirror-image.

"My lord," Sawyer said as they both surveyed the damage. "Where's Rose?"

Athan scanned the bar quickly as they both continued to push through the crowd, wary of any stray fists or tankards.

He couldn't see Rose by the bar, and he certainly couldn't see her anywhere near the main group of fighters.

There was a loud crash at the front doors as they were pushed inward violently. Loud piercing whistles began to blow and Athan turned to see a group of local police push their way into the bar, batons held high, ready to quell the fracas.

"Oh, dear God," Sawyer said.

Athan turned and followed Sawyer's pointing finger over to the far corner of the bar.

Rose lay on her side, half-propped against the wall. Her dress ruffled up around her knees and her collar loose around her neck. Blood was flowing from her temple, and she held her left arm in her right hand.

She was crying.

Zachary was by her side, kneeling down next to her and talking to her softly, trying to soothe her. He had one hand placed softly on her shoulder, while the other was down lower, holding her elbow.

She looked up at Zachary, tears streaking her cheeks, then she nodded, complete trust in her face.

Zachary kept talking, dodging a knee from a staggering patron. He helped her stand and slowly guided her down the side of the bar and away from the fight ring that was now being dissolved by the batons of the constabulary.

Neither looked at the crowd or the fight as they headed towards the back of the bar.

Sawyer took a couple of quick steps, but then stopped, as if he wasn't sure of what to do. His eyes looked wild, and he licked at his top lip.

When Zachary and Rose disappeared out the door to the kitchen, Athan stepped up next to Sawyer and lightly nudged him on the shoulder.

"We don't want to get caught up in all this," he said. "Don't worry, she's in good hands."

It was meant to put Sawyer's mind at ease.

It didn't.

HEIGHT IS AN ILLUSION

"I think this is the last of it," Sawyer said as he carried the broken chair legs to the pile of wreckage by the door.

The hour was late now, and the crowd had dispersed. The fights and brawling had concluded as soon as the local police had arrived on the scene. Those drunkards who escaped the police had stumbled on home, leaving a wake of destruction behind.

Athan leaned on the broom and swept the last remaining pottery shards into the far corner.

"The rest can wait until morning," Sawyer added.

"Will they be able to open again tomorrow?" Athan asked, turning to face him.

Sawyer shrugged. "I have no idea. It depends on when the bar can re-open."

Athan nodded as the conversation stopped.

He didn't want to talk to Sawyer. He didn't like the man. But both of them wanted to help Rose out. Both wanted to ease her pain.

And both wondered what had really happened.

Is she alright?

Is Zach?

Neither of them had reappeared, and Athan was starting to worry about where they had fled to. But he also didn't want to go blundering in and find them in...

In what?

...in a possible situation.

So Sawyer and Athan were left alone to remove and clean away as much of the stains and debris as possible.

It had taken them a while, but they had done a fine job in Athan's eyes.

"I guess that's about it," he said.

Sawyer nodded. He inspected a piece of chair leg with a look of exasperation and shook his head. Athan recalled he was some kind of carpenter. It would probably be his job to fix most of this.

Well, that will keep you busy.

The continuing silence became awkward.

Athan lay the broom down on the bar.

"It's getting late."

"Yes." Sawyer's grimace was unsettling. He sat down.

Quiet again.

"I best be going to bed." Athan pointed over his shoulder, towards the stairs that led to the rooms. He turned around to leave.

"Athan!" Sawyer said the name like a command. He took a quick step forward and Athan saw the man's hand reaching out towards him before pulling back.

Athan faced him, but didn't say a word.

Sawyer's smile looked nervous and worried.

"I was...surprised," he managed.

"Surprised?"

"To find you here today. At the pub, I mean."

"Where did you think we'd be?" Athan asked.

"No, I mean, I was surprised that...ah..." Sawyer's eyes looked around the bar, as if he expected someone else was listening.

"Go on," Athan said slowly.

"You and Zachary. Still here. In town."

"I see."

Silence.

"I thought you— I thought you would be gone."

"I thought you *had* gone," Athan replied.

"I just got back. Came into town and saw the brawl happening. I didn't really know what to do."

Athan nodded, remembering their situations were similar. Remembering the talk he'd been having with Zachary before they walked into the main street, and how he wanted to discuss moving on.

"Why would you think we'd be gone?" he asked.

Sawyer took a step backwards. "No reason. I just thought—"

"We're not going anywhere, not with Zach's eyes firmly fixed on young Rose," Athan added and watched for Sawyer's reaction.

The man stared back at him, blinking quickly, as if trying to wipe Athan or his comment from his mind.

"Rose," he whispered.

"I think you've lost your lady, there," Athan continued, pushing the man for more reaction.

"She's not my lady." Sawyer turned to the bar, busily fixing nothing.

"*Right.*" Athan couldn't help but smile. "I've seen the way you look at her."

He lost his heart long before we arrived...

"I don't look at her in *any* way. And I *don't* stare at women. And I wouldn't be too quick to pass judgement, if I were you, Athan."

"And why is that?" Athan folded his arms and walked to stand at the bar next to Sawyer. He was taller, and it felt good to be standing over him, proving his point and winning the argument.

The man swung around, looked up and stared straight back at him, his lips curled.

"Well, if I've lost my lady, then *you've* just lost your best friend and your only ally in this town."

Athan's smile slipped from his face.

He didn't feel quite so tall, now.

THIS WOMAN, THIS BLOOD

"In here, that's it." Zachary guided Rose to the back of the kitchen. The noise outside, the crashes and shouts, were muffled as the heavy door swung shut behind them.

He led her to the back corner of the large and cluttered kitchen, where the chairs were stacked for the cooks. He spun one chair around to rest near the wooden bench and eased her onto it. He grabbed a chair for himself and dragged it over as she wiped her wet cheeks with her right hand.

A silver tray with three covered bowls sat a little way down the bench, steam issuing from under the metal lids.

Bronwyn's meal.

Rose must've been ready to take it to her when the fighting started.

"Let's have a look," he said, placing his fingers under her chin and lifting her head, tilting it toward the single ceiling lamp at this end of the kitchen.

The blood had run down into her hair on the left side in a thin stream. It wasn't as bad as he'd thought when he first saw her lying there on the floor of the bar. He'd been panicking then.

He felt a sick pressure at the back of his throat as he examined the wound; a wave of horror that had nothing to do with this woman or this blood. He blinked several times, trying to take the sudden blur away from his eyes, to focus on the present. On her and only her.

Rose's face swam into view. Steeling himself, he carefully probed the skin. It was a tiny cut, and it had already stopped bleeding.

"Did someone hit you?" he asked, keeping his voice steady.

She shook her head and didn't elaborate. Zachary didn't press her.

He thought of those people in the bar watching the fight, heedless of the woman they had cast aside.

He wondered what to do with all his anger.

He licked his thumb and smeared the blood from her skin in slow strokes. As he did so, he let everything settle inside him for a minute; his thoughts, his heart-beat, his need to hit something. There was no reaction from her as he tucked a strand of hair behind her ear.

Her arms lay crossed in her lap, the right still gripping the left.

Animals. Bloody animals.

Zachary held out his hand for her injured wrist. She lifted it and he saw that her fingers were trembling. Her skin, always so pale and delicate, looked slightly red and a little swollen.

As he slowly turned her arm to inspect the underside, Rose bit her lip, winced.

"Does that hurt?"

She shook her head and he smiled.

"Of course it does. I'm sorry."

It looked badly bruised, nothing more. She would have to keep it still for a while, let it rest.

He cast a glance around the large kitchen, looking for something with which to bind her hand. "How did it start?"

"One of the rail workers said something about the Three Belles. He wanted to know where the name came from," she said. Her voice was hushed as she watched him feel the bones

176

along her wrist.

"Go on," he prompted.

"A local miner told him and the rail worker laughed and said...something that I won't repeat. Then they started to fight." She shook her head slightly in a gesture Zachary didn't understand.

"And you were caught in the middle?"

She nodded, eyes downcast, and he squeezed her fingers, briefly. They were cold.

"I just got bumped. I was trying to stop it, to calm them all down. I must've slipped on some spilled beer and fallen awkwardly. Perhaps I fell on some glass... It all happened so fast."

He could see a dark, wet stain on the left side of her dress near her hip.

Silence fell between them, and it was then that he realised the commotion from the bar had subsided.

"Well, it sounds like it's quieting down out there, now." He indicated to the door.

There was one last loud *crash*.

"Mostly," he added apologetically.

He dug into his pocket and drew forth his large handkerchief. As he shook it out, a coin dropped onto the wooden bench and spun in gentle, mesmerizing circles.

Tails, he thought, automatically, as the coin slowed. It stopped in jittering throes and lay still, heads up on the bench.

Just as he'd found it.

Zachary swallowed hard. He looked away from the coin to loop the kerchief around Rose's wrist, ensuring the pressure was tight enough to support without cutting off the circulation.

"There."

"Thank-you." Her voice was a whisper.

Zachary thought she looked more beautiful than he'd ever

seen her.

He placed her arm gently on the bench. "I should go back out there and make sure Athan is alright."

"Wait—" Her fingers gripped his arm, drawing him closer to her.

"Shhhh... It's alright Rose," he said in a soothing tone. "It sounds as though the fight is over."

"No," she said, her fingers digging deeper into his skin. "I forgot. I have to tell you something."

Zachary could smell the scent of her hair; see the cotton of her bodice where a few threads were loose at the seams.

"There are police here. In town, looking for you— Well, for the killers. They're inspectors, I think."

The news registered in Zachary's mind. Alarm and fear, but most of all what registered was her nearness.

"You're worried," he managed.

"Of course. For you. If they find you..."

"We'll be alright." He took her hand and ran his thumb across her knuckles. "Do you believe me?"

She nodded and smiled. He could feel her breath on his cheek and everything came down to her right then. Not the inspectors, not Athan, not even Sacha.

Zachary returned her smile and moved forward until their lips touched in a light, careful kiss. Her mouth was warm and dry; soft most of all. He pulled back a little, felt her cold fingers curl around his.

Light-headed, he leaned in a second time.

But her hand pushed his away as she started back, the chair legs screeching on the stone floor. Her cheeks were flushed and her eyes looked away, at anything other than him.

"Ummm..." she began. Her fingers plucked at the handkerchief around her wrist. Once more, they were trembling.

Perhaps more than before.

He reached for the solidity of the table.

"I apologise." He had no other words for his gross misstep.

"No. I just…" she took a breath and stood, moving quickly around him and over to the bench where Bronwyn's tray lay waiting.

Cooling.

Zachary's cheeks heated until he thought his skin would burn. He faced her empty chair, mortified.

What were you thinking?

The noises from outside had stilled leaving the kitchen silent; highlighting every tight breath, every awkward move, every enormous mistake.

The fight was over.

It's not the only thing that's over.

He couldn't look at her. A sickness built in him; shame. He'd destroyed it, what they had. No, what they *might* have had. He should never have kissed her. What was he thinking?

She was moving quickly—wanting to get out of there as soon as possible, probably.

Away from me.

He did look at her then, for maybe the last time.

They'd have to leave. Athan was right. They had to run. There was nothing to keep him here now. They'd be gone by morning.

Rose placed a pitcher on the silver tray and lifted it by the two delicate handles on each side, bringing it around to leave. But her face crumpled and she cried out in pain as she dropped everything abruptly on the bench. The meal clattered on the bench as she gripped her bandaged hand. Liquid sluiced over the white ceramic.

Zachary stood and approached her. "Here, I'll do that."

It was the least he could do.

She nodded, still not looking at him.

"That was stupid," she said. "I completely forgot about it."

"I understand," he said.

You were too busy trying to get away, I know.

He took the tray and slid it from the bench easily. There was a tinny clatter as something dropped to the floor.

Rose bent down and picked up the coin, peering at it for a few seconds before offering it to him.

"Can you..." He meant *'keep it for me.'* She must have understood because she nodded.

"Of course." Rose looked at the coin once more, reading the date, probably, looking at the design. Zachary hoped he'd scraped all the blood away.

He waited patiently, but he too, wanted to leave the room. The sooner they left, the sooner he could get back and thoroughly wallow in his ill-timing, his stupidity. He needed a drink.

He took a single step, but Rose stopped him with her hand. She stepped up close to his side, her hip almost touching his leg, her breasts only inches from his arm. She looked up at him.

Then he felt her touch; on his left hip, then his thigh.

Zachary froze. His breath caught in his throat like it would be stuck there forever, neither drawn nor expelled.

He looked down past the tray he was holding to see her slowly ease the coin down into his pants pocket with two long delicate fingers.

Rose's cheeks coloured dusky red as she smiled. She stepped away and the sudden absence of her body heat felt like a blizzard.

"Shall we?" she asked.

Zachary could only nod.

And follow.

Smalls Worlds Change

"**Y**ou're late," Bronwyn said from behind the closed door.

"Sorry," Rose replied. "Something...came up."

She immediately wished she hadn't said that.

It was impossible to look at Zachary right then, she looked anywhere else. She could feel his body heat as he stood beside her, his arm against hers, his hands still holding the tray.

They hadn't spoken much as they walked across town to Bronwyn's house. Each seemed lost in their own thoughts of excitement and terror, madly processing the events that had played out in the Three Belles.

Did it really happen? Did he really kiss me?

Rose remembered pulling away from him and seeing the look of hurt and destruction in his eyes. She hadn't meant to do it. She didn't *want* to do it; it just happened. In those few seconds her mind was awhirl with fear and love and wonder and hope. Her heart was beating so fast, her breath matching its frantic beats. Pulling back was just a reflex, an instinct that she couldn't control. She at once wanted him and feared him.

Her cheeks warmed with the mere thought of it. The act of putting that coin in his pocket was so...forward. So *unbecoming*. But she was glad she did it. Her actions had saved them from her mistake.

When Zachary suggested they leave through the back entrance of the Three Belles, Rose knew it was so she wouldn't see the chaos in the bar.

She'd agreed, marvelling at his consideration. At that moment, she would've agreed to almost anything.

She led the way, but she didn't see where she was going. Her mind was on other things. The touch of his fingers, the press of his lips; skin on skin.

Zachary.

They'd been polite to each other as they walked down the main street, skirting crowds and ignoring others who passed them by, but the conversation had been stilted, formal, as if they were waiting for each other to take the lead.

"How's your wrist?"

"Feeling better, thank you."

...and...

"Is the tray too heavy?"

"No, I can manage."

The walk across town was the longest Rose had ever taken—and the fastest. Zachary strode by her side the whole way, they walked in unison, but didn't turn to face each other. So close, but aware of the very inches that separated them. His power; his strength, his manner, his body. Giddy, naïve thoughts ran through her head. Childish thoughts. Mature thoughts.

Part of her resented the walk to Bronwyn's house. Rose wanted to be walking and talking with him, going in the opposite direction. Heading out into the fields and lying down on the cold grass like they had done that day weeks ago, when she'd brought them lunch. Athan and Sawyer had been with them on that occasion.

She wanted to disappear with him. Just the two of them, to somewhere they'd never be found. Her small world had changed and she was scared by it, exhilarated by it.

Instead, they were on the front porch at Bronwyn's.

"Who is that?" Bronwyn asked, the door still closed.

"This is Zachary," Rose replied.

"Nice to meet you," Zachary added in a nervous voice.

"Hmph. *Him!*" was the only reply.

They stood in silence, both looking at the closed door in front of them. Rose's flight of indulgent fancy was fast catching up to her reality. After a few more seconds of silence, Rose heard the scraping of the bolt across the latch. The door opened a few inches and Bronwyn's eyes appeared in the gap.

"He shouldn't be here," she snapped.

Rose nodded. "I know, but there was trouble at the bar. I've hurt myself. I couldn't carry the tray."

She held out her bandaged wrist and saw Bronwyn's shrewd gaze drop to it.

The older woman nodded slowly. "I see." It sounded like she didn't believe her.

"Zachary was good enough to offer to carry it over here for me."

"It looks like a wonderful dinner," he added, trying to help.

Rose couldn't look at him. She wanted to, but couldn't. Not here, not right now. She was scared everything she felt would be in her eyes and Bronwyn would see. This was her secret for now. Hers and Zachary's.

Bronwyn ignored his comment. "Bring it inside," she said but her eyes were firmly on Rose.

The door opened wider and Zachary went to move forward. Rose placed a hand on his shoulder and held him back. Their eyes met for the first time since they left the kitchen.

She smiled up at him. "I can take it from here."

"Are you sure?" His eyes creased in concern. She could read him so easily now. She wanted to blot out the world and just talk with him, get to know him more. Get inside him.

Calm down, Rose. He's not the first man you've ever kissed.

She nodded and took the other end of the tray as she walked slowly across in front of him, blocking his entry to the house.

Zachary didn't let go of the tray until she had a good grip. She nodded again, more forcefully this time, and he reluctantly let go. The tray was heavy, and the ache in her wrist burned with a dull fire, but she knew she could carry it for this short distance.

"I suppose I should return to the Three Belles," he said to her.

She nodded. "I promise I won't be long."

He leaned forward until his cheek touched hers. "I'll wait for you at the end of the street," he whispered, his breath touching her ear.

He stepped back off the porch and nodded a goodbye to Bronwyn, before turning and walking back down the path.

Rose watched him go; his broad shoulders and red hair captured her stare and she couldn't break it.

"You *can* come in," Bronwyn called to her, trying to get her attention.

Zachary reached the front gate and slowly turned as he swung it open. He hesitated, then waved to her and ran his hand through his hair.

Just like she longed to do.

Rose's hands were full, there was no way she could wave back to him, but she nodded slowly instead and could feel her cheeks burning.

Bye, she mouthed silently, but she had no idea if he saw it or not.

Finally, as he walked off down the road, Rose turned back around to the doorway.

184

Bronwyn was standing at the other end of the hallway, by the kitchen door, leaning against the wall with her arms crossed in front of her.

"My food will be cold by now," she smirked.

Rose blushed some more as she walked in and pushed the door shut behind her with the heel of her boot.

She tried very hard not to say the terrible thoughts that suddenly came to her.

You're lucky I came by at all. I don't have to, but I do.

"I'm sorry," she said out loud.

"No, my dear, you most certainly are *not*," Bronwyn corrected.

Rose couldn't wipe the sudden smile from her face as she walked towards the kitchen.

Bronwyn reached over and took the tray from Rose, her wedding ring clinking against the metal of the tray; loud in the silence between them.

He's been dead for a year and she still wears her wedding ring... How quickly happiness can slip away.

Rose turned away to hide the joy in her face, hoping she was luckier than her friend.

GROUNDING

When did this room become a prison?
There was only a little whiskey left in the chipped glass and Athan swallowed it, holding the glass to his lips until the last drops trickled down. He was lying down on the bed, a large pillow behind his head that sent a cramp through his neck. He endured because it kept him awake.

He placed the glass back on the side table and filled it with an indiscriminate hand. Amber liquid ebbed at the rim like a king tide.

More than two fingers. More than four.

The lamps lit up the room, their dependable, steady flames unwavering in the glass cases. Solid light that cast small shadows. That was the idea.

There was nowhere to hide in here.

Athan had nothing to do but sleep, wait and drink. He didn't have any hobbies beyond fixing things around his house. He didn't have anyone he wanted to talk to except his wife and that was impossible.

For a multitude of reasons, now.

He was stuck here, in this room that was fast becoming intolerably familiar; the predictable squeak at the upper-right corner of the bed when he leaned over for the bottle, the large open knot in the boards near the wall that let in the cold air and the occasional spider, the slight stain on the opposite wall where something had once been thrown and dripped down to the skirting, the scrub marks and cracks in the plaster where the door and ceiling met, and the number of uneven, uncured beams lining the roof. He knew almost every inch of this small space and the more he knew about it, the more he hated it.

He dreamed at night of clawing his way out of this room; out of himself. They were the worst dreams. Worse than Sacha.

But his nightly thoughts always ended with Sacha regardless of the terrors that came before.

So did Zachary's.

His fingers absently played with the copper bracelet. He'd bought it for Molly the day he'd walked into Sacha's kitchen. Felt like months ago, now. Another life. He could never give it to her. Links broken and repaired, metal tarnished. It was ruined.

Athan heard uncertain steps outside the door, then the quiet turning of the door handle; metal scraping metal. Zachary silently slipped into the room.

A waft of cold air accompanied him.

He was smiling, that was the first thing Athan noticed. Smiling like he was in on the mother of all secrets, a beautiful secret, one that Athan was not privy to.

The second was the quiet murmurs. Zachary was musing joyful thoughts to himself as he walked in, probably expecting Athan to be fast asleep by now. He certainly was *not* expecting the pouncing form of a man whose brain homed in on anything he could hate or fight against.

Zachary laughed a little, a quiet private laugh, then turned to peer at the bed.

Athan lifted his glass.

"Ah, the stranger returns," he said. He could not help the

bitterness in his voice. The sight of that flushed happiness made him curl in on himself.

"Sorry I'm late. I didn't wake you, though, did I?" Zachary's teeth flashed briefly as he grinned. His eyes were bright in the light, full of colour and alive.

He can barely keep the bloody smile off his face.

Athan held the glass up to the light and looked at his reflection while Zachary crouched to untie the laces of his boots.

Athan's eyes looked like black holes below his blond hair, dead.

"No. I was just lying here, thinking," he said, finally answering Zachary's question.

"Oh. What about?"

"Nothing much. How is Rose?"

"She's fine. A lot better than she was, in any case."

There was an odd set to Zachary's mouth as he spoke like he was trying to hold something in. Like when a child lies, or when a person is in love.

Athan held that beautiful secret once.

"I helped carry her tray." Zachary's eyes practically shone with it.

"Did you?" Athan's voice turned mocking; ugly. He heard it and there wasn't a thing he could do about it. He watched Zachary run a hand through his hair and saw the light fade in his eyes.

You are a bastard, Athan.

But he couldn't help it. He was on a roll and Zachary was his only audience in this town or, for that matter, in his life. This life he hated. Like this room.

Silent, Zachary pulled off his overcoat and hung it on the chair by the bed.

Athan sat up. "I said—"

"I *heard* what you said." Zachary shot him a glance that

189

hovered somewhere between injured and irate. He folded the lapels of the coat, turning his back to Athan.

"Do you love her?" Athan asked. He needed to know, because he was sick of playing this game. The rails may have stopped at this town but they were also moving on, stretching beyond this place.

"What?" Zachary snapped, his voice muffled.

"You just seemed... Protective. Durin' th'fight, I mean." Athan slurred a little. It ordinarily would have annoyed him, but he was past caring tonight.

"It was a *brawl*. Did you *want* to see her get hurt? She took us in. We can protect her. We owe her at least that much."

"I saw how you looked at her. Sawyer, too. He's...less than pleased," Athan said, flatly.

Zachary rounded on him. "I don't care about Sawyer." Again, his hand ran through his hair. It was something he did when he didn't know what to say—when he was confused.

"I think you should get some sleep, Ay."

"Not tired. So you get to stay here in this place, find the girl of your dreams, and live happily ever after? Well, this *has* all worked out pretty well for you, hasn't it? *She's* worked out well for you."

He could imagine Zachary's chaste fumblings, her modest acquiescence. Did they hold hands? Kiss? Did he touch her hair? Or more?

No. Sweet Zachary wouldn't.

But when he entered the room, he'd been grinning like his face would split apart. Maybe he was everything Rose had ever dreamed of, here in this little town. The handsome stranger on the run.

A damn Bronte novel in the flesh. Zachary Vaughn. The boy who had it all.

The boy in question was glaring hotly at Athan and Athan

didn't care one bit. Nothing could burn as much as the glass-ful of whiskey he then poured down his throat.

"Don't bring her into this," Zachary said. "She's looked af-ter us. She's given us a room, she's given us jobs—she's even warned me about—" He stopped.

"Warned you about what?" Athan's voice was slowly losing coherence, but his mind was sharp.

Zachary muttered something under his breath.

"Warned you about *what*."

Zachary bit his lip. "Two Inspectors. In town. Looking for the killers of those women."

Athan felt cold fear at the very centre of his soul, like someone had reached in with an iron hand and squeezed.

"Us," he breathed.

"Ay, we didn't—"

Athan dismissed Zachary's words with a sketchy wave. "I know we didn't. You know what I mean. They're looking for *us*. They've got our descriptions, and they're going to get us, too. Do you finally see? We *have* to leave. Now."

He swung his legs over the bed to rest his feet on the floor. The action steadied him, grounded him again.

He looked at his friend, waiting for his point to strike home. Finally, there was a tangible reason of why they shouldn't stay here. The fact that it took the arrival of two inspectors to convince Zachary, however, angered him.

They'd left it too late. Because of a girl, they would get caught. Because of Zachary's infatuation, they'd hang.

I've given up so much more.

Zachary didn't give voice to his objection. He shook his head instead.

So like Zach.

"Christ, Zach. You should've told me instead of going off on your little stroll with that..." He shook his head, trying to find a word to describe the woman and her relationship to Zachary.

He couldn't because he didn't know.

Before Sacha, he would have known. Zachary was his best friend and they shared things like that.

They *used* to.

Zachary's voice was hushed. "She's not the problem."

"Oh?" Athan smiled without humour. "I am, is that it?"

Zachary once again said nothing. He sighed and folded his arms over his chest as if protecting himself.

There was nowhere to hide in here.

"Say it," Athan demanded.

The smaller man sighed and looked to the floor. "I'm going to sleep, Athan. It's been—"

"Say it! You wanna stay for her. You've got it all now and I've got nothing. Thank-you for being there, *friend*."

When Zachary looked up, his eyes were haunted.

And when he spoke, Athan had never heard such anger in his life.

"You've got your *wife*, you son of a bitch. Molly. You just won't go and see her. Good *grief*, she's in the next bloody town. It'll take you less than five hours to get there! But no. You won't. That's your decision. Not mine."

Zachary marched to the door and placed his hand on the cold handle.

His laces were still undone, his overcoat still hung on the chair, but he opened the door and when he next spoke, his voice was soft, even though his body still shook.

"As for being there? *I* wasn't the one who let my best friend fall into a pool of blood. *You* did that."

Zachary left the room, shutting the door as quietly as he had opened it.

That was Zachary. No real temper. No fits of rage.

Athan lifted his feet from the floor and hunched his knees up to his chest.

He didn't know whether it was the alcohol or the fact he no longer had his feet on the floor, but he wasn't grounded anymore.

THE PENNY DREADFUL

January 4, 1889

At first, he didn't know where to walk and he didn't care. He stumbled blindly, his mind filled with conflicting thoughts, his chest aching with mixed emotions; revulsion, sorrow, love and ruin.

For a while, Zachary walked around the town, trying hard to put his thoughts in line, trying to work out how Athan and Rose could rest side-by-side in his soul. There had to be a way. But he didn't see how.

He walked past others in the streets; some hand-in-hand, some solitary like himself, but unlike him, they seemed content.

He knew this life on the run was not for him. It wasn't what he wanted. It was too hard, too stressful.

It wasn't what he deserved. Hiding away from the world would not solve his problems...or Athan's.

Athan had a pathway out. Athan had goddamn salvation, but he was stubbornly keeping from it. He refused to visit his wife, refused to return to the one person who could somehow work this out for him. She was in reach, but he wouldn't even consider the option.

Since Sacha, Zachary realised he was alone, hanging on to the life he had once known, wishing he could get it back, wishing everything could be as it was.

But that life was ending. He felt it in his bones. He felt it behind his teeth as he slept.

He didn't want to lose his best friend, didn't want to be the one to drag them apart, but he knew there was something better here, in this town, something worthwhile. He could make this work. He could erase the horror of his past, if only he'd be allowed to. Rose was his answer, he was sure of that now.

Everything could be solved.

Gradually, the pall of hate and confusion lifted. His shoulders un-hunched and his steps became stronger, longer.

He knew where to go. He turned around and headed back down the street, towards Rose's house.

The air was cold and he wished he'd taken his coat when he'd walked out on Athan, but he hadn't thought much beyond needing to get out.

Zachary didn't like seeing Athan drunk, and he didn't like hearing what Athan had to say. Friends shouldn't be like that. Friends should be supportive, especially after what they'd been through together.

He couldn't really blame Athan, not when he was drunk and scared.

Zachary had made the best suggestion, as far as he was concerned.

Go see your wife.

If he was in the same situation, he would see her. He'd run to anyone he loved. Make it to her no matter what. Fight the world to get to her. Always return to her.

No matter what.

Because she would always be there for him. He knew that for certain. Just as Molly was there for Athan right now. Waiting and worrying.

Zachary walked up to Rose's house. The closer he came, the more sure he was. His fears were left behind, shrugged from his shoulders as he shivered in the night.

Nothing was more clear to him. Nothing had ever been.

She's my way through this.

He walked up the path and headed for the front door.

He remembered when they had first seen each other; the kitchen, the broken glass, the apple and the sugar. The memories brought a smile to his face, as he thought back.

Lives can change over the simplest things.

He ran a hand through his hair and made sure his clothes were straight, his shirt collar was not creased. He licked his fingers and tucked an errant strand of hair behind his ear.

He reached out to knock on the door, but changed his mind. It was much better to slip around the back, over to the kitchen door and see her there again, like they had that first time.

Like it was beginning again.

He smiled. In some ways, it was.

He crept around the house, trying not to make any noise, easing past damp ivy, boots squelching in the muddy path. A flickering light shone through the windows. She was in the back of the house somewhere, probably near the kitchen. He hoped she'd ask him to stay for tea, if she was up to it; if she wasn't still shaken from the brawl in the Three Belles.

He turned the corner of the house and could see the kitchen. It was well-lit with two lamps, and there was food on the table. He couldn't see anyone in the kitchen, but he could hear Rose's voice.

It was a wonderful sound, her voice in the night. Light, almost angelic. The most beautiful sound.

He saw her fill a tea pot with hot water from the kettle on the stove and sit down at the table. She was facing away from him, so he could only see her thin, smooth neck, and her hair tied tight in a bun. Then she turned slightly and he saw her profile, her cheek and nose, the slight press of her lips. She nodded, as if she was thinking to herself, agreeing with herself.

Rose.

He took a step closer, his hand reaching out to knock on the door.

And then he saw the figure. Saw it step smoothly out of the darkness of the hallway. It came quickly towards her, hands gesturing.

Zachary froze, his hand in mid-air, his breath half-taken. Flashes of another kitchen, another woman, assailed him.

Not again.

But the figure passed her and reached towards the kettle of boiling water on the stove.

Zachary blinked, started back.

Sawyer.

Rose turned to face Sawyer as he reached past the kettle and grasped the china pot, carrying it over to the table, his hands tipping it forward, filling two cups with the hot tea.

Sawyer said something to her and she shook her head. She looked annoyed, but finally, she smiled. Then he reached for a cup and saucer and handed it to her. She took it and Zachary watched as their hands touched lightly, for the most fleeting of seconds.

Why?

Sawyer knelt by her then; knelt down by her side and looked up at her, his eyes wide.

Rose looked back, intently, as the sandy-haired man's lips moved, sincere and calm.

Zachary couldn't hear what he was saying but he didn't want to know anyway. Sawyer didn't stop. He kept talking and Rose said something in return. Sawyer nodded.

Zachary took a step back, letting the air leak from his lungs.

Suddenly his chill was gone. He was hot, cheeks burning, sweat breaking across his forehead and prickling across his back. He looked to each side, although he didn't know why. Her house was isolated.

I could kill him now. No one would know.

But who was he kidding? He could no more murder a man than Athan.

He turned back to look at them. Sawyer was still kneeling—

Get up, damn you!

—and still talking to her. She said something back and then lifted her arm, placing her hand on his shoulder, touching him.

Holding him.

No! No, no, no, no, no...

He whirled around, off balance, his hand reaching for the side of the house, his feet spastically trying to gain purchase as he dashed from the door and the sight of them.

He had to run, he didn't care to where.

It can't happen like this. It CAN'T!

It wasn't fair.

He sprinted from her house and down the road, half-hoping and half-praying a carriage would round a corner and take him under the horses hooves; ending his life there and then. He ran blindly, trying hard to stop the tears welling in his eyes.

When he couldn't hold them back any longer, he let them fall. He careened into the side of a store, his shoulder hitting the wall hard, and he slid down into a crumpled mess of despair.

I trusted her...

But what promise had she given him? What right did he have to blame her for her choice?

He didn't know how long he stayed there. The tears seemed

never ending, the crying erupting from the deepest part of his soul. He didn't care how long it took, or who saw him. He couldn't go to her now, and he couldn't go back to the room to face Athan, not after what he'd said to his friend. He'd laid it all bare, gambled with his heart, but he'd made the wrong bet.

What would Athan think? How can I tell him he was right and I was so so wrong?

Once the tears subsided, Zachary picked himself up and brushed off his clothes. The night seemed colder now, more empty than before. Heartless. Barren.

Like his life.

He almost smiled at the melodrama that was playing in his head like a story in a penny dreadful.

He walked towards the remains of the Three Belles. Inside he would find the solace he needed.

Everything we touch we destroy. Everywhere we go, we leave havoc.

No. Everything I touch.

Zachary understood now how Athan felt. They were both hurting, both grieving a loss they could not retrieve.

Athan was right; had been all the time.

Zachary wondered if he'd misread the situation between Rose and himself. But he knew he hadn't. He remembered what she'd said and what they'd done. What she had done. Her fingers so bold at his thigh.

How could I misunderstand her intentions?

He pushed open the door to the bar and walked inside, knocking aside the broken chairs and tables. Within a few seconds he'd found an unbroken bottle on the shelves behind the bar, one without a label. He uncorked the top, pulling the reluctant stopper out with his teeth and spitting it into a shadowed corner.

This seemed to work for Athan. Every night the man escaped into one amber haze or another.

Zachary didn't bother with a glass or a chair. He cleared an area on the floor and sat down in the middle of the broken debris.

Broken too, he swigged at the bottle and wondered if anything could ever mend his soul.

EARTH HANDS, WHORE HANDS

Emma shivered and pulled her shawl closer around her hunched shoulders. She had been walking around the sprawling town for almost an hour, unafraid and unhurried, the only woman walking alone.

This didn't bother her. She knew this butcher; she just had to find the next victim. She also knew the next victim was not her.

The papers had blared headlines for the first few weeks, then settled to the occasional comment. It was enough to keep people afraid. Editors couldn't afford to let the story die just yet.

They were hoping for another body to fall and they wouldn't have long to wait.

The shift in power between her and her two charges intrigued her. More than her intrigue, however, was her thankfulness. She was no longer a tool for them to use, but a woman with some authority. Edward would never respect her, but he was wary and that was good enough for now.

Her thoughts drifted, as they always did, towards home. George was an officer at the Yard. He could help her, just like he'd said the night she left.

"Why not call the Yard? I'll help—"

Someone had to stay with Lucy—someone who was stronger than she was, who could handle their emotions.

So she thought about him, she wrote to him and she wept for him when she could. She searched doggedly, despite what Edward thought, for an end to this because the sooner she finished this, the sooner she could get back to her family.

Providing she lived through it.

Before supper she had left the Three Belles, knowing Edward was prowling around a garden at the edge of town. She had requested Douglas go; he seemed the more...sensitive of the two.

But Edward, still smarting over his enforced stay in the local lock-up, grabbed Douglas' umbrella and stormed off into the night claiming that he could watch the antics of a recluse thank you very much.

Douglas let him and then retreated to his room without a word.

When Emma left for her walk, she'd had to creep past his room. His door was ajar and she saw the comforting orange light of a desk lamp emanating from within. Curious, she paused and peered inside.

Douglas sat hunched over a piece of paper, his thin face softened in the light, his black hair falling into his eyes. In his hand was a pen and further over, a bottle of ink. He chewed thoughtfully on the end of the pen and continued to write. He was already a quarter of the way down the page.

Emma wondered who he was writing to and why his expression was so desolate.

She stepped back and continued on her way down the stairs, walking on her toes to avoid the tell-tale clip-clop of her boot heels. Passing through the dining area, she warmed herself briefly by the double fire-place and then slipped out into the night.

She walked carefully along the wet streets of Oak Ridge, taking her first real look around the town. Planks for the ladies to walk between buildings sat upon the thick mud where the townsfolk had not yet laid gravel or pave, and a few well-fed dogs roamed in a friendly pack, skittering at her approach.

She confined herself to the paved areas and watched each building-front as she walked by; light filtering through clouded windows. There were two Inns almost opposite each other; the Three Belles being the largest and most appointed. Newspaper sellers, a general store, soap sellers and hardware sellers all locked in together along the main street.

At the end of the street, a corral for hoofed animals and sparse chicken coops for tomorrow's meals.

The wind blew freely, making the ornate signs that hung beneath the shop fronts swing on their heavy hooks. The gas street lamps lit the town adequately in the centre, but their numbers decreased as the settlement sprawled to the west, away from the mountains. That's where she headed, walking slowly, enjoying the solitude.

There, in the quiet of the lit streets, in the shadows of the alleyways, she found peace; no men telling her what was best, no customers looking at her with wide-eyed gratitude for the lies of happiness she told of their future.

Walking alone, there was no expectation of ending such an enormous legacy, the breadth of which was bathed in blood.

The night sky was overcast, the air crisp. She felt her way through the town, one hand firmly clutching her shawl, the other running along the leaves of willow, pine and ivy. Touching wet, segmented bark, waxy leaves and smelling sharp sap that freshened her every breath.

A light misty rain began to fall and she lifted her face, smiling at the sheer vitality of it.

As she reached the opposite end of town to where Edward now crouched, she came upon a plot of several Birch trees and stopped.

Their white bark gleamed in the distant lamp-light and she leaned forward against the thickest trunk, hoping it would cleanse her as effectively as the rain that was now starting to pour in earnest.

The Oak endured, the Ash healed but the Birch comforted.

Her eyes closed and she stood, unsheltered beneath the naked branches, feeling the solidity of the tree, brushing her fingers up and down its damp, soft bark.

Then she heard the smash.

Emma spun to face the sound, grabbing at the tree behind her for support. The killer they sought could not hurt her; but other things could. Men could. Her heart sped as she saw a man in the lamplight down the hill. He stumbled after the bottle he had just dropped.

She would have sunk back into the darkness and waited until he had gone but for his red hair.

She knew him. One of the two men who was always around Rose.

Zachary?

Edward and Douglas made a point to know the names of the two men and comment on their similarity to those seen fleeing Sacha. Emma had shrugged at their diligence. The men that fled Sacha's house all those weeks ago were innocent and therefore not Emma's concern.

She took a breath and pushed off from the tree, walking the dozen or so feet to the road. When she stepped onto the road, her boots were loud on the slick stones; their din unavoidable.

Zachary straightened, swayed and fixed his gaze upon her.

His red hair was starting to look dark brown in the rain that was growing heavier by the second. She felt water culminate at the ends of the curls at her neck and trickle down the back of her dress.

"Are you alright, sir?" she asked, keeping her distance for now.

"I...dropped the bottle." He gestured to the broken mess with his right hand.

"So I see," she said.

He kicked the glass off the road and into the trees. It took him several attempts as he clumsily tried to remove all the shards from the stones. His efforts took him onto the mud at the side, into the trees a little.

"Are you lost?" she asked, speaking to his back.

"No," he shook his head. Then he turned and smiled. "Yes."

It was a bitter smile, she thought.

"Can I be of some assistance?" She took a step, wanting to get closer, to see if he was her link; the answer to it all.

"No...Miss..." He squinted at her, through the rain, the needles of the pine almost obscuring his face from view. "I know you, don't I?"

"We haven't met." She had to raise her voice a little to be heard. "Though I have been reading palms in town this last week. My name is Emma." She almost said 'Mrs. Godley' but felt his addled brain would cope better with a first name.

"Zach. *Zachary*," he said. He offered his hand, something he probably would not have done had he been sober, and she took the last two steps that brought her off the road to him. The toes of her boots squelched in the mud. He wore one ring and they shook hands, no gloves, skin to skin.

Emma felt the chill of his fingers and knew it was the alcohol. He wore no overcoat and the laces of his boots were untied. She felt a rush of pity for him.

"You're out late," he said. He withdrew his hand and stepped back, overstepping and stumbling a little, he caught himself with one hand on the trunk of a young pine.

"I could say the same."

"I'm..." A pained expression flashed across his face briefly. "I'm thinking. About a certain quandary I have." His words were not slurred as she expected, though his body swayed with his inebriation.

Emma nodded. He was not the one she was searching for, she was sure. "I'm thinking too. Is there perhaps anything I can do to help with your current consternation?"

He shook his head and laughed without humour. "No. Not unless— No. My thanks for the offer, though." He blinked rapidly against the water running down into his eyes. "You read palms?"

"I do. For money, mostly," she tried to smile, but didn't quite make it.

She hated the charlatan aspect of her work, the 'fortune-telling.' Her mother had found it most distasteful; her readings were clinical, mediated and steeped in the science of line, shape, dimension and rigidity. They were about the person, the personality, the fibre of a being and the means in which to handle events.

She'd taught Emma the same. Anyone claiming to see fortune or tragedy, her mother said, bore the burden of both superstition and ignorance. Glimpses, yes; absolutes, no.

When it came to the family 'duty' however, fortunes were indeed told; it had little to do with dark strangers or pots of gold. It was blood.

Lucy, too, had the family 'gift.' Emma just prayed she would never be called upon to use it.

"You any good?" He sniffed.

"Well, some would say so."

"Right then," he shrugged and held out his left hand, and she took it, his rain-slicked skin sliding across hers.

"We should move into the light," she said, using her grip on him to gently lead him back to the road and into a pool of lamp-light.

There, she patiently switched hands to take his right instead—he'd gestured with that hand, he'd moved to steady himself with that hand. It was his leading hand and she needed to see where he was going, not where he'd been.

He shrugged and she lifted the palm into the light.

"How old are you, Zachary?"

"24."

He had earth hands, a strong balanced palm, a deep attachment line that made her mouth curl up involuntarily.

Just like George...

She looked to his line of destiny, from childhood to adulthood; now and beyond.

What she saw made her flinch.

The amount of breaks, the damage across that solid line, made it look like a train track—and the breaks started now. Around the age of 23 to 24. Protective squares lined up one after the other like cinder blocks. Four of those squares were close together, the rest further apart.

Her shawl slid from her hunched shoulders onto the ground. Zachary made to retrieve it, but she held him fast.

She read him for a few minutes, hearing the unspoken question in the way he held his hand, tense and rigid in her own.

What do you see?

Fine lines covered the Mount of Venus, going in all directions, crisscrossing and spreading outward like a web.

He's losing her.

Finally, Emma looked into his glazed eyes. For once, she told the truth. He would be either too drunk or too worried about his lost love to remember what she said and she had spent days telling people what they wanted to hear. Lies came easy to her lips in this place and she hated the taste.

This man was suited to truth. She would honour that.

"You've travelled a long way. You are following, but mostly you are leading. You are not, by nature, a leader, but for some reason, it is you who are setting the path. You have found love..." She swallowed, hearing a hollow groan from the man. "You have the *promise* of a perfect love, one you should try to keep. This love, if given a chance, will flourish because you are steadfast in most instances. You belong here. But there are other forces at work that can destroy that love. Mostly in yourself. You know a woman..." She frowned.

Another square of protection—but not on any of his main lines—away . Away from it.

"A woman close to you is—" She stopped.

My God, was I wrong?

And then she saw it; not the lines, nor the furrows, the whorls, the loops or the stirrups. She saw it happen.

The lines faded and his palm became a tapestry of image.

"Blue ribbons. A woman with blue ribbons. This woman with the blue ribbons is in trouble. I see death, Zachary. I see...blood."

Zachary jerked his hand from her, just as the picture began to clear: a room, the blood. A picture. Zachary in the picture. Framed in metal. Ribbons.

It all dissolved when their palms separated.

He stumbled back from her like she was the devil. His face went sickly pale and his blue eyes blazed in that complete absence of colour.

Shaking his head, he laughed. It was a harsh and quick sound. "A trick, right? This is what you do? *Play* with people?"

"No. I—"

"Do you want me to throw coins at your feet? In payment

for your *entertainment?*"

The last word made her feel like a whore.

"I know what I saw."

"Leave me alone! You don't know!" He was shaking his head now, his eyes welling with a horror that was all too familiar to her, and made her take her own distancing steps backward.

Zachary's chest heaved with breaths that seemed to pain him. A rough, rasping sound came from his throat and he held out a hand to her, warding off any approach she might make.

She wouldn't approach him. Like her, he was damaged by a dead woman staring up at him.

Zachary turned and ran and Emma watched him go.

Her hair and dress slowly soaked through as the hammering rain came down.

It was a few minutes later when Emma realized she was shaking from the cold. She picked up her waterlogged shawl, wrung it out with cold-reddened fingers.

The lamps would lead her back to town. Emma held her face up once more to the rain and let the water wash over her eyelids hoping it would cool the images that burned so vividly there.

She began to walk, taking her time, enjoying her last moments of solitude.

Zachary was nowhere to be seen as she walked into the main street; not hunkered under the sodden beams of the porch of the Three Belles bar as the rain poured off the awning in glass-like sheets and filled the water butts. Nor was he crouched by the fire places drying off like so many others, hands outstretched, palms out, for warmth.

She swallowed hard as she walked up the stairs, leaving wet boot prints in her wake.

211

Zachary was not the one; he didn't do anything.

But he was surrounded by death and he could not escape—no matter how far he ran.

MR GODLEY,

I am using this rare opportunity to impart to you my gratitude and recognition for your patience and understanding in these last many weeks. Your wife, Emma, has been invaluable to our search and has, surely not to your surprise, carried herself with grace and courage throughout this long and arduous journey.

Although my words are a poor substitute for your wife's more gentle musings, I feel compelled to impart this message of her safety and wellbeing.

I am also moved to express my regret at the way in which her leaving has obviously affected her, yourself and your daughter. The taking of Emma, particularly the abruptness of manner and the speedy departure is something for which I am in no small part culpable.

And something which I so desperately regret.

I speak of your wife in the highest terms. I have seen exhibited a heartsome spirit and determination due in no small part by her fervent desire to return to you, her devout husband, and also her only daughter.

Language is insufficient to convey to you the importance of our purpose and your wife's place in it.

Her Spirit and Will lead me to believe there are some grander mysteries still left in the Human soul and, though this path is a treacherous one, not all such things are as confounded as I had once thought.

I cannot tell you what it is we seek. I can tell you that any prolonged exposure to suffering and violent death, seems to render men more heedless and neglectful.

We have been both of late and I, at least, heartily regret my own behaviour.

I do not know what Emma has communicated in her private correspondence to you, but my own observations are that she is in good health and good spirits and will no doubt impart many a tale upon her return, including the temporary incarceration of myself and Edward, the telling of which, I am positive will bring you no small amusement.

I am writing to you on this night, Friday, Inst., in the private hopes that this pursuit will be at an end soon or at the very least will pass from our purview so that your dearest wife may return to you.

In God we place our trust & abide His will.

Yours very sincerely,
Douglas Chisolm

One Night Wouldn't Matter

Zachary's brain told him to go to bed, but his body walked him doggedly up the muddy embankment. Slipping, falling and scrabbling with his fingers, he clawed his way to the top of the mound where the vegetation grew thick. He tried to tread quietly, but he knew his footfalls were loud, his breath hoarse.

The ground blurred beneath him, but his eyes stayed focussed on his boots. He didn't want to look anyone in the eye, and he didn't care if anyone saw him. He stumbled on until he was standing at the open mouth of the railway line, its teeth broken and jagged, where that day's work had ended.

The line lay before him, metal cold and misted in the mottled light from the half moon. The rails stretched off into the distance, disappearing into the woods, and he wished he could follow them.

Just disappear.

He turned and looked behind him, where the rails would soon be laid. The workmen had stacked up most of the timber, but other sleepers lay where they fell, ready to be picked up the next morning.

Zachary's gaze slipped lazily over the tents the workers slept in. He could see the steam engine that ferried the wood to the site, but he couldn't see anyone watching him. A few lanterns dotted through the tents. Some workmen unable to sleep, others writing letters home.

He turned away, half-staggering through the first row of tents, mindful of the guide strings and makeshift campfires outside the tents. He heard murmurs and snores, and he could see silhouettes of men inside some of the tents. As he walked he was sure he could hear someone crying nearby. He stopped and listened, but suddenly everything was quiet once more.

He walked over some misplaced wooden trestle until he was walking along the sturdy, constructed line. He walked straight down the middle, as if the rails stopped his swagger, his drunken meander, bordering him and giving him direction. The way he should go.

To leave all this.

His path took him by the locomotive and the ballast wagon sitting off to one side, toward the mine. The locomotive's big driving wheels, grimy oiled sides and soot-coated cab looked out of place in the treed setting.

Like me and Athan.

He ran his hand along the side of the engine, feeling the dirt and grime, the grease and oil. Small hisses and pops came from its slowly cooling boiler, the piping still warm under the touch of his fingers.

It could be a way out for us.

The night was cold and quiet, and he knew he had to get back to the Three Belles, but he was torn between returning to what he knew, and just running. Running and never stopping. Or running with some purpose.

His breath clouded before him as he stared at the rails, those two ribbons of steel, once a life-line, now...

They stretched into the darkness undulating between the trees on either side, before adopting a lazy curve that took them out of his sight.

216

His eyes dropped down to his side, and he stared intently at the rails in the half-light. Suddenly he heard a noise to his left. He looked up in time to spot a fox as it dashed across the line in two bounds. It paused on the other side, eyeing him intently before jumping through the bushes and out of sight, quickly gone, the animal no more than a flickering afterimage burnt into Zachary's memory.

He's free. He knows where to go, what to do.

And it was at that moment Zachary made up his mind.

Athan should be going. But if he won't, I will.

The rails gave him the idea, allowed him to gauge the distance.

Athan may not be able to save himself, but Zachary knew he had one chance to make something right.

Molly could save him. Molly was their only hope.

He stood, prepared to run, to follow the fox and run blindly through the night. But he stumbled, over-balanced, his arms swinging wildly as he fell to his knees.

I'll go. I'll get there, he thought. *I'll go. Just not now.*

One night wouldn't matter.

Nothing could change in just one night.

COME AND GET ME

It never used to be a sad place, but Bronwyn felt sadness in her house, now. It seeped from the walls like sweat from the sick.

Rose had left over an hour ago and took with her any remaining light of day. The night had settled and Bronwyn was alone again.

Trapped. Allowing herself to *be* trapped.

It annoyed her to distraction most nights.

Bronwyn loved her house during the day; the halls and rooms filled with the heady scent of Boronia, Daphne and Jasmine in the spring, pine and orange in the autumn.

The house lived in the day and she came alive with it.

She could create in the day, mould her clay and capture his image. She could look out and see changes in the weather, the trees. She could hear the clattering of the carriages as they headed out of town, the chatter of others returning. People living their lives unaware of how lucky they were just to be outside.

At night the house closed in around her. The street lamps outside were the last to be lit in town, and sometimes they were not lit at all. The row of elms obscured most of their light anyway, so when darkness fell—and it fell fast in this season—her house was swallowed by the darkness. And she along with it.

She walked the house each night, checking the rooms, the shutters and the bolts, travelling in an indolent fashion before it was time to sleep.

Every floorboard, every frayed rug edge, every peeling door frame and every chipped china cup were oppressive in their familiarity.

Most nights were silent except for her footsteps or the metallic shudder of the boiling kettle against the stove-top. She walked the halls like a caged cat in the London Zoo; back and forth, restless and listless at once.

The same pictures, the same pieces of clay, the same smell, no surprises.

The same sherry that Rose brought in a flagon every week. Sweet sherry, not expensive in a large town, but over-priced here. She didn't have to worry about such things. Not money.

What she wouldn't give for something mundane to concern herself with. Anything to let her know she was still alive, that she still existed in the minds of others. A bill to pay. A meal to cook.

And what if Rose stopped visiting one day?

She smirked without warmth. At least that would be something different to the routine that ground her down like the dust from her sculptures.

The only surprise she ever received was when she lifted the lid on the dinner tray Rose brought her each night.

A cooling and congealing meal of limp vegetables and chewy meat. Bread, sometimes. Sometimes pudding.

Surprise.

Bronwyn opened the curtains at the back window, sweeping them right then left. She sipped at her sherry and gazed out the clear pane to where her beloved statues waited, whole and naked, glazed and fired and cemented so they could withstand the day, the night, the elements. Everything.

A small smile tugged at her mouth. She leaned forward a little until her nose almost touched the cool glass, until her breath fogged it so much she could no longer see out.

She stepped back and erased the cloud with her hand.

Damn cold and surrounded by men.

Edward had to smirk. The situation was ludicrous. He knew he didn't have to be here. He could've sent Doug or the woman to do it, but he wanted to make a point; make them understand things from his point of view.

Now he found himself standing in a line of statues, in some woman's garden.

He looked around and rubbed his arms, trying to keep warm. The statues stretched in an arc, right around the back of the house, rimming the garden and the path that went by it. He counted fourteen statues in all; all wide-eyed, soulless and deathly still. It unnerved him, standing there, but he certainly wasn't going to show it.

This is easy. Simple.

The statue closest to him stood bent slightly forward, its arms behind its back, palms out, as if it was expecting to be paid from behind for something. Once the rain had stopped, Edward closed his umbrella and rested it across the hands of the statue.

At least now you're good for something.

The statue looked as if it was offering the umbrella up to Edward.

Even Douglas would laugh, Edward thought, especially as it was his umbrella in the first place.

The woman who made these must be a right nutter.

"Damn cold and wet," he whispered as he peered out from

221

behind the statues, using a low hanging branch from a Hazel tree to remain hidden.

The house looked quiet. He couldn't see any movement from inside, but the warm glow from the windows told him that she had to be in there somewhere, and he was going to prove to Douglas and the woman how wrong they were.

Nothing beats experience.

He shoved his hands into his pockets and took out a handkerchief, wiping sweat or rain from his brow; he wasn't sure which. Both.

At least these guys don't talk back. They just sit or stand, they don't even move. Some people could take a lesson from that.

He smiled again.

Best company I've had in months, maybe even years.

Although none had been so unruly as this latest one. She was like a thunderstorm that wouldn't be calmed.

I'll tame her, given time. She's not with her husband or kid now. I'll tame her or break her—one or the other.

He placed the handkerchief back in his pocket and leaned across to the statue on his left. This one was standing to attention, saluting the night.

"At ease," Edward whispered as he smiled.

His eyes darted from one window to the next, looking for any movement in the house.

Why doesn't she do something?

"Took Emma long enough to tell me where I had to be," he whispered again to the statue. "Then she wanted Douglas to come here instead, do you believe that? Like I wouldn't be able to handle the situation. One thing's for sure, if she keeps it up, I'll handle *more* than just this situation."

He rubbed at his nose, the smell of bacon still on his fingers.

"Douglas says I shouldn't hurt her, but I can tell you, there

are other ways to get a woman to do what you want her to do. You don't have to hurt her."

He turned to face the statue.

"You know what I mean? She's got a husband and a young child. There are other ways."

He smiled at himself, then.

"I said at ease, son."

He chuckled and turned away to face back to the house.

I'll give her five more minutes or else I'm calling off this witch-hunt.

He thought of his bed, the warmth of the Three Belles, taking off his boots and massaging the corn on his right heel.

He thought of relaxing. Of sleep. Of a final end to this whole sorry matter.

If only...

Then he thought of Douglas and his endless worry; the hand-wringing, and his young companion's own self doubt.

Finally, he thought of her, of her endless nagging, her strength, her growth and power over the past few months.

Things could so easily get out of control...

He saw a movement out of the corner of his eye. The curtains parted on the left side of the kitchen door. The woman leaned forward, stared out at him, then wiped at the window.

He stepped further back into the shadows and held his breath.

Let's get this over and done with.

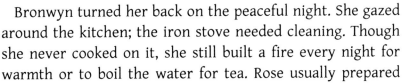

Bronwyn turned her back on the peaceful night. She gazed around the kitchen; the iron stove needed cleaning. Though she never cooked on it, she still built a fire every night for warmth or to boil the water for tea. Rose usually prepared the wood and the paper, the coal in the scuttle. She'd been preoccupied lately and Bronwyn didn't have the heart to take the role of Lady of the Manor when Rose was so happy.

Tomorrow, she thought.

She sniffed and walked briskly to the cupboards above the large kneading bench. Up on the top shelf sat a smaller bottle of sherry, the best she had.

She didn't bother dragging a heavy chair over, instead, she stretched high on her toes and reached up until the tips of her fingers tickled the glass. The muscles along the back of her hand burned, but she eventually coaxed it forward until it fell heavy in her hand.

She refilled her glass, feeling a small sense of achievement that didn't last beyond her re-corking the bottle.

Continuing her walk, she moved past the parlour and into the hall, her routine unfolding like a well-read periodical. Her husband's image was rife. He stood, reclined, slouched in every corner. On every surface, there were parts of him.

She picked up a raw piece—a foot—inspected it, and placed it gently back. She wiped her fingers together, enjoying the gritty feel before wiping the clay dust onto her skirt.

The route took her slowly upstairs, past her bedroom, into the room where Josiah lived in earnest. Here, his figure was not so brutally glazed as outside. Here, he was clothed, painted and life-like. His image was here, his body, every-thing she could remember of him. A hand curled limp in his lap, the tendons of his neck taut against his clay skin.

She toured the room, knowing she would return late to-night to sit in the single chair with her blanket and lamp.

It had been months since she'd slept in their bed. Sleep would not endure an entire night in that bed, not anymore. She would always wake up, search the cold side for him with frantic fingers. But find only the cotton sheets and emptiness.

The garden was the only place she felt at peace, the only place where she could venture out. The iron spikes of the fence not imprisoning her, but protecting her. Not far, mind. Not to the end wall with its grappling ivy and mossy base, but at least into the gravelled pathway that looped into a wide arc before bringing her back to the patio.

Finishing her sherry in one sweet and burning mouthful, she made her way down the stairs, the ninth stair squeaking as she knew it would, as it always did, as her foot came down.

She stopped, looked at it in resignation and lifted her foot to continue down, hearing it squeak again at its release.

No surprises there.

The kitchen was still warm from the low fire in the oven as she opened the parlour door, feeling the chill breeze sting her ankles, smelling the freshness of the rain.

The sheer scope of outside made her blench. But Bronwyn prided herself on being a strong woman and, after a moment, she stepped resolutely out onto the wooden patio.

She looked side to side, the patio's expanse on her left and right swallowed up by the darkness four feet in either direction. Such space. Like she would fall off the edge of it if she went too near.

But it was forward she wanted to go. She lifted the lamp from its iron hook and took a step before pausing.

Step. Pause. Step.

In this strange slow waltz, she made her way across the boards, down the sodden steps and onto the safety of the path, heading deep into the closed comfort of her garden.

The path was made up of quartz and limestone, white and cream-coloured stones that illuminated well even in the near dark of a crescent moon.

It was this path she followed. Each statue she met along the way had a different meaning for her. Josiah had been a good man, but weak of will in many things. She loved him dearly, but it was in these statues his flaws were allowed to surface. A statue with its head in its hands, one with its neck on a tilt, a gesture he would acquire when he asked her what it was he should be doing.

His faults showed in these men. Hands clasped behind his back, head down. Sightless eyes peering quizzically because he didn't understand.

Bless him.

She touched each one, caressing the rough cheeks, holding the sturdy fingers and slipping her hand along the broad shoulders and the strong necks that belied the uncertainty she had sculpted within them.

Along the line she walked, knowing each by feel, knowing this path so well, she blew into the lamp's glass case, extinguishing the comforting flame to walk in darkness, each statue calling up a different memory and a different—better—time.

That's her? She's the one?

Edward shook his head.

He watched her walk down the porch steps and into the garden. He craned his neck to follow her as long as he could, before the statues blocked his view and he lost her in the darkness. She carried a lantern with her, so he knew he would see the glow of the light if she got too close to him. No need to worry.

He didn't know if it was anger or disappointment, at himself for believing Emma, or in her abilities.

How could she be so wrong?

Nothing would be happening here tonight, he was sure.

Then he began to think that maybe, just maybe, Emma was still toying with him. Sending him out to a dead end, a chase that led nowhere, just so he would be away from her and Douglas.

But why?

To turn Douglas against me? To try to convince him to side with her?

Or worse...

Betrayal?

Edward didn't like his line of thought. He knew he would have to return to the Three Belles and make her pay, let them both know that their performance wasn't up to scratch, that there was more at stake here than egos and bruised pride.

His eyes scanned the back of the house once more, looking for her returning figure or the glow from the lantern. The back door was still open, and there was no sign of her or the light.

Or of anyone.

Come on, go back inside and go to bed, luv.

He pushed his hands deeper into his pockets, the cold night air settling about him and making him shiver.

It was a rare thing to be ahead of these killings, to have a chance to be ready and waiting, instead of arriving too late, a day, a week late, having to build the pieces from the shattered and torn remains of the victims.

A rare opportunity indeed, and that was what made him so angry; that what they thought was a chance of ending this scourge was just another dead end, a false trail, a lost hope.

If she's playing with me, leading me down here just to get me away from her and Doug, I'll split her in two, myself.

They had been too late for Mary, for Sacha too; so close and yet so utterly useless. He couldn't remember all their names or their faces, as there was never anything much left to look

227

at, but he could remember each and every situation. Each dark, bloodied room, each dim-lit street corner or faeces-ridden hole he had found them in over the years.

He closed his eyes and sighed deeply.

"When will it all end?" he whispered.

Suddenly he was very tired; his whole body and very soul were drained from the days, weeks and months, from the endless travel and the lack of knowledge, from the congealed, sticky blood of the victims to the stench of their rotting corpses.

He didn't want to see another life ruined, but he knew there would be more. Maybe one, maybe ten...maybe countless numbers yet.

And she sends me on a fool's errand.

"I'll teach her to come into my room and tell me I don't know how to do my job..."

Emma had told Douglas she was certain the girl from the Three Belles, Rose, wasn't the next victim, even though she'd seemed pretty sure she was when they had first arrived in the town. She'd changed her bloody mind and practically demanded that Douglas go check out this loner on the edge of town.

How can any of us be sure of anything anymore?

Edward had objected, but Douglas said, "I'll go."

On her side—again. Maybe they are working together.

Edward wasn't going to give in that easily, especially if they were both in agreement, so he took charge and told them he'd go, storming from the room.

"You better take this!" Douglas called after him, holding out his umbrella. "It's raining outside."

Edward said nothing. He'd just grabbed at it and marched out.

He wasn't going to let them win. But now, as he stood half-frozen in a shut-in's bizarre statue garden, he wondered if he'd done exactly what they wanted him to do.

They'd played him; made him look like a fool. And they were probably laughing at him now. Together.

"Damn them to hell," he said, anger taking control.

I'll tear them both to pieces.

He stepped out of the clearing.

Right into her path.

Her fingers slipped from one slick, glazed hand to the broad shoulder of—

Bronwyn froze and opened her eyes. Without the lamp light, she could only see the silhouette of a man.

This man wore clothes.

He did not have Josiah's build.

And he was warm.

She leapt back, pushing at the figure as she did, hoping it was a trick of her imagination.

Did Josiah come to life?

The figure grunted and fell back, pliable, malleable.

Flesh.

Bronwyn didn't scream, but the skin of her back turned to ice and she dropped the lamp, hearing the glass case smash on the gravel as she turned and ran for the rectangle of light that meant safety.

She ran, fearful of his hands grabbing her, grasping her shoulders, holding, hurting.

She fell up the stairs, still slippery with the rain and clawed her way into the familiar kitchen. Iron. Warmth.

Grasping the door, she slammed it shut, driving the bolt home and sliding down the heavy surface, her breath loud in the sudden silence.

Someone was in her yard.

A man. A rail worker? Was he lost?

She held one hand to her throat as all the gossip of Rose's visits caught up with her.

Maybe two men? Like the papers said?

She eyed the long hallway opposite, expecting to see the sharp silhouette of another figure already in the house, waiting.

Nothing.

She scrambled away from the door, afraid the figure in her garden was right behind it, smashing it down, forcing his way in.

Getting to her feet, she ran down the hall to look in each room, her hand at her stomach as if it would stop the sick feeling that broiled there. Where she found an open shutter, and there weren't many, she slammed them shut, locking him—them—out. Where she found open curtains, she closed them, overlapping the material where it met in the middle.

Yet the more she shut herself in, the more she hated herself.

Why do I have to do this alone?

Because Josiah left her alone. Because she was now as weak as he had been. Because he died.

She cursed him for it.

Once upstairs, in Josiah's room, she shook out a cigarette from the silver tin and smoked it until it was gone. She smoked a second, becoming calmer, listening for any signs of anyone trying to gain access. Holding her breath, listening for any noise, any creaking floor board, and squeaking doorknob.

Nothing.

But they knew where she was. They could take their time...

Bronwyn looked to the nearest Josiah. He stared back at her, a keen and penetrating expression on his face. A loving look. He was always strong in this room.

Right then, she hated him for it.

He was strong in his death-image, but he was still dead.

She was left here trapped in this house with men outside who...

What? What did they want?

Or...what will they offer?

It was like a voice in her head. Bronwyn felt as if cool hands were running down her hot cheeks, soothing her. She lifted her own hands to her face to make sure no one was there. She was suddenly sick of it all. Sick of hiding and of being trapped. She was sick of Josiah's face, dead and at peace.

Why do I always sculpt *him at peace? Why does he deserve peace and not me?*

Mostly, she was sick of being afraid of *out there.*

She reached out and pushed at the nearest Josiah, watched him tilt back, then forward, then back once more before toppling to the floor.

He shattered, heavy blocks of him shooting from the clothes he wore, splitting and spinning across the floor, spreading their soft, powdery dust in all directions.

She moved through the room, pushing the rest over, enjoying the noises they made, the solid thumps as their backs hit the floor, the brittle cracks of their more delicate extremities.

Numb, she watched their destruction.

Then she ran down the stairs and through the rest of the house, flinging open the windows, the shutters, the bolts, some of which hadn't been worked in over a year. Her closeted life was at an end.

It was time to get out.

He ran faster than he had in years and faster than he thought he could. He sprinted through the garden, knowing he couldn't scale the iron fence, and leapt at the rear wall. Quickly he clambered over it, his skin and nails tearing on the bricks, fingers grasping and stretching for purchase, blood and dirt and grit combining.

Once he was on the other side, he sprinted down the side of the house and out into the front lawn. He knew if he could get away from there, she wouldn't follow him. She couldn't leave the house.

He just needed to get away, well away, so she wouldn't be able to see him, point him out, or describe him.

Damn it.

He didn't think she saw anything more than a fleeting glance of his face. He was sure the shock would mean she wouldn't be able to describe him. He could control the situation and no one ever need know, as long as she couldn't recollect his features.

She's a shut in. No one's going to believe her anyway.

He slowed to a walk as he reached the road, not wanting to draw any suspicion out in the open like he was.

He just needed to keep calm and in control. He tried to slow his breathing as he tucked in his shirt and wiped the grime and dirt from his trousers. With a shaking arm, he dabbed at the sweat on his forehead with his sleeve. His nails were torn and grubby, his hands were bleeding from the climb over the fence. Wiping them on his clothes, he gasped in pain. He studied his hand to find a deep gash bleeding profusely across his left palm.

With shaking fingers, he wrapped the wound in his handkerchief. He stopped for a moment to compose himself. He

232

looked behind him to the empty street and let his shoulder relax.

Made it.

He'd only taken two steps before he stopped in his tracks.

The umbrella.

He turned to look back the way he had come, back towards her house, remembering the statue that was leaning forward, its hands at its back, palms out.

I've left the umbrella!

"Jesus Christ Almighty."

Finally, the house was completely open to the darkness, chilled to its corners with the crisp air.

Bronwyn slumped in a chair facing the open patio doors, flung wide to reveal the absolute darkness.

She was unable to get out, but she *was* able to let them in.

"I'm ready," she said. "Come and get me."

LUNATIC OR PARAGON?

Zachary stared out the window of the tea room. He squinted through the morning sunlight, willing the head-ache that broiled his brain to go away. Every noise from outside, footfalls, laughter, the sound of horse hooves and cab wheels on the cobbles, was magnified.

He fingered the cuff of his shirt and ran his tongue over his teeth. They were rough from the drink he'd consumed the night before, but he didn't care. Pain was all that seemed to register right now.

Wherever I go, it's there. I cause it.

Of course, he had a chance to stop someone's pain—Athan's. Of all the jumbled thoughts from last night, all the blurred images, that thought was the clearest. Molly.

Zachary rubbed his eyes, feeling them sting beneath his fingers. He had decided to go to Molly and tell her about Athan. He'd bring them together—make *something* good come out of all this.

He planned to honour that silent promise.

It took all his strength to make it out of his room and down the stairs into the tea room to obtain the strongest brew available. He almost fell on the stairs, and once thought about turning around and heading back, but he couldn't stay there, not while Athan was in there.

He hoped his stomach would be able to keep the tea down.

He'd been offered food by the cook, but that was the last thing he wanted right now.

The cook was already in the kitchen of the Three Belles, ready for any customers, but the wreckage from the brawl almost guaranteed business would be light, even though the tea room had escaped any damage. There was the Vernon tea house and Leather Apron up the road.

"Here." The cook nodded as he placed the tea on the table in front of Zachary.

"Thanks," Zachary replied carefully.

He turned back around to watch the cook walk around the ordering table and head for the kitchen.

She hasn't shown herself yet, he thought. *I wonder if she will.*

He ran his hands through his hair, almost believing he could feel the throbbing of his head in his palms. He couldn't remember everything from the night before, but he could recall enough.

Rose and Sawyer in her kitchen.

The door to the corridor swung open and Zachary's eyes darted to it, expecting her to appear.

But instead, Athan appeared. He looked tired and un-washed, but Athan's usual sparkle was in his eyes as he walked across to the bar.

Why is he hale and hearty and I feel like death? How can he handle a night like last night and I can't?

Athan leaned against the ordering table, picked up a small bell and rang for the cook. The cook stepped from the kitchen and Athan talked with him. It was almost as if he hadn't seen Zachary in the room at all. Or was ignoring him. Athan and the cook seemed to know each other pretty well. Zachary wondered when that happened.

He thought about walking over there, saying good morning and testing the waters with his friend, but he wasn't sure he could stand up and make it all the way across the room without his head hurting even more.

He could remember the argument they had the night before, but not the particulars. He knew they had both said things they would—did—regret, but he couldn't pinpoint what they were. His mind was too busy fending off his nausea. All he wanted to do was sit in his corner and wait it out.

They had work today. He wondered how he'd cope.

He stirred the tea in front of him, watching the bitter liquid swirl around and around, going nowhere. Never ending.

The door opened again. He hunched over a little, hoping and dreading at the same time. But this time Emma walked inside with a worried look on her face.

A shard of memory slipped across his mind.

Her. Last night...something.

But Zachary couldn't find her through the fog of thoughts.

I saw her. Talked to her...I yelled, I think.

He shook his head slowly and raised the cup to his mouth, swallowing the hot liquid and letting it burn his lips and tongue. Why would he raise his voice to a lady? He can't have, surely. He watched her, but she did not look at him. This morning, it seemed, he did not exist.

He tried to remember what happened after he'd fought with Athan. He knew he left the Three Belles and went to Rose's house.

But *he* was there...

After that, it was all a blur.

Walking. I walked. Where the bloody hell did I go?

There were railroad ties...something smashed... Ribbons, blue ribbons... Something important, he was sure of it.

Molly.

That was all.

And then Rose entered the room.

He watched as she walked through the doorway, a grin on her face as it turned to the side. She was saying something over her shoulder to the person following her.

Sawyer?

But it wasn't Sawyer stepping into the room after her, it was another man, the younger one who was always with Mrs. Godley. He nodded, doffed his cap and said something back to her, and Rose laughed.

She looks so happy.

Rose walked happily over to Athan and the cook. The younger man hesitated, then marched purposefully towards Mrs. Godley who had taken the table at the other end of the tea room.

Zachary watched the young man sit awkwardly, playing with the cap in his hands. Another moment of hesitation, then he said something and she smiled back at him. They both laughed; the man's laugh containing no small amount of relief.

Happy, Zachary thought. *At least someone is happy.*

"Good morning."

Zachary turned to find Rose standing next to him, looking down at him and smiling.

He grunted and turned back to stare into his tea. He was staggered by his own rudeness, but seeing her smile at him like she'd smiled at Sawyer made his insides twist.

"You didn't sleep well?" she asked.

"You could say that," he replied.

"Nothing troubling you I hope," she sounded concerned, but he knew better.

"Nothing I can't deal with."

The conversation died and Zachary felt as if everyone in the room was listening, waiting to see what happened next.

He looked up from his tea and scanned the room, but no

one was watching them.

"I'm about to take Mrs. Belle's breakfast to her," she continued.

He didn't reply.

"Would you like to walk with me?"

"No, thank you," he muttered.

"Oh." Rose moved away, but then leaned forward and whispered to him. "Are you sure you're alright? You look well peaked."

"I'm fine," he closed his eyes, unable to meet hers.

He kept them shut, trying to wish her away, wanting to wish the town, his headache, his problems, Sawyer and Athan, everything away.

He wouldn't open them. Not now. Slowly, he started to count as time slipped by.

"Need a hand?"

Zachary heard Athan's voice across the room.

He opened his eyes and managed a smile. He knew his friend would be there for him. As always. No matter what.

He opened his eyes to see Athan walking towards the bar, smiling at Sawyer who stood with a pile of wood in his hands.

"I know there won't be too many people in here today," Sawyer was saying, "but I've been out to get a stockpile of wood to keep the fires burning. Could you help me bring them inside?"

"Certainly," Athan replied. "Just lead me to them."

Sawyer turned and walked back towards the bar, Athan following.

Zachary was left alone.

He watched the swirling dregs of his tea spin round and round, and he just wanted to die.

"They're not coming back tonight?" Athan asked.

"They are not. We'll be closing the doors after sunset. They've been told," Sawyer replied.

"The local constable take care of that?"

"And the Sergeant," Sawyer replied. "They were both up here."

"Not those other two—the Inspectors?"

"No. Then again, it wasn't a *murder* was it?" Sawyer looked pointedly at Athan.

"No," Athan said, evenly. "Official casualties?"

"Four tables, 11 chairs, 35 glasses, 9 mugs. Miners have four blokes who won't be hauling rock today. Rail workers have two who won't be laying track."

"And Miss Doyle?"

Sawyer's face turned grim. He looked at Athan whose casual line of questioning had snuck up on him.

"A small bump to the head. A sprained wrist. Ask your friend. He'd know better than me." Sawyer's voice lowered to a murmur as he turned away. "I have to work."

He moved further up the bar and grabbed the first piece of wood that came to hand.

Athan leant back in his chair and played with the cuff of his newly-pressed shirt, eyeing the solid back of the other man. Athan's fingers snagged on the bracelet he wore and he peered at it, scraping his square nail over yet another weak link. Broken again.

The atmosphere of the Three Belles was subdued, even for this early hour.

Inside the entrance-way and further into the bar, a pile of broken glass and ceramic shards from gin tumblers and beer mugs lay, swept high, in a corner away from the foot traffic.

Broken chair legs, those splintered beyond repair, were stacked near the coal scuttle ready to burn.

The only real noise was Sawyer planing a piece of timber, his carpenter's belt swinging, laden pockets knocking the bar top with muted metallic thuds.

The bar top, centrepiece of the establishment and pride of Bronwyn's former husband, was hidden under shelving, fresh timber and buckets of nails.

The smell of coffee brewing and bread baking did little to cover the odour of souring liquor in the carpeted entrance to the roped-off dining area.

A crude sign that said *"Boarding Clientele Only!"* hung, suspended by a dirty stable rope.

It was behind this barrier, at a table near the cold fireplace, Emma and Douglas sat together, taking tea.

They seemed to have reached some kind of understanding and were deep in conversation over a fresh pot, voices lowered, upper bodies at an intimate, yet not improper lean.

They had assured Rose, before she left on her errand, there was no hurry for their breakfast and, unlike previous mornings, it would be just the two of them.

They sat, sipping from china cups, Douglas periodically glancing toward the stairs leading to the guest rooms, his frock coat still fully buttoned like he was expecting to leave at any moment.

Zachary, pale and slow walked into the bar area. He passed a tin cup of tea to Athan who was now perched on one of the few undamaged tables. The blond man took it in silence without looking up. Placing it in the centre of the table, he went back to squeezing the links closed on his copper bracelet. He'd borrowed a flat knife from the kitchen for leverage.

The occasional 'clink' of cup on saucer, the sound of sharp plurals and consonants in Emma and Douglas' muffled conversation and the steady planing were the only sounds for a good 20 minutes.

241

Until the door opened with a quiet creak.

Rose closed the door carefully behind her, turning the handle fully and pressing the heavy door closed. She paused for a moment, one hand flat against it before turning and walking into the foyer, hugging a tray against her. Her shoulders were shaking.

She headed straight for the space between Zachary and Sawyer. There she leaned slightly, not looking at either man.

After a few seconds, she let the tray lid drop to the floor, her hands rising to cover her face. The sound of the crashing tray caused everyone to jump. Emma's hand came to her throat like she was stifling a scream of fright. She smiled apologetically at Douglas who briefly glanced her way.

Athan glanced up from his tinkering and frowned.

Rose started to shake all over. Soundlessly and without histrionics, she slowly came apart. But she refused to cry. Her hands fell from her face and worried her skirts.

The two men on either side, watched each other, unsure.

Sawyer took a small step toward the stricken woman, but stopped and rethought. Zachary's sickly pallor had gone. Two spots of colour warmed his face and he stood a little taller, suddenly sure of himself.

Sawyer nodded slowly and dropped back against the bar.

Zachary approached her and gently stroked her hair from her face and placed a supporting hand under her elbow. His fingers then moved boldly to the metal studs of her frock collar and undid the first two, his ring catching on one of them, briefly, before he manoeuvred it free.

"What is it?" he asked, his voice gentle.

"She's dead," Rose said. "Killed." She looked down at the empty tray, then back up at Zachary who had taken an involuntary step backward, stopped only by the fact he still held her arm. He shook his head in wordless denial.

Emma and Douglas exchanged troubled glances.

"Who's dead?" Sawyer finally asked. His tone was careful, like he was trying not to upset her.

Rose shook her head, the movement slow like she had a migraine. Her eyes were still free of tears, of any emotion altogether except maybe shock.

"Mrs...Br-Bronwyn," she said. Though the name took her two attempts, her voice was still calm. "Blood everywhere. I...couldn't touch her. I think her eyes were open. I should have closed her eyes. That would have been proper..."

"Jesus," Athan said it first and Rose mechanically made the sign of the cross at the utterance. Her mouth formed the words, *Father, Son, Holy Spirit.*

Zachary refused to look at Athan who was staring at him intently. He went to work, instead, calming Rose who seemed unaware of where she was now that she had imparted the news. Her breath hitched in her chest as she leaned against the bar and her hand moved to her stomach and pressed tight.

Sawyer rounded the bar and expertly poured a brandy, handing it to Zachary, who tried to coax Rose to drink.

Emma looked pointedly at Douglas, leaned forward.

"Where's Edward?" she asked, quietly.

He shrugged. "Asleep?" He asked it like it was a guess and she had the answer.

She leaned closer. "When did he return last night?"

He shrugged again.

Sawyer drifted towards Athan, the only other person not doing anything. He stood over the blond man as if waiting for an explanation. Athan drank his tea in one swallow resolutely ignoring Sawyer. Soon, both men were watching Zachary and the girl.

Rose calmed a little. She drank the brandy and told Zachary

that she had run to the police shed on her way. The two In-spectors from the Yard were 'taking care of it.'

She was the first to look up when the loud and confident footsteps came clomping down the stairs.

Edward reached the bottom of the stairs, looked sideways into the tea room where he spied Emma and Douglas at their corner table. He peered at the elaborate set of dishes between them.

"Tea, eh? Fortifying, I'm sure. I'm going for breakfast, want any?" He asked it like he didn't mean it—and he didn't.

Silence. Emma shook her head in what looked like disgust and Douglas opened his mouth, but nothing came out.

"*What?*" Edward looked at them scornfully.

"What happened to you?"

Edward turned. The red-head, Zachary, had asked the ques-tion from the bar area. The boy was standing over the cham-bermaid with one hand on her shoulder like he owned her. The lass looked pale.

Everyone looks pale.

He looked down at himself. Scuffed boots, dirty shirt, torn vest pocket and his hand wrapped in a bloody kerchief.

"Oh," he said. He'd forgotten the state he was in. He smoothed a hand over his head, flattening down the sleep-knotted hair. He managed to look chagrined. "I had...an acci-dent."

Douglas stood and moved to stand by Edward's side, the faithful dog. He touched his smudged jacket sleeve and Ed-ward jerked his arm away.

"Leave off. I'm fine. I just haven't bathed yet."

"What about that blood?" Sawyer said, stepping between

244

Edward and his view of Rose. Edward noticed the deliberate move and sucked his teeth, trying to bite back words he would regret.

Sawyer continued to look at him like he was a criminal. Edward's lip curled slightly and the skin of his neck grew hot with an angry flush. "Cut myself, what's it to ya?"

"The recluse is dead," Emma said softly. She, too, stood, easing out her full skirts from under the table so they fell straight.

"What?" Edward's voice was a whisper, but everyone in the room heard it.

The colour left him. His neck and cheeks, flushed with anger at Sawyer, now bleached at the news. His brain spun with last night's events and his head felt it would burst.

She was fine...

He left her. He didn't believe Emma—or didn't want to, he admitted that—and he left her. He could have stopped it. But he was too proud and he didn't like being told what to do by a—

He finally let out a breath.

He'd botched it.

His fault.

They were all looking at him and he realized that only Emma and Douglas knew about his 'mission.' The rest...

He recovered quickly from his terrible shock. His eyes swept the room, locking on Sawyer.

"You're all just flaming lunatics if you think it's me."

Rose blinked rapidly and sank back against the bar like it was the only thing that was holding her up. Zachary caught her, one arm going swiftly around her slim waist, and eased her into the nearest chair.

She nodded her thanks and Edward despised her for her frailty. They were all so *weak*. It was so damn hard to keep them alive.

Emma approached and Edward stabbed the air in front of her before she could get too close. There was blame in her eyes and he wasn't ready for her serve on top of his own.

"I was in bed," he reiterated loudly for the benefit of every-one.

"Oh? I thought you were supposed to be doing your job," Emma shot back.

No one saw it coming. His arm moved fast and he back-handed her before Douglas could react. The sound of his hand against her skin was meaty and thick.

Emma reeled back a step but steadied herself, her hand moving to her cheek, her eyes blinking, languid in those moments before shock bled away and the pain hit.

Some of her hair slipped from dislodged pins.

Douglas moved to her side. Shaken, he hesitated a moment before gripping her arm in a gentle fashion. Sawyer also stepped closer to Emma, not quite between them yet, just as he'd done with Rose.

What a paragon you are, boy.

Sawyer held the heavy plane in one hand, hefting it with loose and ready fingers.

Edward ignored him; he watched Emma instead, a familiar thing.

She wasn't going to cry, he could see that. He gave her credit for it. She just held her face and took a breath before looking at him. None of the blame had left her. On the contrary, it was nicely complimented with a solid dose of...

Pity.

Edward blinked.

Be fucked.

He turned away, sucking air into his lungs in a long hiss.

Athan watched the entire proceedings, looking at each of

them with dull eyes and no invested interest. He seemed to be somewhere else, thinking about something or someone.

Must be nice not to care.

"That was uncalled for!" Douglas said harshly —the nearest he'd ever come to yelling at Edward. Edward faced his two... partners and saw Douglas had drawn Emma to his side in a brotherly, comforting manner.

An allying manner.

Edward glared at them as he literally watched the pendulum swing against him. It would be slow to return in his favour.

"She didn't deserve that," Douglas said.

Edward didn't look at Douglas. "I wasn't the one with the smart mouth," he said to her.

Emma shook her head, her loose ringlets swaying against her swelling cheek. "No, you're the one with blood on his hands."

HORRIBLE WAY TO GO

"Rabid dogs, Sir?" Collins turned to face Foster, who was still standing near the gate in the garden, looking up at the body impaled on the high fence spikes.

Foster continued chewing his tobacco before turning away and spitting it into the bushes. "Nope," he replied, shaking his head. "She lost most of her blood in the house. Whatever happened, it happened inside. Dogs would have to get inside somehow, and they would be heard, cause a commotion. Nothing like that was heard last night."

"Then how'd she get up there?" Collins continued.

"How indeed?"

"Was she pushed? Did she jump?"

"Long way to be pushed." Foster turned to stare towards the windows on the second story of Bronwyn's house. The middle one was flung wide. "If she jumped—ran and jumped—from that window, she *could* impale herself on the fence."

"Sweet Jesus, you think a suicide?"

"A possibility," Foster shrugged his shoulders. "Or maybe, Sergeant Collins, that's what we're *supposed* to think."

Collins stared blankly for a few seconds. "I know what you mean. I was thinkin' that too. We're missin' something, I'm sure of it."

Foster pointed at the body hanging from the fence. "Look at her again. Tell me what you see. Maybe you see something different than I do."

Collins squinted in the morning sunlight and focused his attention on the body. The woman was on her back, the four spikes spearing right through her, each sharp bloody tip coated in drying blood. Her legs were splayed on each side of the fence, the soles of her bare feet stained with blood and clay. On the closest side her arms hung backwards, swinging slightly in the morning breeze, as if she were reaching out towards them for help.

Her face and hair were covered in blood—most of it originating from a horrific and deep gash across her nose. Her arms were too, as if the skin had been carefully removed, but with force. Long strips of skin, sinew and muscle hung from her, entwined with the shreds of her torn and bloody dress. Her eyes were dark holes, the result of either her last few minutes alive, or from the two crows circling nearby.

What clothes remained were torn in deep wet strands and the pool of blood slowly congealing at the base of the fence made it clear that this horror had been visited upon her only very recently. Her final breath taken while skewered, impaled on the fence that had protected her for so long.

"She's all ripped up," was all Collins could manage.

"And?" Foster prodded.

"Ah..." Collins tried to find anything, searching for what he was missing. "I don't know, Sir."

"See a pattern?"

"A pattern to what?"

"The killings, Collins. This is like the other one, and the one before that. The same marks, the same cuts, the same way."

"Yes, I know that," Collins agreed. "But it's not helping us, is it? We need to find this animal before he strikes again. Who is he? And how do we stop him?"

Foster sighed and turned away. "Too many questions," he

replied. "And we don't have even one answer."

Foster walked back towards the front of the house, running a hand through his tight curly hair. Collins followed him close behind. The local coppers were surrounding the house, trying to keep the onlookers and children away.

Kids shouldn't see this. It's unseemly to have them here.

Word had got out, like it always did, and the townsfolk were coming to see if it was all true.

Another one. Damn it. Another one.

Constable Nash walked up to them and met them on the path to the front door. "Found an umbrella, Sarge. Hanging on one of those statues. And...a lady over here says she saw a large man running from the property last night. Seems he was in a hurry to get away. She says he was all bloody."

Foster nodded. "Anything else?"

Nash looked confused. "Sorry sir?" He looked back toward the growing crowd on the street.

"Did she say anything else? A name? Where he lives?"

"No sir, she doesn't know him. Says she hadn't seen him before."

"A stranger then," Collins interrupted. "He must be a stranger, Fred."

Foster nodded as he glanced at Collins, ignoring the lapse in form.

"Plenty of them about with the railway going through. *And* one of them is missing an umbrella," Foster replied. Then he turned back to Nash. "Good work, son. Keep her nearby. I'll talk with her soon."

Nash nodded and went to leave.

"Hang on a minute," Foster called.

Nash turned back to face him.

"Get someone out near that body to keep the birds away."

"Will do, Sir."

251

"There's not much of her left, but we don't want the crows getting at her, too."

"Right, on to it."

With that, Nash left them and Foster walked into the house with Collins by his side.

They walked up the hallway and stepped around the large blood stain, trying hard not to interfere with the broken chair and the confusion of footprints and smudges along the hall. Blood was splattered along the walls and floor, and deep red palm-prints stretched frantically halfway up the stairway.

"Did she try to escape, Collins?" Foster asked as they walked.

"Couldn't. She was a shut-in."

"Might have tried though. She could've run to the door and been attacked there, then dragged back."

"But there's blood and mess everywhere, footprints and destruction all over the house."

They turned and started walking up the stairway to the second floor.

"I know, Collins, but did you notice anything else? Look at the footprints."

Collins stopped on the stairs, bent down and re-examined the bloody tracks.

Footprints everywhere. Bare feet.

It took a few seconds, but then it hit home.

He stood and nodded at Foster. "There's only hers," he said. "No one else's."

A smile stretched across Foster's face. "Exactly, Sergeant. Exactly. Now, I find that quite interesting, don't you?"

"I do," he nodded. "Yes, I certainly do."

They walked across the landing and into the room where Bronwyn Belle's statues once were housed. Around them now was nothing but broken shards of plaster; pieces of statue, arms and shoulders and legs and feet, mixed with splatters of blood and strips of real flesh. Some tools were neatly stacked on a nearby bench, chisels and hammers, a pile of needles, and bloody handprints streaked the walls.

Collins pointed to the tools. "You know, Sir, something's not right about that."

"What exactly?"

"Think about it." Collins walked across to the bench. "You're bein' attacked and you fear for your life. You manage to get away from your would-be attacker, and you run upstairs and into a room where these tools are...lyin' out in the open."

"Go on." Foster was listening intently.

"You've got some time; not a lot, but a little, right? Why wouldn't you grab one of these tools and defend yourself? They're sharp, some very sharp. It's a weapon, why not use it?"

Foster shrugged and turned away.

"I just don't get it," Collins muttered to himself, looking at the tools one last time.

"Maybe she was paralysed with fear? Or maybe she did fight back with one of her implements," Foster replied. "Maybe he overpowered her and took it from her. Used it on her and then got rid of it. Or took it with him."

"*Bastard*," Collins cursed.

Carefully, they walked across to the open window. The bloody footprints stopped with two clear prints on the window ledge. The shattered and broken face of a man was beneath the ledge. The face looked so life-like, almost real except for the destruction.

Foster and Collins both leaned forward and stared out of the window, looking down at the prone corpse skewered on the fence below. Nash was beneath her, shooing at the crows

with a horse-blanket, trying to keep them away from the body. The crows circled above, waiting patiently.

"Horrible way to go," Collins muttered. "No matter if she were pushed or forced to jump."

"I know," Foster replied.

"Who do you think did it?"

"I still have no idea. It could be anyone."

"Why murder a shut-in?" Collins asked.

"Why indeed." Foster pulled more tobacco from his pocket and started to chew.

"Did she know somethin'?"

"Possibly."

"But *what*? What could she know that was so important? She was a shut-in."

"I know, Collins, I know. Maybe a shut-in is the perfect person to tell your secrets to."

"Sir?"

Foster turned to face his partner. "Yes?"

"What do we do now?"

"We question any large stranger who can't account for his whereabouts last night."

"No, no. I mean, about her." He pointed over his shoulder and down towards the widow Belle.

Foster shrugged. "You get her down from there, Tom. Get her off that fence and away from here before we have a riot on our hands."

He turned to walk from the room, leaving Collins by the window.

"But how, Sir?" Collins called to him. "How?"

How indeed.

"The inspectors are at the house," Emma said to them as they walked down the street. She paused as she considered her next words. "They're...removing her from where she... fell."

"Yeah. Fell. Right," Douglas said.

"Quiet." Emma whispered as they turned to watch Edward marching towards them.

Douglas looked over Edward's shoulder towards the wall running off a small, narrow laneway. He noticed the policeman kneeling in the lamplight, rubbing from the wall the remaining words written in chalk.

...The miners are the men...

...that will not be blamed for nothing...

By then, Edward was by their side.

"Did you—" Douglas began, but Edward cut him short.

"We should go tonight—do it before they clean the place up," Edward said in a rushed tone.

"We're not going to get near the place, now," Douglas replied.

"*You* are not going anywhere." Emma's tone towards Edward was final.

"What?"

Douglas saw some of his old fire light Edward's eyes.

"I didn't spend all this time and effort to—"

"You're *not* going anywhere near it," she repeated. "Not after the...scene before. Not after what was said."

Edward opened his mouth, then closed it. He nodded and looked back towards the policeman as the officer finished obliterating the scrawl in the laneway.

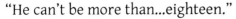

"He can't be more than...eighteen."

255

"No," Emma replied. She controlled a shiver and tightened her shawl around her shoulders. It wouldn't help. She shivered at night in her bed, unable to feel warmth no matter how many quilts she drew over her.

She had thinned considerably since this started. Her bodice no longer hugged the swell of her breasts. Eating was the last thing she wanted to do despite the pangs of hunger that hit in the evening. Every morning she woke feeling like someone had been sitting on her chest during the night. She just couldn't get any air these days.

Her wedding ring slipped from her finger only this morning sending her scrabbling for it under the wooden bed. That simple gold band was all she had of him.

She fingered the band now. Feeling it slip up to the knuckle with ease, she clenched her fist. Young Constable Nash, the object of Douglas' scrutiny, stamped his feet twice on the widow Belle's patio.

She and Douglas stood under the shelter of a large oak, in plain view; just another couple of curious onlookers pausing to witness the silent, looming face of the large house. Most had wandered past them before the sun went down, paused and looked. They murmured softly, wondering what horrors lay inside, what remnants of butchery were not yet cleaned up.

"I'm sorry, Mrs. Godley. You're cold." Douglas' voice was soft. Not kind, just quiet.

Emma turned to look up at him. She hoped her utter incredulity was not apparent.

"I mean...I'm sorry you're out here. You shouldn't be. This is no job for— I mean, you're a..."

Lady. Lady is what he's trying to say and can't even muster that.

She shrugged dismissing him and his comment. "It's nothing I can't bear. For the short term."

256

Too much more of this and she would waste away, she was sure. Or cease to care. And which would be the worse fate?

Douglas shifted, uncomfortable. "The street is clear now. We should go in when he does his next round."

"You mean *I* should go in." She didn't take her eyes off the constable. Nash *was* young. She wondered if George had looked like that when he first started in the job. Surely not that young.

"No," Douglas said. "We'll both go. I'll keep an eye out for Constable Nash while you're..." He trailed off, then nodded to himself. "Well. There it is."

Constable Nash lifted his mug to his mouth and drained the contents, flicking the last few droplets onto the geraniums with a quick flick of his wrist. He placed the cup on the patio rail, straightened his collar and pulled his jacket down with a sharp tug.

"Ready for action, our boy is," Douglas murmured, sounding like Edward when he said it.

Nash walked stridently down the steps of the patio and wheeled right, walking along the front before wheeling again and disappearing into the shadows. Soon after, they heard the side gate swing open.

"Shall we?" Emma asked, even though she was already stepping onto the street, heading towards Bronwyn's house. She heard Douglas follow her, but wouldn't have cared if he stayed behind. They soundlessly opened the small gate and ran across the lawn, avoiding the stones on the path. Emma lightly ran up the steps to the front porch. In her rush to get inside, she tried the door. There was a sharp sound as her wedding ring hit the metal handle.

Both she and Douglas froze.

Stupid!

She felt Douglas' eyes at her back as he waited. In her

257

mind's eye she saw him reach for his home-made sap.

She shook her head quickly. "No. It's alright."

He was silent for a few seconds and she braced herself for the blow.

"If you're sure."

She let out a breath and turned the handle. To her dismay, the door simply opened.

"Why...?"

"Go on. Go, go," Douglas hissed, briefly touching the small of her back to move her inside. Once in the dark corridor, he shut the door quietly and retreated backwards until his heel hit the first stair of the staircase that lead to the second floor.

"I suppose they thought that boy was enough to deter any violation of the house." He turned a relieved smile on his face. "I reckon they were dead wrong."

Emma nodded once, not really listening. She stepped back from him.

Over his shoulder, she saw the first of the blood.

She felt that weight once again settle in her chest as the air left her. The light from the lamps outside crawled across the interior like smoke. Not enough to see detail, just black shadow smears behind him.

They were halfway up the wall. Finger streaks, palm smudges; the last signature of a woman fighting for her life.

Emma took a breath.

There was a surprising absence of odour in this place.

The air was static in here. It wasn't like Mary in her noxious shack; heat from within and draft from without mingling in the centre of her room. Nor was it like Sacha's breezy kitchen or her cold and odourless grave.

The sheer weight of the air seemed to dampen any smell. For that, she was extremely grateful.

Douglas titled his head.

258

"What is it?"

"Behind you."

Douglas' eyes widened in horror and he spun, his foot gathering the hall runner as he did.

"God."

"It's dry," Emma said, dully. She was becoming accustomed to the sight of blood, violent smears of it, pools and prints. That wasn't healthy, surely.

"There's so much of it," he said, his voice hushed.

She remembered his face in Mary's alley and felt a certain kinship with him that she would never have with anyone else. He'd seen. Up close. Edward hadn't.

"They move around a lot," Emma said. "I don't know why. The ferocity of the attack, probably. It's never quick. Our killer is patient, predatory. Lets them run away a little."

The thought of the victims no longer terrified her. It simply made her sad. She looked to her right, feeling her eyes sting at the thought of it.

A long, dark corridor stretched into darkness. It was oppressive with wall hangings and thin tables laden with Bronwyn's clutter. Emma touched the nearest. It was once a beautiful polished wood, wonderfully made; now splashed with perfectly round droplets of dried blood. An oil lamp sat in the corner, metal and glass smudged where bloodied fingers had turned the flame down. Emma swallowed hard. She'd check the lamp on the way out.

"I should never have seen this," she whispered. "No one should see this."

She moved past Douglas, walking carefully on the tightly-woven rugs so her feet did not make too much noise. Boards would squeak in a house this old. She only hoped that Constable Nash wasn't listening too closely. He would have finished his circuit of the house by now.

The blood started at the base of the stairs; dark, large pools and elegant splatters that arced up the walls. The pattern of spray and motion of blood was becoming familiar to her. A new language she had learned.

In the middle of the large hall runner was a strange void; a portion of carpet in all this blood that was untouched.

The smears began at the base of the stairs where Douglas stood—where Bronwyn would have grabbed at the wall for support after the initial attack.

Why had she run upstairs where there was no way out? Was there perhaps a room up there that she might have barricaded herself in?

Emma forced herself not to think about the 'why.' Her duty was no longer to Bronwyn but for the one who came after.

They'd missed it. *Edward* had missed it. There was someone else now who needed saving if they could.

She gathered her skirts and began to walk slowly up the stairs, hoping the light from outside reached the second storey.

Wordlessly, Douglas followed. The dried trail led them up to the landing. It was clear Bronwyn had slipped and fallen, gripped the banister to pull herself up. Skin on lacquered surface.

Emma forced herself to bend down and peer at the myriad hand prints on the floor. Smudged. All smudged. She swallowed down disappointment. She did not want to be the one to report back to Edward that they lost the trail.

"Anything?" Douglas' whisper was harsh. He may as well have spoken aloud.

"Nothing."

"Right. You're doing fine."

She stood, feeling a faint dizziness as she did. Forcing herself not to grip the stained banister, she continued on. The room where Bronwyn had clearly entered was well lit from the lamps in the garden. Here was the scene of her final struggle.

A large room, big enough to take up half the upper floor, stretched out before her. But for the debris on the floor, the room was mostly empty. A chair in the corner. A large wooden work-bench like the kind carpenters' used in work-shops, sat squat in the corner. It was covered in tools, cloth bags and ceramic basins. A series of unfired hands lay in a row at the back.

White hands.

On the floor, the statues that had once stood in the room lay destroyed; tipped, smashed, shattered. Chunks of clay man had spun to almost every corner of the room and into the hall where Douglas stood, waiting.

She turned and raised an eyebrow.

He shook his head. His courage, apparently, went only so far.

Emma almost smiled and walked into the room, carefully stepping over the decimated figures.

There was blood in here, but not enough. Footprints only. The inspectors with their heavy shoes and Bronwyn's bare feet. Blood in the dust. Useless.

Give me something, woman.

She made her way to the window, its swing-panes open and swaying slightly in the gentle breeze of night. Emma smiled. There, on one flat glass pane was a perfect handprint. Back-lit by the garden lamps, it was translucent and more detailed than any print she had ever seen.

She knelt on the floor and peered at the fine brown lines, pulling the window closed with a soft "snick."

Bronwyn had long palms and long fingers. Slender and creative, hundreds of fine lines that told Emma immediately

Bronwyn was highly emotional. Sensitive. Vulnerable. She was accustomed to caring—and being cared for.

It's not fair.

The intellect and fate lines were joined at their inception, making her cautious or fearful. The poor woman had been scared every second of her time here.

She had good reason, it turned out.

Two marriage lines, the lower of the two, long and deep. She pined for someone.

Emma knew what that felt like and thought once more about slipping away from Douglas. He wasn't like Edward. She doubted he had murder in him.

But looking at Bronwyn's palm made her want to stay. Someone had to help these people.

Like the times before, her peripheral vision seemed to darken until all she could see were the lines. Rushing fate lines, harrowed marriage lines, water hands and hands full of puzzles.

Portraits in tin frames. Cheap, but simple and not un-sightly. A woman curling something through her hair. Zach-ary, his face static, his feet stopping on a broken timber deck and turning, his face surprised. The rictus of an old woman. Dead and lying in a pool of her own fluids. Dying pansies in a pot. The railway. The town, the blood that always accompa-nied—

Emma fell backwards to the floor, catching herself with her hands.

"Are you alright?"

"Yes." Emma dusted her hands off and clambered to her feet. "Quite fine." Douglas had not moved from the doorway.

"Did you get...did you see what we came for?"

"I think so, yes," Emma said quietly. She didn't care if he heard or not. Something bothered her. Bronwyn *was* the woman she saw in Sacha's palm. Without a doubt.

And yet...

"Go wait downstairs, Douglas. Let me know when our callow policeman has finished his rounds." Douglas obeyed, stepping backward and out of her sight with a slight deferential nod.

Edward would have stayed, knowing what it was she had to do, but Douglas had a trust that Edward didn't.

Emma looked through the room once more. She looked at the blood-smirched glass, the broken men around her, the dust.

She approached the work-bench and, one by one, she lifted the chisels, the small hammers, the sewing needles. She looked at the ceramic bowls, clear liquid on top, fine silt on the bottom.

The bedrooms, though unblemished by Bronwyn's desperate escape attempt, held jewellery, trinkets in pewter and iron. Emma made sure she did her job—like she would have had Edward been at her shoulder with a shotgun in his hand.

She finished her search of the house and crept carefully up the hallway toward the door.

There's nothing here, she thought with some relief.

"He's off, Emma," came Douglas' harsh whisper.

"Then so are we."

As she passed the side-table in the hall, she ran her hand across the cold metal of the oil lamp she had seen when she first arrived. Her heart sped up as she did so.

Douglas met her at the door. He raised his eyebrows.

"No."

"Edward *is* going to be pleased." He peered out of the crack in the door. "Alright. Go." He swung the door wide and ushered her through. They retraced their steps until they were safe on the other side of the road under the shadow of the oak.

A few minutes later, Constable Nash walked around the right side of the house, his steps quick and nervous as he emerged from the darkness.

"We'll all sleep soundly tonight with him on duty," Douglas chuckled.

Emma looked at the house, its dark windows, closed on this side. The secrets it held...

"Are you alright?"

"Hmm?"

"You seem...I dunno, you seem..."

Douglas' voice faded into the background as Emma thought about what she'd seen—and what she hadn't.

A woman surrounded by men, yes. White hands, yes. Smudged dresses, tintypes and metal; in the windows, the fence, the brackets of the tables, the lamps.

It all fit with what she'd seen in Sacha's hand... But Zachary's reading puzzled her. It, too, was valid. He'd touched this killer. He was part of the trail, he'd had contact.

So...

All through the house there was material, dust, clay, men...

But there were no blue ribbons.

Not one.

"...Mrs. Godley?"

"I'm fine, Douglas. Let's get back."

The Truth, This Time

January 6, 1889

"**A**nd the blood?"

"Excuse me?" the man snapped.

Sergeant Collins would have stood were it not for the subtle hand at his elbow. He cast a glance at his superior officer.

Foster raised a suspicious eyebrow at the subject of their inquiry as he leaned back in his chair, his body relaxed. His entire manner said, *Talk to me, son. We're here to help.*

Collins envied the Inspector's patience. The man opposite them was obviously on some kind of drug that addled him. He didn't smell of whiskey so it was not the horrors of the drink that assailed him. Laudanum? He was withdrawn, irritable. His skin was pale except for two points of colour on either side of his neck and there were obvious tremors in his hands.

"You had blood on you this morning," Foster said, changing the question slightly. "Care to explain?"

"I don't have to explain anything to you," the man said.

"I'm afraid you do. A woman has been found murdered. Crime like that'll certainly have you gibbeted. You won't even make the treadmill."

"It wasn't me," he mumbled.

His name was Edward. Edward Baker. The only other time Collins had seen him was when they first put him in the clink after the tip-off from one Sawyer Evans. It hadn't panned out then, but this time Edward was looking guilty as sin.

Collins saw Foster nod slightly and took his cue. "Listen, mate," he began, his voice deceptively calm. "We got you in a hotel foyer the mornin' after the attack with blood on your person. We got you discussin' the deceased in that foyer. We got a witness description that you most *certainly* fit and," he raised his voice, making Edward start, "we've got you strikin' a woman! Now what kind of man does that *make* you?"

Collins slammed his hand down on the table. Standing, now, he looked at the man in front of him. Edward would not or could not meet his gaze. Collins despised him for that cowardice.

He'll hit a woman, but he can't look at me. Damn prick.

"What kind of man would do that, eh?" Collins continued, nostrils flaring, but voice calm.

"That was different," Edward said. "She said... She wouldn't—"

Collins shook a finger at him. "There's never a good enough reason to strike a woman, *sir*. Not ever." He resumed his seat.

There was silence for a long minute. Opposite their calculated and unified veneer, Edward Baker played with the frayed cuff of one jacket sleeve. He stroked his moustache occasionally, finger underneath the bristles. Right, then left. He did nothing to wipe away the sweat that stood out on his forehead.

Foster leaned forward. He titled his head in an artful nod of approval to Collins. When he spoke, his voice was friendly.

Collins envied his patience once more.

"You see how this looks, Mr. Baker? *Edward*. You're a stranger in town. You're in the company of another male individual—also a stranger. Prove to me that you weren't in the deceased's garden. Give me something."

"It was horrific," Rose whispered, wiping her eyes yet again.

"Calm yourself," Sawyer replied, kneeling down next to her. "Stop thinking about it. It only upsets you."

"Why does everyone tell me to stop thinking about it? How can I stop thinking about it? Every time I think of Bronwyn, all I can see is her...pinioned there on that fence, the crows pecking at her face. Her arms outstretched towards me, her eyes looking right at..." Her voice sunk to a whisper and her chest heaved with further sobs of distress.

Sawyer reached for a nearby stool, grabbing it from under one of the tables. He sat and reached out towards her, but hesitated. He settled for resting his hand on the arm of her chair.

"The more you think about it, the more upset you will become, that's all I meant. There's no use getting into such a state. What's done is done, Rose." Even to his own ears the words sounded, at best, flippant.

Her eyes rose to his and she stared deep into them. "She was my *friend*, Sawyer," she replied in a cold, level tone. "My best friend. She was taken from me in a most appalling manner. That counts for something."

He nodded and sighed, looking around the bar, checking no one was listening in. It was a reflex action used whenever he talked with Rose. But today no one was listening. No one was there.

"I understand that," he continued. "I'm just trying to help."

"Well, *don't*."

"Rose, I—"

"What do you expect me to do? Do you want me to *forget* about her? Forget about the monstrous thing they did to

267

her?"

"No, no I don't." He reached out to her now, but she pulled back; just as he'd expected. "All I'm saying is that it is the talk of the town. People everywhere are gossiping about what happened. I simply don't think it will do you any good to become so emotional about it all. It won't solve anything. It won't bring her back. If you continue like this, people might connect you to this horror somehow. You will become their new focus of attention. You don't want that."

"They already know I take her meals every day. They know she was a friend of mine. What does it matter if they know I found her? I'm already connected to her. I'm allowed to grieve, Sawyer. We're all allowed to grieve. We have to. Otherwise, we're no better than dumb animals."

Sawyer looked away, suddenly feeling uncomfortable and unsure about what to do. He tried a different tack. "Can I get you something?"

"No."

"A drink? A meal?"

She shook her head. "I have to get ready for opening time. People will be arriving soon."

Sawyer half-smiled. "Oh, Rose. No one will be eating here tonight. Don't worry so much about that."

"I have to. It's almost time for dinner. I have to get the meals ready. Get Bronwyn's tray—"

She stopped abruptly, her hands reaching for her open mouth. She didn't say anything more, just closed her eyes and let the tears run down her face.

Sawyer stood and slowly backed away from her. As much as he wanted to touch her, he held off.

She needs time, that's all. The wounds will heal.

He turned around at the sound of footsteps approaching. The door into the bar opened. Sawyer readied to usher the customers away, to tell them no food would be served to-night.

A crowd is the last thing she needs right now.

The clairvoyant woman, Mrs. Godley, rushed into the room. Her cheeks flushed and her hair tousled. She let her skirts fall from where she had held them to prevent them from being mussed. She looked wildly around.

Sawyer liked her. She'd had splendid things to say about his future when he'd asked her to read for him days ago at his workshop. He didn't dare believe her predictions, though. That kind of hope could destroy a man; the promise of true love. But she had been kind and he appreciated manners.

"Are you alright Ma'am?" Sawyer asked.

She looked right through him for a second or two before he registered to her, then her eyes locked on his.

"Sawyer," she said in a rush of breath. "It is *Sawyer*, isn't it?"

Almost as if she was expecting someone else.

"Yes. You read my palm a couple of days ago."

"I remember, yes."

"We won't be serving meals tonight, unfortunately," he continued.

She shook her head. "That's alright. I'm not hungry."

"Can I help you with something else?"

"I very much doubt it."

"I could try," he said, needing to do *something* useful.

He stepped towards her but she darted around him, spotting Rose and dashing to her side.

"Is she alright?" she asked over her shoulder to Sawyer as she squatted down next to the crying woman.

"Yes," he replied, without turning around, his eyes focussed on the back of the bar.

Women can be so complicated...

269

"Rose?" he could hear her saying. "Are you alright, dear? It is about Mrs. Belle, isn't it?"

Sawyer kicked at a large splinted piece of wood still lying on the floor from the brawl the night before. It was long and sharp, probably broken off from a chair leg.

All in pieces...every single one.

He slowly bent down, his back still towards the women, and picked up the wood in his hand. His fingers wrapped around the thick end as he weighed it, judging its strength and feeling its texture on his palm.

He turned around to face them both. Rose was staring straight into Emma's eyes as she knelt before her. They were talking in hushed tones to each other.

Sawyer took a quiet step forward, slowly inching towards them until he could hear their conversation.

"I know..." Emma was saying. "But it's not over and I need you to be strong."

Rose nodded. "I will."

"It could be anyone. Even someone you know. It's not safe here, Rose. Be on your guard, promise me you'll be on your guard!" As she talked, Emma's hands roamed along Rose's arms, lightly touching the fabric of her clothes, as if she wanted to smooth them out. She stopped only twice, once at Rose's hands, where she held them tight for a few seconds, lightly brushing her bracelet and the ring on Rose's finger; and then again along Rose's cheap silver buttons on her sleeve, one by one, fleetingly, but with purpose.

Sawyer took another step closer. They hadn't noticed him yet, too intent on their own private conversation.

"I'm trying to make it stop, to go away. But I need your help, Rose."

"But what can I do?"

Sawyer was behind Emma now, leaning forward, right over

her.

"Emma!"

The shout tore across the room.

They all turned quickly, facing Douglas in one fluid movement as he moved to join them.

"Did you have any luck?" Emma asked him.

"No, Mrs. Godley," Douglas replied, regaining his manners as he reached them. He was puffing and red of cheek. "He's nowhere to be found."

"Who?" Sawyer asked.

"You're *absolutely* sure?" Emma ignored Sawyer, something he was used to.

"Yes, no one knows where he is." Douglas doffed his cap and wiped an arm across his forehead.

"Who?" Sawyer asked again.

Emma turned to face him and seemed surprised he was standing so close to her. She let go of Rose's hand and stood.

Sawyer took a step backwards, giving her room.

"Edward," she replied. "We don't know where he is." Then she turned back to Douglas. "Did you check his room?"

Douglas nodded. "Yes, he wasn't there either, Ma'am."

"And you asked around the local establishments?"

"I did."

"I don't understand," she replied. "Somebody must know something!"

Sawyer tried to hide his smile. "I know where he is," he said.

All three turned to face him. Rose had calmed considerably. Sawyer was grateful for that.

He said nothing more.

"*Well?*" Douglas prompted. "If you know where Edward is, *please* tell us!"

Sawyer looked back at Emma and waited.

"It *is* important," Emma urged.

He smiled slightly.

"Those inspectors from the Yard have him," he told them. "Came earlier. Took him away."

Emma turned to face Rose. "Is this true?"

Rose shrugged and looked worried. "I...I don't know. I've been—"

"It's true," Sawyer replied. "They've got him at the local nick. You can go check if you don't believe me."

Douglas grabbed Emma's hand. "Quick, we have to get there."

But she didn't move. She stayed in her place.

Douglas looked at her, surprise registering on his face. "We must get him."

Emma shook her head. "Let him sit a while. If he's with them, he can't do any more damage."

Douglas considered it. Sawyer could see he was wavering.

"He's been gone quite a time now," Sawyer added. "A few hours at least. No telling what they've done to him by now."

Douglas' resolve returned. The fire was back in his eyes.

"Please, Emma," he insisted. "We *must*."

Slowly, she nodded, and sighed deeply. Before they left, she turned once more to look down at Rose. "Will you be alright?" she asked.

Rose nodded.

"Don't worry about Miss Doyle," Sawyer said, stepping to Rose's shoulder and placing his empty hand on it. "She'll be safe with me."

"Right, then," Douglas said. "Good. Don't go anywhere. We'll be back as soon as we can. Until then, don't do anything...foolish."

They both nodded as Douglas and Emma hurried from the Three Belles.

"Horrific times we live in," Rose said softly, her voice sounding so sad.

"Yes," Sawyer agreed. "Horrific indeed."

"I don't have anything. I wasn't there."

Like a perfectly hit cue in a theatre production, Collins flipped Douglas' umbrella onto the table.

Edward's mouth dropped slightly before he could stop it. They picked up his reaction like midges to bare skin. As one, they leaned forward. Collins' hatred was evident. Foster was looking at Edward like he was a puzzle to be solved.

"You recognise it then?" Collins asked. His lips pursed in satisfaction.

"Yes," Edward whispered. He had nowhere else to go. He'd bollocked everything. He'd lost his temper, the shut-in was dead. Maybe he deserved this.

"What did you say?" Foster asked. "Speak up, son."

"I said, yes. Yes, it is my umbrella." Once he said it, everything else just followed. It felt so good to simply say it. "I *was* in her bloody garden—only it wasn't quite so bloody then, was it? She was fine when I left. *Alive.* I got sprung so I ran. I climbed the fence, cut myself, came back in a state and slept it off."

"You went to sleep?"

"Yes."

"Just sauntered back to the bar and went to bed?"

"*Yes!* There wasn't much more I could do, now was there?"

"Then you woke up," Collins said casually, "Belted a girl..."

"She *deserved* that!" Edward hissed. He would *not* apologise for that.

"So you're telling us you were there," Foster said. He

dabbed the tip of his pencil against his tongue and flipped open his notebook.

"Yes. I was there."

"In the garden with this." Foster patted the umbrella.

"Yes."

"Right." Foster scratched his hair. "Why?"

Christ.

Edward looked at his trembling hands. He wasn't scared of these two or the law or their threats, their accusations. He knew the truth. He was scared that the ghost of Bronwyn, the woman he'd terrified so much before running from her garden, would haunt him for what he did. What he failed to do.

Ghosts most certainly existed.

He was scared of all the future victims that he would fail to save if he was locked up. He had a job to do. He saw himself as the two officers saw him. Guilty. And he was. But not for the reasons they thought.

"I was watching her," he said. "I was watching her because I thought she might be the next to die."

Their eyes fairly gleamed with anticipation.

"Why did you think that?" Foster asked carefully. They were handling him with kid gloves, now.

Edward didn't care how it made him look. He started talking. It was just him and these men. Same jobs, different masters. Surely they would understand.

"The woman we travel with…"

"The one you—"

"Yes." Edward glared at Collins. "*Her.* She has…a *gift.* She can see things we can't. She saw a woman die who fit the description of that shut-in."

Foster cleared his throat deliberately.

"Sorry. *The deceased.* She saw her in a palm-reading and I was in the *deceased's* garden to make sure she was alright,

274

see? I was there to help." He took a breath. "I failed."

"You're not wrong there," Collins murmured.

"You, this woman and the other gentleman," Foster continued, "just *happened* to be in this town?"

You're clever, Inspector. Sharp. Like me.

"No. We arrived here with purpose. We are hunting the killer, same as you."

"Killers," Collins interjected softly. "Plural."

Edward nodded, cursing his oversight.

"Yeah, killers. We...uh. We've been looking for a while. We... knew one of the previous victims. Emma—that's the lady's name—"

"Mrs. Godley, actually," Collins said pointedly.

As you like, son.

"Yeah. She has this talent and we asked her to come with us to help us find them."

"She doesn't seem too happy with you," Foster said.

"No, well, we...got off on the wrong foot. A *lady* shouldn't have to see the things we see, should she?" He looked at Collins. "Should she?"

"No," Collins said tightly. He took off his glasses, pinched the bridge of his nose, then replaced the thin frames, hooking the wire stems over his ears.

Edward nodded. "So she's a bit upset. Gets a bit hysterical, she does."

Foster carefully placed the pencil on his notebook. Edward saw he lined it up with the spine. Meticulous man.

"If I ask Mrs. Godley what it is you're doing here, she'll tell me the same thing?"

"She doesn't like to advertise her gift. People...don't understand. She's had problems in the past so she keeps it a secret."

"Ah, but if I tell her you've already told us...?"

"Yeah. Yeah, she'll tell you the same thing. We knew someone. Someone special who was taken from us by these killers.
We want to see her avenged."

The "family of the victim" story had always been their fall-
back. Always worked no matter what. He could put real emotion into the words because he'd seen the most recent victims. And, no matter what Emma might think, he *did* have a
heart.

"Let us suppose I believe your incongruent tale, Mr. Baker,"
Foster said. He was leaning back again. Relaxed and in control. "Now that you failed to save this woman, what now? Has
Mrs. Godley had any more...*insights*?" His lips twitched in a
smirk.

"I don't know. She just left to..." Edward scrambled for a
phrase that didn't involve Emma and Douglas breaking into
Bronwyn's house to search her belongings. "Commune with
the spirits," he finished lamely.

"Is that right?" Collins sounded like he wanted to spit.

"Yeah. Sometimes it works, sometimes it doesn't."

"And I suppose you'll let us know when she has another...
spell, then?" Foster asked.

"Of course."

Not a chance, you Scotland Yard toad.

They must have read his thoughts as they exchanged yet
another glance and then Collins moved right into his face, the
spit from his ire flecking onto Edward's cheek.

"You really think we'd believe that fabrication? It's like
somethin' out of a penny bloody dreadful! It's ludicrous!"
Collins shouted. His smartly-cut moustache quivered over his
lip.

"We've got enough," Foster said, calmly.

"We got enough to have you hanged!" Again, Collins
slammed his fist on the table and Edward flinched.

Foster shook his head, looking pleased. "You were in the vicinity of this ghastly murder, Mr. Baker. You're a stranger to this town. If we ask the good people of St Leonard's or Oak Ridge whether someone matching your description were seen in the area of the other victims, what do you think they will say? Or the ones before those? You think that might shake someone's recollection?"

"*I think it might,*" Collins said.

"Yes, I heartily agree. And do you think if we really harangue the woman she'll tell us what's really going on—maybe even dump you right in it, eh?" Foster leaned forward and Edward looked from one to the other.

He had a job to do. He could not afford to linger here, let alone hang. They'd do it, too. They'd been working on this too long—he knew the look. The desperation to finish, to achieve *something*, even if it was only a temporary and false victory. A result. Enough to let them breathe. Oh, he knew the feeling all too well.

Bloody hell.

He swallowed once and it hurt his throat.

But not half as much as his next words.

"Alright. I'll tell you what happened. The truth, this time."

"Then?"

"I'll kill him," Athan said. He meant it. At least now, he did. He'd never really hurt anyone, let alone committed murder. He'd struck a man once. He'd killed chickens for food. He'd punched a fence post and split his knuckles, leaving a white scar on his right hand.

What the killers had done to these women was obscene. It was an affront to nature. To kill out of rage was one thing, this was... Athan didn't know what it was, but he was tired.

He didn't want to run any more and he didn't want to hide here. So the best thing to do was *not* hide here. Come out. Be seen. Track this evil bastard down and stave his head in with a shovel or brick. A quick death. Bloody merciful compared to the mercy he showed those women.

His fingers quickly laced his boots and, as he pulled the laces tight, one snapped in his hands.

Dammit!

He let out a slow breath and began to unlace the boot. He intended to relace it without using the first four eyelets at the top. It was something they had done many times when they were running.

Zachary, whose shocked silence spoke volumes, said quietly, "You can't just...kill someone, Athan. Besides, there might be two of them, like the papers say."

"Zach," Athan said patiently. "The only reason the papers think there's two killers is because the papers are describing *us*. And they're wrong. One man did this. No partnership in the world could be based on such depravity." He shook his head at the thought. "He's here. I mean, it's like he's following us, Zach. I know he's not, but..."

"Probably followed the line, same as us."

"Either way. He's murdered again." Athan shrugged. "I find him and we can—"

"You won't. It's not in you."

"No. No, no, no, my friend." Athan chuckled briefly, but there was no humour in it. "It *wasn't* in me. But he's ruined my life. He's murdered innocent women."

Despite the broken lace and the disapproval in his friend's eyes, Athan felt happier than he had in weeks. His eyes were clear and free of the constant stinging. His hands were free from the quivering of a drinking man—something he had never been before Sacha. A broken lace would have flown him effortlessly into a rage only yesterday. But Bronwyn's murder had somehow brought a sense of clarity to him; levered him out of the rut in which he had been wallowing.

"You can't," Zachary repeated.

"It's the only way, Zach. The Inspectors clearly can't find their own—"

"Athan, you'll hang!" Zachary shouted.

Athan stopped pacing. His chest moved with deep breaths. The sheer desperation in Zachary's voice startled him.

"Zach," Athan tried to gentle his tone. "I don't *intend* to seek out murder. I'm intending to seek *him*."

"We've seen what he's done, what he's capable of. If the Inspectors can't find him..."

"You're right. It's very likely I won't even cross his path. There are dozens of strangers here. Any of them could have arrived when we did or before or after."

Athan tugged the short bow tight and let his foot drop to the floor.

"I'm sick of hiding. I'm sick of running. We have been unbelievably lucky the Inspectors haven't yet targeted us for their inquiries. Do you comprehend how lucky we've been? They're from the *Yard*, Zach."

"I know." Zachary slumped against the wall and shoved his hands into his pockets.

"They're busy with the shut-in—"

"Bronwyn."

"Yes. I apologise. While they are otherwise engaged with seeing to the poor woman, I can investigate the town. I can *find* this man."

"I'm leaving town."

"You're—" It took Athan a few seconds to catch up. "You're what?"

279

"That's what I've been trying to tell you. I'm going to leave town, travel for a day or so, clear my head, come back..."

"No." Athan shook his head and stepped back from Zachary. His boots felt too tight around his feet, like they were pushing all the blood to his head.

"Why not?" Zachary asked. He arched his back and pushed off the wall. "Do you truly think I want to stay here and watch you kill someone—or get killed yourself?"

"I'm not going to get killed! Zach, I'm doing this *for* us. So we can get our lives back."

"Why don't you come with me? We could go up to Long Gully..."

"No."

"Do you truly believe Molly would think you a killer?"

"We went to Sacha's to pick up our shirts. She knows we do that. Our descriptions are in the paper—"

"*Vague* descriptions. Our *names* are not in the paper. Which means she hasn't gone to the authorities to relay any suspicion she might have."

Zachary spoke the truth. Vague descriptions at best and nothing really to pin on them but for the fact they were two strangers in town. Molly may not have told—she was loyal—but she would certainly suspect. She had to. "No. I will not bring this...butchery to her doorstep. Not until we're free. If I find this man, I can clear our names."

Zachary half smiled. He nodded as if affirming something to himself. "I understand, I do. You need to know that it's alright."

Athan looked at his friend. Shorter. Thinner. He imagined him on the long roads alone, camping and in the dark, wandering and trying to find a peace that wasn't there.

"I don't understand you. First you don't want to leave even though your life—*our* lives—depended on it. Now you can't

280

wait to get out of this picturesque little podunk. Why?"

"Because you had a life before all this happened. *I* had a life. I just want to remember what it was like to be free and on the road. I need to think and then I'll come back and I'll help you. I promise."

Athan sighed. Guilt was what drove Zachary, now. God bless him, it was guilt. But the gesture was appreciated. "And what of your life?" he asked quietly.

"I...can make a life here. I can."

Athan watched Zachary carefully. For a man besotted, he looked miserable. Zachary hadn't accompanied Rose to Bronwyn's this morning, and that in itself was strange. But it could have been his hangover. He was probably regretting that now. Athan would have regretted it too, in his position.

"Okay." Athan smiled sadly. "You go. I'll clear our names. I can tell you right now, I'm not going back to Moll until I am a free man. She deserves—" His voice simply stopped for a moment as the full weight of it hit home. "She deserves better than that."

"She *deserves* her husband."

"She needs a *free* man, Zach. Until I'm free, I can't go back. If I went back now and she looked at me with distrust or worse, in fear...I think that would end me. No, I have to finish this before I go back. So you go, then. Think things through. Camp under the stars." Athan was surprised that he actually meant it. He was not afraid to look for this murderer. He was not afraid for himself. Just for Molly. And for Zach.

"Take care of her while I'm gone?" Zachary asked.

"You're...?"

"I *am* coming back." Zachary grinned and it was like they had been before, not a care in the world. Work, shirts, pay and houses with welcoming hearths.

"Alright, then."

"I just have to sort through things and I need to be certain of Rose's well-being while I'm gone. Will you do that for me? Look out for her?"

"I will," Athan said, solemnly.

"I'll be back in a day or so."

"I'll look after her. Like she was my own sister. Good luck to you, Zach."

"You, too." Zachary nodded and extended his hand.

Foster and Collins watched Edward walk out of the small interrogation room. The man was so confident he even waited for the constable to open and close the large metal door for him.

Smarmy git.

"I'll be watchin' you," Collins grated. "Don't leave this town."

Edward paused briefly. "No, Sergeant. I surely won't."

And he was gone.

Both policemen listened intently for a few seconds.

"You don't think it's 'im?" Collins asked, once Edward's footsteps had receded. His tone was incredulous while remaining respectful.

"No." Foster flipped his notebook closed.

"Why not?"

"Just a feeling."

Collins rolled his eyes. "Don't *you* start, Fred."

"It's not him, Tom. But we should keep an eye on them anyway. All of them."

"You *believe* 'im? That first crazy story—and now this second one?"

"I don't know about the first. I hear they're using a psychic back in London right now. Percy told me when he came up with the extra men. Some fop who claims he's seen the killer in a 'vision.' I hear some of the senior officers are taking him seriously in private." He tapped the table, thoughtfully. "In public, he's a madman, of course..."

"We should be back there." Collins fingered the umbrella. "Bigger case."

"This is just as important."

"Yeah, I know." Collins sighed and leaned back in his chair. "What now?"

"We have a royal decree. We've been given the money, we know our job. We do what we have to. If we have to follow these killers to *Scotland*, we go. Luckily," Foster stood, buttoning his dress coat over his waistcoat, "they're *not* in Scotland, my friend."

Collins smiled. "Right. Let's go pick 'em up."

Douglas followed the street towards the police station. He'd seen that small building become a thriving hive of lawful activity in the last 16 hours. A few tents, a carriage-load of men from the nearby town of Banrock and a few from London, besides. Important men, some of them. Of course the *real* important ones had already had their likenesses taken, their quotes verified. They were headed back to London, leaving the plods to do the work, here.

They'd be back to take the credit if an arrest was made.

Douglas crooked a finger and ran it around his collar to loosen its relentless grip on his throat.

They had never been so targeted by the local law. They were always so careful. They'd had to be. If Edward hadn't struck Emma, if he hadn't made such a scene days before,

they would not have been under any scrutiny now.

They would have blended in, like always. Observed, collected their facts and moved on, always ahead of the police, but always behind the murders.

But no. Edward had left his post and a woman had died because of it. There was no sugar-coating that fact. Not even Douglas could defend him. One mistake in an entire career of exemplary service and that one mistake...

It's enough to drive you mad.

Douglas was worried about the arrest of his partner. But he was worried most of all for the mission.

Stop the killings.

Douglas had been doing this since he was 20 years old. It was a long time. A lot of blood between when he'd started, a callow and naïve man with a thought to change destiny, and today; a seasoned and cautious man, still young, still affected by what he saw, but less able to see the hope in things.

He stopped near the bake house to view the police station.

A few people were gathered similarly, simply watching, trying to catch a glimpse of something they could relate to others in the future; something to make their lives seem more important. Douglas didn't want important, anymore. At the start, he had. Now, he wanted to get Edward out of jail somehow. He wanted to be at peace with Emma and help her find the killer. Stop it all and go home, start his life proper.

As it stood, now, he could not have a family until this was over. He could never love, never pause in a town long enough to establish any connection or roots.

Douglas sighed.

Better get this over with, then.

He walked toward the station, the story fresh in his mind.

To his utter surprise, the door opened and Edward strolled out. The man paused in the doorway for a moment, before

ducking his head and walking out, pausing for a cart that rolled past, spraying dirty water on the hems of Edward's trousers. He didn't even step back to avoid it. Instead, he slipped his hands into his pockets and walked across the road.

Douglas jogged up to him.

"What happened? I thought you were arrested! Sawyer told us that they'd—"

"It's alright, Doug. Everything's fine." Edward looked at Douglas briefly.

He was not himself. He looked positively ill; shaking and pale. It was as if between the time they'd seen him last and now, he had been taken with ague.

"Edward, are you alright, mate?"

"Fine." His voice was slightly hoarse, but he managed a smile. "I'm fine."

"They're not arresting you?"

"No, they're not." Edward's shoulder lifted in a shrug.

"That's a relief," Douglas exclaimed, letting out a relieved breath.

Edward didn't answer.

They walked in silence back along the rain-soaked streets, back to the Three Belles.

I HAVE NO AXE

January 7, 1889

The flowers were dying. Zachary looked down at the tattered bouquet, the drooping paper and the loose bow. Crooking his leg slightly, he rested the bouquet on his knee and quickly re-tied the ribbon. It was not a perfect bow, but it would do. The Lilies were the only flowers left intact. The rest were tilting on the stem.

Zachary lifted the brass knocker and tapped it three times against the door.

He listened for sounds from inside; footsteps, movement, anything.

The petals were wilting—especially the Pansies. He plucked the two most pathetic blooms from the bouquet and flung them into the nearby lavender bush, shoving them down deep between the long stems before turning back to the door.

As he rearranged the remaining flora, he hoped they wouldn't remind her of a funeral bouquet especially with her mother so ill.

Or maybe she has already passed.

In a way, he now wondered if his decision to take the flowers from the front of Bronwyn's house was the most prudent plan. But the cemetery was on the other side of town and, as he ran past, he'd seen the abundance of floral offerings from the townsfolk—those guilty of not caring while she was alive; not visiting, not even acknowledging her. It was easy for them to drop a card or a bouquet in front of the dead woman's house and move on, thinking they had really given a damn.

The bouquets were surprisingly colourful against the cold fence. Pansies and Camellias; violets and yellows, blacks and pinks as well as Christmas Roses, their green-tinged centres not yet aged to pink.

He'd grabbed the largest and most colourful bunch he could find and ran, stealing some Snowdrops along the way. There was no-one around except the police who sauntered around the back in units of two as if the answer to the woman's death would simply...manifest. Zachary quickly ran his hand through his hair, hoping the grime and sweat from running would not make his face unrecognisable.

He knocked again, using his knuckles this time.

After a short while Molly opened the door.

His welcome smile slid from his face as he looked at her. Her eyes were gaunt, her skin sallow. She seemed shrunken, smaller, and she had not slept soundly, it seemed, for a long time.

Her once-golden hair was tied in a tight brown ball at the back of her head, and she looked through him with a ghostly stare.

"Yes?" she asked in a tired voice.

"Molly?" It turned into a question as he tried to reconcile the image of this woman with that of the one he had known.

"Yes," her forehead furrowed. "What do you want?"

"It's me," he stepped forward, his free hand reaching out towards her. "It's Zachary."

She blinked slowly.

"Zachary," he said once more, his voice a whisper.

"Zach?" Her hands strayed to her hair and then to the creases in her skirts, smoothing them down quickly.

He held out the bouquet to her.

"Flowers," he said.

It sounded so out of place, so bloody simple.

She looked at them and tried to smile, but couldn't.

"I brought them for you, Molly," he continued, feeling his courage dying like the flowers in his hand.

"They're..." he tried again.

"Dead."

"...they're from Athan."

She looked at the flowers with no expression. "Are they?"

Zachary swallowed. He withdrew his hand and let the flowers hang by his side. More petals dropped to the stone.

"What are you doing here?"

"I've come to see how you are. Athan... He's concerned for your wellbeing."

Molly looked down, her mouth curved in a smile that he did not understand.

"May I come in? I've travelled quite a distance."

Molly looked at him a long time. She licked her lips and he noticed how dry they were. Cracked, with one tiny split on the lower left lip.

She nodded and stood aside to let him pass.

Zachary eased past her into her house. It smelled of old tallow and sawdust. Stale smells and closed windows. Heat. Odours. Sickness.

"Excuse the state of the house," she said as she closed the door. "I wasn't expecting company."

"That is...understandable." He set the flowers down carefully on a side table, moving aside a small glass bottle so as not to let the flowers fall to the floor. The bottle's rim was almost obscured by small strands of web that cocooned down into the neck. Zachary leaned closer until he could see the dull black shadow of the spider, curled inside.

"Please, come in," she said.

He nodded and followed her into the sitting room. It seemed bare, empty; a single chair sat near the window, a small coffee table and a lamp its only companions. The fireplace held a healthy fire. The only healthy thing in here.

Small indents in the sitting room rugs revealed the absence of other furniture. A sofa. A dining table.

"Do you have a vase?" he asked.

"For what?"

He was about to remind her about the flowers when he re-thought. She truly didn't know.

"Nothing." He stood beside the chair. "Athan really did want to come."

"That's fine, I understand, Zach." Her hands twisted in front of her.

"Molly, sit, please."

She licked her lips again and sat in the chair, back rigid, arms protectively across her chest. "Say what it is you came here to say."

"He loves you deeply."

There was another long silence between them. Molly stared at the floor.

Zachary swallowed. This was all wrong. This was not how it was supposed to happen. "He wanted me to tell you that he loves you."

"If he *really* loved me, he would be standing there in your place." She did not look up.

"We're in trouble, Molly. He can't travel here. At least not at present. He wants to, he truly does, but he can't. He *does* lov—"

"Then why isn't he here? Why is it you can travel here without incident yet he cannot?"

"We've been on the run, fleeing the law."

"I know."

"We didn't—"

"I know." Molly sighed and finally looked at him. She was about to speak when a loud clatter sounded from the back of the house.

"Molly! Molly, dear..." The old woman's voice sounded both weak and sharp at once. Molly straightened reflexively. She stood, once more smoothing her skirts.

"I have to tend to mother. Wait here."

Zachary nodded and she swept out of the room, down the dark corridor. He was alone.

While she was gone, he stood and walked the small, bare room. Pacing a little, trying to figure out how best to speak to her when she returned. He knew Molly. Knew her well and they'd had happy times in the past. He'd been at her wedding as Athan's best man. He'd watched them smile and laugh despite the fact they couldn't afford a good suit for Athan and the weather had been less than clement.

He paced past the mantelpiece and spied a pitiable stack of pictures; tintypes, daguerreotypes... He leaned forward. Her parents, a small painting of her grandparents. An image of the old homestead in the south. A picture of her and Athan, posing quite austerely under the oak tree at their home in St. Leonard's.

He saw upon the dust of the mantel the tiny footprints where their frames used to sit. She'd sold them, too, probably.

Oh, Molly.

The only picture still sitting in a frame was that of him and Athan. He remembered the day well; beautiful sunny weather. The fair was in town and the Ferrotype cost them more money than they'd cared to spend. They stood, Athan's hand on his shoulder in a bear-like grip. Dressed neat, pressed shirts and fitted waistcoats. The image was in a cheap tin frame. She couldn't have got much for it even if she did try to sell it.

He heard her in the kitchen and quickly sat back in the chair.

She returned to the sitting room with a large tray that held a pot, two cups and strainer.

"As you can see, there's hardly any left," she said as she handed him a cup of tea. "This has lasted me at least five pots." She poured. "The dogs have even run off. We've nothing to feed them. I hope some kind soul has taken pity on them."

"Oh." Zachary didn't really know what to say. He took the tea, the cup warm to touch. Glancing left, he eyed the abandoned bouquet in the foyer, the long, blue ribbon trailing down toward the floor in a delicate spiral.

They should've cheered her up, given her some solace.

Things were bad. Worse than he'd thought they could be.

That said, he'd been lucky. He'd not really expected her to be here. He came this way on a chance she might be. It had been many years since he had been to this house, just after Athan's wedding. It seemed like a lifetime ago now.

Hearing Athan talk about her mother being so ill, he knew Molly would not abandon her. But if she had died, Molly would be back in St. Leonard's and out of his immediate reach.

"She won't recover," Molly said, as if she'd read his thoughts. "It's just a matter of time."

"I'm so sorry to hear that, Molly," he whispered. "Athan would be too."

"He wouldn't know..."

"It must be hard on you."

The corners of her mouth turned upwards in a mocking

smile. She didn't say anything for the longest time. They finished their tea and she stood, collecting their cups and walked out into the kitchen.

Slowly, Zachary followed and stood near the long bench, saying nothing as Molly placed the tray near the window. The kitchen was mostly empty, a thin layer of dirt everywhere. The cupboards were bare where the crockery once sat, and the door to the meat locker hung open and at an angle, one hinge missing.

He thought about how he and Athan had been living these past weeks, after their initial flight from Sacha's. The comfortable beds, the warm food from the Three Belles, and welcoming smile and guiding hands of Rose.

Rose...

He knew he had to make things right. This was his only chance to make sure something good could come from all of this. He walked back to the foyer and grasped the flowers before returning to the disorderly kitchen. He reached down and picked up an overturned empty jar, blowing the webs from inside it and dropped the bouquet into it.

While she was piling the cups into the nearby tub, he placed the jar of flowers on the table.

"I can offer you bread for supper, but not much else," she said.

He nodded. "I understand. Things are not easy right now, for any of us," he lied.

"There's not much wood left," she continued, ignoring his comment, as she opened the stove door, stoking the fire and placing the kettle on top for more hot water.

"I can chop you some," he offered.

"No," she replied, still turned away from him. "I have no axe."

"Molly, *please*," he said. "Tell me. What has transpired?"

"What do you think?" she said. "My mother is ailing, my husband missing and I have no income. There's no money, no means and no time. The landlord still appears each week, no matter what circumstances his tenants find themselves in and the constant ravings of my mother I can do nothing about."

"What? What are you talking about?"

"It doesn't matter. It's not anything I can control. I'm used to it now."

"Molly, if only Athan knew."

"Yes," she sighed. "If only he knew. But then, he does not care to witness this, does he?"

"I promise you. He will return. I'll *make* him return."

She turned around to face him then, her eyes wet with tears. "You shouldn't have to *make* him, Zach. He should be here. He should *never* have left. If he truly loved me he would never have run. He would've stood by me."

Zachary stood quickly, rushing to her side as she buried her face in her hands. He grabbed her, holding her close to his chest, tightly as she sobbed on his shoulder.

Athan must see her. He must see what we're putting her through.

No matter what it took, he would bring Athan back to Molly. No matter how much Athan complained or refused to come or beat him down with logic and delusions of altruism. He'd go back, he'd see Athan, he'd explain to Rose.

Rose...

He would tell her his feelings and dreams and hopes. He had to protect her heart from the broken ones around her.

"I promise," he whispered in Molly's ear. "He will return."

She nodded, still crying. "But when?"

Zachary thought fast. He calculated distance and minor delay. He imagined having to coax Athan out of a warm room and into the cold. But then, once Athan knew what was happening here, he'd come willingly, surely. They would run like they had before and make it to Molly's in plenty of time.

Zachary took her by the arm and eased her down onto the nearby chair.

"This place is a mess." She wiped her hands through her hair. "*I'm* a mess. I'm so embarrassed..."

"Here. Shhhh..." He leaned over and untied the ribbon from the bouquet. He rounded the chair and tied it into her wispy bun. Walking back around, he smiled. "That's better."

The blue contrasted with her eyes. She gently touched the curls of the ribbon.

"Thank-you."

"We'll be back before supper tomorrow. Athan and I."

"You can't promise that." But her eyes held a question of hope.

Can you?

He smiled. "I actually can."

He took her hand and guided her to the sitting room where he picked up the tin frame, his ring clinking gently against the side.

He handed it to her. "Think of this, Molly."

"I'll try," she said, taking the picture frame and hugging it close.

"Before supper. I promise you."

Zachary left the house. His heart was heavy with both hope and despair. His thoughts were a confused blur that made his head ache.

I will persuade him to come... This will all work out. I'll have fixed it.

He walked slowly down the unkempt path toward the

winding track out of the gully.

He paused and tilted his head.

He could have sworn he heard her call his name.

He listened intently, eyes closed, but heard nothing but the twitter of sparrows.

Zachary debated his course of action.

Then he turned and walked back to Molly's house.

CAUGHT

He ran his fingers along the rough ends of the metal. Four of the fence posts had been sawed clean through, presumably to hoist the body off. The spikes ended at head height, the posts on either side continuing to their full height above him.

The constable on duty had lit the side and back lamps. Even in the dim light, Athan could see the dried pool of blood below the fence. They hadn't even bothered to wash it away.

He looked around once more, making sure the constable was nowhere to be seen. He knew the sun would soon rise, and his time hidden from sight in the dark shadows of the garden would be over.

He'd laid awake in their quarters for hours after a perfunctory first look around the town. He'd found nothing, just as Zachary had said. His mind raced, thoughts swinging from hate to depression to sadness to despair. He missed Molly. He wanted so desperately to see her and hold her again, kiss her, tuck her beautiful golden hair behind her ear. But he didn't want her involved in this appalling state of affairs.

He couldn't remember how many times he'd tossed and turned in his bed, switching to his side, eyes open, hoping Zachary was awake so they could talk. But all he saw was the empty space where Zachary should have been.

He's out pulling himself together, he thought to himself. *And so should I.*

He'd dressed quickly for the second time that night, slipped from the Three Belles as quietly as possible. To begin with, he just walked aimlessly, with no plan or objective other than to make sure no one saw him. At that time of the early pre-dawn, there were few about. The butchers, the bakers, the lamp-lighters ready to douse the flames of night, the stable boys at the Livery.

All of them quiet and furtive; scared, like him, of what lurked in the darkness.

Or who.

The killer was here somewhere. No matter what Zachary said, Athan knew he'd kill him if he had the chance. Athan was strong and he was fast. This murderer was not prepared for a man's strength, he was certain, considering the vulnerability of his prey up to now.

He kept well away from the main street and the railway, even though he was sure that somewhere out there the killer hid, probably waiting for his next victim.

It won't happen again. I won't let it.

Then he found himself at Bronwyn's house. He wasn't sure how long he'd walked, or in what direction, but he was standing there, looking at the two storey abode in the lamp-light.

He didn't think he would've recognised it if not for the large numbers of flowers out the front, laid and strewn in the darkness like thoughts and prayers; offered up but unaccepted.

The constable was asleep on the front balcony, his legs stretched up on the railing and his snore echoing in the silence. It took Athan only a careful moment to slip past him and down the side of the house, creeping towards the large gap in the iron fence where they had retrieved Bronwyn's remains.

Taking the fence posts with her...

He didn't know why he was there, standing in the growing morning light, his arms and chest cold in the night air, his hair and forehead wet with the cold sweat of his fear and exertion. It was as if he wanted the house to tell him something, give him a clue, point him in the right direction.

Or maybe he just wanted to let Bronwyn know he would fix things.

He never met her. But he knew how she died. He'd seen that in Sacha. He couldn't help Sacha, then. Maybe he could avenge Bronwyn instead.

Or maybe he thought the killer might still be there, hiding in the darkness, watching and waiting, hoping to find his next victim in the same place.

No. She was a recluse. There were no other victims here. Besides, why not take the constable?

For obvious reasons. He only kills the women.

Of that, Athan was sure. But no more.

Tonight, tomorrow or next week, I will exact vengeance on him. Make him pay for the lives he damaged and destroyed. For my life and Zach's.

The wind ruffled through the trees around him and he turned to the left; his eyes searched the darkness for any movement, but he couldn't see any.

His hand slipped around the gate and he turned the drop handle and pushed the gate open. Hesitating for only a moment, he took a step through into the backyard.

His eyes darted from statue to statue, making sure none of the white figures hid anyone, making sure none of the figures *were* anyone. He waited, letting his eyes dance between them, focusing on each, carefully examining them for any movement.

There were no lights from the house, still no sign of the

constable in the backyard. His fears evaporated as he stepped farther into the backyard. He didn't know what he was looking for, but he was sure the answer was here somewhere, either in the yard or in the house.

Something the police had missed. Something that would lead him to the killer.

He took another step forward. He could do this. He was sure that he only needed to think, to put himself in the mind of a fugitive—something that was not difficult for him.

He heard the sudden pounding footsteps and the rapid breathing too late.

Athan turned around but didn't duck in time.

The fist connected at his jaw, sliding across to his nose, sending stars exploding across his eyes.

He reached out to grab hold of something, anything, but his hands found only air as he tumbled backwards.

He hit the ground hard, and darkness engulfed him.

ALL FOR YOU

When he was released from gaol, Edward had not spoken. He skulked into his room without acknowledging her presence. Emma had talked to Douglas for a few minutes in the corridor, but he was none the wiser.

She knocked on Edward's door, unafraid of any wrath her intrusion might bring.

Silence. She knocked again, harder this time.

Eventually, Edward's door opened and he peered out at them. His face was pale, but still held that familiar, contemptible scowl.

He ushered them inside and gestured for them to sit down.

"Have out with it then," he said, not sitting down, but leaning defensively against the side-table near the bed.

"What happened?" Emma asked. "With the Inspectors. We thought— We were worried."

"Things got slightly out of control. They're fixed, now."

"How do you mean?" Douglas asked.

"The police are close, too close. They could jeopardise everything we're doing."

"What did you tell them?" Emma asked.

"Nothing," he replied sheepishly. "Nothing...certain."

"How do you mean?" Douglas pressed. She gave him credit for that. There was a time when Douglas would not have asked Edward such a question.

"I just...let slip some information, moving their investigation away from us."

"And?" Emma asked.

"*And?*" Edward looked mad again, his scowl deepened until his eyes squinted.

"And," she repeated.

"Nothing! There is no 'And'," he replied as he grabbed his hat and coat and charged towards the door.

"What did you tell them, Edward?" she called after him.

He spun. "I— Look, we cannot lose this trail. We are closer, closer than anyone has ever come. Don't you comprehend that?"

Emma knew then what he'd done.

"You didn't..." she said, standing, angrier than she had been in a long, long time.

"Go to hell, both of you! You don't get to judge me." Without a backward glance, he stormed from the room, slamming the heavy oak door behind him.

Douglas stared at Emma, and she stared back. She watched the pieces of the puzzle connect in the younger man's mind, saw his disappointment.

In the end, it was Douglas who broke the silence.

"I better go after him," he said. "In case anything *else* happens."

With that, Emma agreed.

After he left, she stood by the window, looking out across main street to the gaol, watching the comings and goings, watching the policemen scurry this way and that.

Only early this morning before the dawn, in that same street, she'd seen the constable return from the hunt with the one they sought. Athan. He'd put up a struggle, fighting off the officers, pushing and punching at them, but as the small crowd surrounded them and the abuse began, he was pushed and pulled inside. She saw a flash of his blond hair before he was swallowed by the heavy doors.

It seemed as though she'd stood at this window forever, staring at the weather.

Lucy was born on a day like today. A chill afternoon where the sun was pale and high and the wind cut through the streets.

Emma stood at the window of her room, looking across the main street of town at the carriages, people and children.

Life was so simple, so normal for them.

She couldn't help her thoughts. It was times like this, the quiet times, when she wondered, imagined what it would be like to be back at home with George and Lucy. To be a happy family again.

She longed for them both so much; the fire in George's eyes when he smiled, Lucy's laughter as she skipped through the garden. She wanted to see them both so much, to hug and hold them, smell them once again. Would she ever get that chance? To one day return to them?

To live life normally again, once all this was over.

If this ever ends.

Her fingers played absent-mindedly with the last button on her glove, her thoughts slipping from the family to which she said goodbye, to the family she now had; Edward and Douglas.

Her curls brushed the nape of her neck as she shook her head, her eyes scanning back up main street, looking for any sign of Douglas returning from his search for Edward. She wondered what the next few days or weeks would hold for them, and how they would all cope now.

"Such a betrayal," she whispered. "He had no right."

She turned to look at the clock in her room. It was just past midday, lunch would be served, now. She hoped both men would be back in time to eat.

Edward and Douglas had been gone for hours—too long—
and she was beginning to worry something else had gone
wrong. Had Douglas lost him? Had Edward done something
foolish?

Her eyes scanned the main street, her fingers picked at her
glove.

*What would I do if they don't return? Go home to George or con-
tinue without them?*

She didn't know the answer, and she didn't like to think
that she may be in that position soon.

Her eyes focussed further into the distance, trying hard to
see Douglas or Edward, their puffed faces red from arguing,
or their pants and boots spattered from the mud of the street.

Instead, her eyes latched onto a flash of red hair, slipping
between two cabs and behind a third. She squinted and leant
forward, her breath fogging the glass.

She grabbed for the curtains, straining to see.

Zachary darted out from behind the third cab and ran to
one side of the main street, walking along the veranda of the
stores.

He doesn't know.

Zachary could run into Edward or Douglas at any moment.

Or worse...

She dashed from the room.

"You were there!"

"I—"

"You were in that poor woman's bloody garden and I want
to know why! Tell me WHY!" Foster spat the words in Athan's
face. It was the first time Collins had heard his partner use
profanity in this interview—this town. It was a dire result

when Fred Foster's method of expression became common.

The suspect, Athan Stowall, sat in his chair. He looked like a shell of a man, his skin was waxy, his sweat sour and full of fear. His blond hair hung limp, his shirt sleeve was ripped from the scuffle. His left eye swelled and blackening.

Stowall did not look up.

One thing struck Collins as he glared at the blond man; he did not profess his innocence upon capture. He was not full of babbling explanations and reasoning as to why he had been found where he was.

None of the other suspects had looked so...guilty.

All had sat in that chair at various times during the last day and night. All dragged from employment or slumber or drink, confused or resigned or simply reluctant.

Edward Baker had an attitude that radiated culpability, but his story had not fit with what they knew. Fred was certain of his innocence. The owner of the livery had been belligerent and uncooperative. He also had an alibi for the murder in London. The lamp-lighter also had an alibi; and had been promptly arrested for the burglary, readily admitting to that charge rather than the hanging offence of murder.

But Mr. Stowall... After Collins had almost knocked himself silly tackling the man from the side of the deceased's residence, they had telegraphed the Yard.

And what they had found... There was no doubt as to the man's guilt. None at all. The only thing they needed to know was *why* he'd done it. How could so innocuous a man be such a monster? Where was his collaborator in these killings?

"I didn't touch her. I didn't touch any of them," Stowall said. His voice, deep and soft, was barely audible even in the echoed expanse of the spartan room.

"Then what about this!?" Foster shook a piece of crisp, new paper, fisted in his right hand, at Stowall's face. "This is a report from the Yard, telegraphed a mere hour ago to this very station."

Foster looked at the paper. Collins knew exactly what it said. Every broken sentence, every stop line. They'd sat together for an hour over two cups of poorly-brewed tea, reading the words over and over. From that moment, Foster's hands held a slight tremble which Collins saw now in the fluttering of the paper's corners.

Foster took a breath. "Says here you went missing from your place of employment in St. Leonard's the same week Sacha Turgenev was murdered. Care to explain that, Mr. Stowall? Care to *explain* how your best friend of childhood also left his place of employment that very same week? Care to *explain* how your descriptions match those men who fled the scene of Mrs. Turgenev's murder? Can you *explain* how you got that scar on your forehead? Can you *explain* why you were in Bronwyn Belles' garden? Can you? *Can you!?*"

Athan sat and trembled. Collins watched his Adams apple rise and fall. Again. Again. Like the man was trying to swallow all that guilt.

"And what of your wife, Mr. Stowall?"

At this, the man looked up.

Foster nodded and continued. "They sent someone, you know. The house is deserted. Did you—?"

"She's at her mother's."

"Is that right?" Collins said. He didn't mean to interrupt, but he was picturing Athan's wife, cut up and dead like the others, but curled and leathered from the months she'd lain undiscovered and unavenged.

How many others had they killed? How many had escaped the Yard's notice? The force was split in two right now. Most—more than half—in London and the rest combing the counties and shires, the hills and valleys and forests that had made up the killing ground for this man here.

And the other one still out there.

Foster creased the telegraph in his fingers. He folded it three times before running his fingers up and down the fat square, squeezing it shut. "At her mother's?" he asked. His tone tight and restrained. Collins frowned.

"Well be at ease," Foster said. "We'll send someone to validate your statement—make sure the poor woman is still in one fucking *piece!*" He flung the paper at Stowall who flinched in the chair.

Foster was trembling with rage and Collins put a hand on the senior officer's arm.

"Fred," he murmured. Anger was his role to play. Anger and instability; he was the hot-tempered one. But Fred had taken these killings to heart, it seemed. Soon, the whole bloody world would.

"You did it," Foster said, nodding and licking his lips as he sat down. He didn't look at his Sergeant, but nodded, calmer.

"You and your friend. Now where is he?"

Zachary straightened his collar once again, trying hard to hide his face from those around him. He was tired and thirsty, and his feet ached but he knew he had to find Athan as soon as possible. He couldn't stop now. This was too important. He was elated and anxious at once. Molly was waiting for them. Once Athan heard about her state, her need, he would depart from this place and start his life over, Zachary was sure. But he had to find him and get him there before supper tonight.

He'd promised. They could make it back there in a few hours if they ran like they used to. It was midday, now. They had time.

There seemed to be so many people out in the streets. He didn't know if it was because he was being paranoid, or whether he just hadn't noticed them before. People, groups of people, all standing around and talking to each other, whispering, reading and pointing to the newspapers.

When he arrived at Oak Ridge, he'd gone straight to the field where they had been working, expecting to find Athan there at this time of the day, but he was nowhere to be seen. He was sure his friend had probably drunk too much the night before and had another hangover.

Just like him, too.

It didn't slow Zachary down. His right hand still held the earring wrapped in a piece of blue ribbon. Molly had called him back for it, handed it to him on the doorstep.

"Give him this," she'd said. "Tell him I need him."

"I will," he'd replied. "We'll be back before tomorrow supper, I promise."

He hadn't released his grip on the earring from that moment. Even as he stumbled and fell, waded through waters and climbed hills, he'd kept it tight in the palm of his hand. He was sure the ribbon would be soaked through with sweat, and that the earring was probably bent out of shape, but that didn't matter. What *did* matter was the thoughts—the hope— that came with it.

And so he'd run, hadn't given up.

When Athan wasn't in the field, Zachary had simply turned around and headed for the Three Belles. But he hadn't counted on so many people.

The Three Belles brought thoughts of Rose to his mind, made him dizzy with both romantic feelings and conflict. He could see both her and Athan, he reasoned. He had the time.

Jumping between two cabs and then following a third, he

cut across the street to walk swiftly along the veranda of the stores. He could see the Three Belles in the distance. He was almost there.

It was an effort to slow down so as not to look suspicious. His eyes darted back and forth, making sure he didn't recognise anyone who could stop him getting to his goal.

Almost there.

He walked towards the entrance of the Three Belles just as Mrs. Godley was leaving. She passed him and he barely recognised her, not until he heard his name and felt the hand grab his arm, spinning him around.

"Excuse me!" he shrugged off the grip and pulled away.

She reached out and took his shoulder, turning him around and marching him quickly through the doors and into the bar.

"Mrs. Godley, I really don't have the time—" he began.

"I must speak with you."

"I can't, not now. I'll apologise for my rudeness, but I must be on my way."

To his utter surprise, she sat him down at a table, her strength taking him off-guard. He watched dumbly as she pulled up a chair and sat next to him, smoothing her skirts so she could lean forward to speak.

"Not yet," she said.

"I must find Athan."

"You won't," she shook her head and looked behind him toward the door before meeting his eyes once more.

Zachary frowned. "I have news. I have to talk to him."

"He's not here. You won't find him here."

Zachary looked properly at her for the first time, saw the tiredness in her eyes, the sadness behind them. She was a beautiful woman, delicate, and clearly strong.

"What do you mean?" he asked, leaning forward, the rough

surface of the table catching at his cuffs as his hands rested there.

"He's not here, Zachary," she continued, looking uncomfortable. "Things have...progressed...since you left."

"In what fashion?"

"It's not safe for you to walk the streets or be seen now. You're lucky you made it here without detection. You are a wanted man."

Zachary's eyes widened and the colour left his cheeks. "I'm— Rose? Oh God, is she alright?"

Emma nodded, reached out and took his hands in hers. "Yes, Zachary, she's fine."

"She's not hurt or unwell? Attacked again? Another brawl."

"No, no," she said in a quieter voice, her hands opening his fists, touching and stroking them carefully. "She is fine. I spoke with her this morning. Everything with her is fine."

He leaned backwards, releasing his hands from hers. But his palms were empty. Now Emma held the ribbon and earring.

"So what is it, then?" he asked.

"It's Athan," she replied, turning the small blue package over and over again in her fingers, all the while still looking him directly in the eye.

"Do you know where he is?"

"Yes," she replied.

"Where? Tell me, I must see him. I have a message from his wife in Long Gully. She wants him to return to her. I'm to give him that earring. He's to bring it back to her."

Emma's eyes dropped to the wrapped jewellery in her hands.

"He's not here," she replied.

"Then where is he?"

"The police have arrested him for the murder of all those people."

"WHAT?" Her words made no sense to him.

"He's in gaol, Zachary. He's going to hang."

"The press will be here on the next train." Foster was leaning against the back of his chair, his tight grip making the wood creak. His curly hair stuck to his forehead in places, damp with sweat.

"They don't normally use a half-finished track, but they're making an exception in your case. All for *you*."

Collins took his cue, standing, he felt his shirt sticking for a moment to the small of his back. They'd been at this for hours. No respite. No tea. Not even a chance to piss. He cleared his throat softly.

"All the journalists are in London right now, but the telegraphs are starting to come in, *boy*." The word seemed to slide easily from his lips. Stowall was only two years younger than he—if that—but the height from which the blond man had fallen made him seem like a babe. It made Collins feel like he'd lived a hundred years.

He lifted the stack of papers that rested on the spare chair and flung them across the table where they slid and hit Stowall's folded arms.

"The London Gazette, The Daily Chronicle, Lloyds', the New York times—even the bleedin' Railway Press'll be 'ere tonight." He leaned over the table; it was fast becoming his favourite tactic.

"Your name'll be all over the country by the end of the week. You are the monster that people fear far worse than anything that's happenin' in the city. You *travel*. You take your despicable murder to our *homes*, you don't just prey on a bit of totty in a back alley, mate." His voice softened to a murmur. "You're the nightmare that's going to frighten our children for generations to come. You're goin' down in history, son."

He sat down, watching the man's lips press together until they held no blood. Stowall's shoulders sagged and his body looked like it had no strength.

But it *did* have strength—Collins had seen the way the Belle woman had fought. You had to have strength to hurl a woman out of a window the way he did. To pull her around her kitchen, touching almost every surface...

Collins imagined Stowall's face on those days and wondered what expression it held while the victims were bleeding out their last.

It was the only time in his life he'd felt like killing someone. But he wouldn't with the Inspector here. He would not belittle himself in front of his mentor.

"I hope it was worth it," Collins said softly.

"I didn't harm anyone."

"We've heard that already, son," Foster suddenly said. "Repeatedly. Now, where's the other one?" He straightened and walked to the back wall, leaning against it with a weary aspect. "Where's your accomplice?"

Stowall shook his head. Foster moved quicker than Collins credited him. In a second he was around the table and lifting Stowall by the lapels.

"We don't have time for this! Where's your accomplice! Where is he?"

"I don't know!"

"Run off, did he?" Foster dropped Athan back to the chair and stepped back, placing his hands in his pockets. "Leaves you to hang while he runs free? Will he think about you when you drop, Mr. Stowall? Will he be disappointed he can't watch you fall those six feet to the breaking of your bloody neck? Is

312

he somewhere else? Killing again?"

"No!"

"Then where is he?"

"I... He left. I don't know where."

"But you're so *close*, Mr. Stowall. You and Zachary. Friends for years. Closer than most, considering the barbarity of your mutual inclinations. Close enough to trust one another so much. Why? Why do you do it?"

"I don't!"

"So it's *him*? You were just...swept along with him, is that it? Why does *he* do it!"

"He doesn't. He *wouldn't*."

"Really. Zachary Vaughn was in St. Leonard's for Mrs. Turgenev. He was here in Oak Ridge, for the widow Belle. Was he in London, too? Where is he *now*? How do you know he didn't do this?"

"I..."

Collins watched, torn between admiration for the Inspector and now pity for the guilty man whose face held a horror that seemed unsuitable to human features. Stowall's eyes welled with tears and he groaned, leaning on his elbows and fisting his hands in his hair.

"He can't have... Why?" Stowall murmured quietly.

Collins knew he wasn't answering the Inspector's question. He wasn't even aware they were in the room anymore.

The Inspector nodded. "*Why* is the question, Mr. Stowall. And you'd better have a fucking answer by tonight or your precious neck won't make that rough noose. Do you understand my meaning, sir?"

Athan Stowall simply shook his head.

Collins caught himself before he did the same thing.

PROMISES

January 7, 1889

The only decoration in Emma Godley's room was a square of cloth; a shawl, Zachary thought, that was neatly laid on the bed.

Her only photo was in a small wooden frame on the side-table, facing the bed, not the room. It was of a man whose expression was serious and poised. He had a moustache and wore some kind of policeman's uniform. She had tied a red ribbon to one corner.

Zachary paced from that side table, past the window to the far wall and back again. He wore no boots, having taken them off at her behest so he would make no sound.

As yet he had seen no sign of her charges; the ill-mannered fellow who spoke his boorish thoughts in front of all, regardless of their sex. And the younger one—the quiet one who Zachary had thought kind.

He presumed that she had sequestered him in her room to hide from the law and her companions, neither of whom seemed the forgiving type.

And so, he paced. Occasionally he glanced out the window to where he could see the corner upon which the gaol sat. It was still a hive of activity—mostly due to the locals who milled around either on its very step or on the other side of the street, keenly watching, but trying to be unobtrusive.

The door opened and he looked up, expecting Emma but

dreading the police.

He was surprised to see the small, familiar figure that framed the doorway.

"Rose..." He took a step, suddenly feeling naked and short in his stocking feet.

Emma appeared behind the young woman, coaxing her into the room.

"Quickly," Emma said, smiling briefly at Zachary. She pressed the younger woman's hands in hers and turned to leave the room in a whirl of black and blue fabric. The door closed quietly behind her and all Zachary could hear was the dull thud of blood in his ears. He forgot all about seeing Sawyer with her that night. He forgot everything.

He took another step. "Rose, I don't know what you've heard, but Athan is innocent."

Rose closed the gap to meet him and took his hands in hers. Her grip was strong and anxious. "I've heard everything, Zachary. I know he's not guilty—and neither are you."

"Me?"

"Yes. *Both* of you are equally accused. They are looking for you, too. They don't want you for mere questioning, nor to simply bear witness against him, but to have you hanged as surely as he."

"But..."

"They have *your* name and your descriptions, where you sleep.... I don't know how. I told them nothing."

"Sawyer." It was out before he could stop himself and he saw her eyes steel.

"No. I asked him that, myself."

"You believed him?" He turned from her.

"He is a man of his word, Zachary. As are you. I believe *you.*"

Zachary found it difficult to draw breath as she spoke. She

stood so close, he could feel her skirts brush his toes.

"You must listen. They have had Athan in custody since almost four this morning. He has been questioned and found guilty by the police here and the inspectors from London. He will be sent back on the next train to trial, such as it will be, then to hang. The inspector said that they have also sent for more men to look for you. They will be here by evening. Zachary, you *must* hide or get away from here. Please? I won't see you caught for something you did not do."

"You really believe me?"

"Of course!" She sounded so indignant that he almost laughed. She stepped closer still, one of her feet sliding between his own. She eased one hand from his and placed it delicately at his cheek.

"I won't see you hanged. You must hide."

Zachary watched her mouth, mesmerized by the way her lips formed the words. None of what she said made sense. He couldn't leave, now.

"I love you," he said quickly. He couldn't help it.

Rose's eyes widened and a blush flamed across her cheeks. Zachary's brain was already scrambling for ways to apologise when she smiled at him.

"Do you?" she asked with a slight catch in her voice.

"Yes." He grinned. The smile felt good after so many weeks of worry. It soon faded. "But I can't leave this town without Athan. I won't let him die for a crime he did not commit." He ducked his head a little. "I hope you understand."

"I do." She lifted his chin with her knuckle. She was still smiling and it seemed surreal to Zachary that they could have this moment, this pocket of complete happiness when outside his name was striking terror into the hearts of the populace and his best friend was about to be judged and hanged for being a killer.

317

Zachary nodded. "I must see him safe. We're already late—I promised his wife that I would bring him before supper."

"You intend to break him free?"

"I have to."

There was a knock on the door. Both Zachary and Rose flinched and turned. Zachary kept tight hold of her hand and stepped a little in front of her as the door opened. Emma peered inside.

"They're searching the hotel," she said.

"Go." Rose pushed him a little and he turned, not letting go of her hand as he walked to the window. He carefully opened it and peered out a little. It was deserted on the west side of the hotel.

"I can climb down," he said, straightening.

"Then climb *now*," Emma urged. She had shut the door carefully behind her. Zachary could hear voices from along the hall, the sound of cupboards being opened, furniture scraping above the resentful protest of the occupants. Careless feet in heavy boots moved closer and louder.

He sat quickly and pulled on his boots, not bothering to lace them. Emma stayed near the door, listening to the sounds from outside and watching him with a worried gaze. Her whole manner screamed at him to hurry.

Zachary stood and turned to Rose, his heart racing with both fear and ardour. He had so much to say and no time at all to say it.

"Go," she whispered, nodding her head as if to encourage his flight. She looked resolved, but her hand moved in his, restless.

"I promise I will return," he whispered.

"I know." She nodded, but her eyes brightened with moisture.

"No, Rose. I *promise*." He held her gaze until he was sure she

318

understood.

Despite their audience, he pulled her to him and pressed his lips to hers in a firm kiss.

This time, she did not pull away. He felt her hand, delicate and cool at the back of his neck.

He suddenly knew how Athan felt. He would do anything to keep Rose from harm. He would run. He would kill.

After a few long, treasured seconds, Zachary drew away and nodded at her. Then he turned, not looking back. He wanted to keep the image of her, smiling with delight, her cheeks warm with the kiss and her eyes full of promise and worry.

Zachary carefully eased out onto the main trellis and gripped the ivy-tangled wood hard. He could feel the wood, weathered and rotting in places, move beneath him. The ivy was probably the only thing that held it upright.

He began to climb down and heard her voice above him.

"Be careful, Zachary."

He smiled and dropped the last few feet to the ground. There was a gap in the hedge-row that he and Athan used to gain access to the fields out back. He slipped through the leaves and walked along the path that would take him around the back of town and to relative safety.

There, he would wait and come up with some kind of plan. He'd free Athan from prison, and fulfil all his promises.

As he walked, he touched his fingers to his lips.

Emma walked up to stand beside Rose. The girl shook; fearful or impassioned, Emma could not tell. Likely both.

"He told me he loved me," the girl whispered.

"He does indeed." Emma felt a pang of jealousy and quickly

subdued it. She would be home, soon, she felt it.

"You read my palm," Rose said, her hushed voice holding a question.

"I did." Emma did not see the future in ordinary people only corpses. She saw, if she was lucky, glimpses of a possible future. It's all she'd ever seen.

"And...?" Rose prompted.

Emma sighed. "And, *if* he returns from his adventure, you and he will live happily together. If he returns."

"He will return."

"I cannot say—"

"He will." Rose smiled and touched her fingers to her lips. "He promised."

"Only a couple more hours now for you," Constable Nash said as he lifted his head from reading the paper. "Soon every paper in the country will have your name on the front page."

Athan said nothing, he just stared through the bars to where Nash was sitting. The constable had unbuttoned his coat and was leaning back on his chair, both feet up on the table in front of him. His smile was one of self-satisfaction, even though he'd had nothing to do with bringing Athan here.

Smug bastard, was all Athan thought.

He leaned back against the holding cell wall, the rough brick biting into his back. By now, he didn't care about the pain, he didn't care about anything.

Foster and Collins had made it right clear. He was going to hang for something he didn't do. And Zachary would hang with him, if they caught him.

Oh, but Zachary can't be found. No, no. He's conveniently disap-

peared.

Athan kicked at the floor, his boot scraping away at the dirt, the already deep gouge lengthening. He wished he could dig himself out of there just as easily. But it was no use, there was nothing more he could do.

"They're right pleased in ol' London," Nash continued, his smile broadening to a toothy grin. "They've needed a good news story for some time, so the top brass is very pleased with what we've done."

Athan closed his eyes, willing and wishing for Nash to disappear, to fall silent and no longer taunt him.

"Course, that is if we can get you ta London in one piece. As the news spreads, it's going to be harder for us to protect you. They'll want your blood and they'll stop at nothing to get it."

Go away!

"Lucky the police special is comin' for you."

Shut up!

"Should be heading up that track in no time. You think we'll hear its whistle from here?"

Nash hadn't said a word while the other police were in the lockup. He'd got them tea and fetched them notebooks, as any local policeman should, but now the others were out, searching every building and every home in town, Nash was acting as if he'd brought Athan in single-handedly.

"Get a promotion, I will," he continued. "I'll be able to say goodbye to here. Maybe end up at the Yard, working on all those famous cases."

No you won't.

"There's only one case more famous than this right now. Still, so many people want to see you hang."

Athan tried hard to get angry, to spit something back at the Constable, but he couldn't find the energy. He didn't have the strength.

The questioning had seemed to last for hours on end, with no breaks, no time to rest or get a hold on the jumble of thoughts in his mind. From the moment they'd caught him trespassing, he'd been jostled and punched, kicked and yelled at, pushed and pulled and thrown and hit.

The left side of his neck burned with scratches and his nose was swelling where Collins had tackled him.

He honestly couldn't find the strength to be mad at Nash. Not when he was so angry with others.

At Foster and Collins. At Zachary.

Oh yes, Zachary.

The one who had escaped from it all yet again. Just in time.

That's who Athan's anger was really reserved for.

If I see him again, I'll kill him. I swear, I'll kill him.

"I'm gonna telegraph me mum." Nash was talking to him again. "She'll be ever so pleased to hear the news. To know I captured a killer."

"Stop it," Athan whispered, his eyes holding on Nash's.

"Excuse me?" Nash said, dropping the paper as he kicked free of the table. Standing quickly and walking towards Athan. "Did you say something, killer?" he asked.

"I said stop it," Athan said as his gaze held firm. "I'm tired. I don't want to talk anymore."

"Oh, excuse *me*," Nash feigned shock. "I didn't know I was disturbing you, *killer*. My apologies." He turned around and headed back to the desk. "No use sleeping now, you're a long time dead, you might as well enjoy what little time you have left. *Killer*."

"It won't happen you know," Athan replied.

Nash put his arms on his hips, but didn't turn to face him. "What?"

"I said it won't happen."

Nash laughed and turned to face him once more. "You listen to me, you bastard. It'll happen. They'll take you back on that train tonight and they'll try you in London. No jury is going to let you loose on the streets, you'll be found guilty, you'll hang, and we will all celebrate the death of you."

Athan was shaking his head, a lopsided smile on his face. "That's not what I meant."

"Oh really? And what did you mean?"

"I meant you," Athan replied.

Nash looked puzzled.

"You getting to the Yard," Athan continued. "It'll never happen. You may think you're the best detective on the force, but I see how those others look at you, talk to you, order you around. They think nothing of you. You're never leaving here. You're as trapped as I am."

Nash's face turned red with anger. "Shut it," he said.

"You're no better than those you arrest. You're gutter scum like the rest of us."

"Shut it, you bastard!" Nash yelled, reaching for his truncheon.

"Or you'll what?" Athan asked. "Beat me? What will your *superiors* say?"

"I'll tell them you attacked me," he said, taking a step closer to the cell.

"They won't believe that."

"They will."

"No they won't."

"I'll make them."

"You'll end up in here with me, and what would your mother think of that?"

Nash lifted the truncheon high above his head and raced towards the cell.

"You bastard!" he shouted.

Athan stepped backward, waiting for the loud clang of

323

wood on metal, but it never came.

Instead, all he could hear was a loud bang and a young voice screaming, "Quick, sir, quick!"

Nash skidded to a stop halfway to the cell. His eyes were wide as he turned to face a young boy who had dashed into the lockup. The boy's small chest heaved as he struggled to catch his breath.

"I seen 'im," the boy said. "The one you're lookin' for. The red 'ead."

"Where?" Nash asked, his arms dropping to his side.

"He's out in the field off Eddowes Road. He's hiding in a big maple, right up the top, near the turn into town."

"How do you know this, lad?" Nash was grabbing his hat and heading towards the boy.

"I was walkin' home when he called to me from the tree. Wanted me to get closer and to buy 'im food from town. I got scared and ran. I thought he was gonna kill me!"

"Good lad," Nash patted the child on the shoulder. "You're sure it was him? It's black as pitch out there."

"Yes, sir, I'm sure. I got close enough to see he's exactly like how my dad said he was written about in the papers."

"Go home now and lock the doors," Nash ushered him out. "I'll have my men arrest him now."

The kid ran off and Nash watched him go, taking his time leaving. When the boy was out of ear-shot, he turned and smirked at Athan one last time.

"Looks like you're about to have company," he spat, putting on his helmet and snatching a lantern from the Sergeant's desk. "And *I'm* going to the Yard."

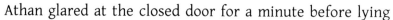

Athan glared at the closed door for a minute before lying

down on the mattress, hearing the rusted springs moan. He shut his eyes for only a few seconds before the door opened.

There was the sound of soft footsteps and keys, but he thought nothing of it.

If it's Zachary, let them lock him in with me. If it's Nash, let him try to gloat.

But after a few seconds, the sounds stopped and the room was quiet again. It became unnerving. Athan opened his eyes and looked up.

Emma stood beside the Sergeant's desk; the cell keys were in her hands.

She watched him, her head tilted to one side, her brow furrowed.

"What are you doing here?" Athan asked, the surprise echoing in his voice.

"I'm here to get you out," she replied, looking over her shoulder to make sure she was alone before walking to the cell door and nervously trying to fit the key in the lock.

"But why?" Athan sat up on the bed.

"No, time," she replied, trying the next key. "You have to get out of here before he gets back."

"I don't understand," he replied.

"You don't have to," she said. The third key slid into the lock and turned. The latch slid free.

"Just leave while you can. It's late, there are not many people around, but the police are still out searching."

He grabbed his coat and hat, patted down his pants and nodded. "Thank you," he whispered as she opened the cell door.

"*Go!*" she motioned to him. "Out the door and turn left, walk down the side of the building and head out across the field. You'll be safe that way."

He walked past her and turned to say something else but

was lost for words. Their eyes met for only a second before she turned away and closed the cell door.

"Quickly," she said again. "Before we're both caught."

"Thank you, sir," the boy said, counting out the six coins in his hands.

"Nothing went wrong?"

"No. The copper fell fer it. He ran out of there like 'is pants were on fire. Last I saw of 'im, he was running down main street like he couldn't get to the other side of town fast enough!"

"Good. You did well."

"Nah, it was worth the six crowns. Thank you, sir."

Zachary ruffled the boy's hair before he turned around and started to run home. His eyes then focussed on the back of the lockup. The clear sky and the near-quarter moon allowed him to discern figures and shapes. He watched the shadows.

"Come on, Emma," he whispered. "Hurry."

He didn't have time to save anyone else.

A few more minutes went by before he saw movement. At first, he didn't trust his eyes, but as the figure lumbered closer, Zachary could easily make out that it was Athan running towards him.

His happiness was tempered by the fact that Athan looked tired, more tired than ever before. His friend looked thin and pale, his hair a mess on his head.

What happened to him? What did they do?

Whatever had transpired didn't matter now. Not while the police were still out on the streets and the train was due soon.

Everything could wait until later.

As Athan drew closer, Zachary stepped out onto his path.
"Athan, stop."

At first, Athan didn't see him in the darkness. He came to a sudden stop at Zachary's voice and simply looked at him.

"Athan, it's me," Zachary said. "It's Zach."

"You," Athan whispered.

"Quick, we have to leave." Zachary took a step towards his friend, but Athan stepped back.

"What is it?" Zachary asked.

"Don't come near me," Athan snapped.

"No, Athan, you don't understand."

"I think I do perfectly," he replied. "You're the friend who left me *just* when the coppers came looking."

"No, no, I—"

"You ran off to hide."

"It wasn't like that."

Athan shoved his hands in his pockets and marched past Zachary, his shoulder clipping Zachary forcefully as he did so.

Zachary turned to watch his friend walk away. He held his arms out at his side. "Ay, let me explain," he said. "There's not much time."

"I don't want to hear it." Athan kept walking.

"Yes, you do," Zachary replied as he followed his friend into the forest, trying to catch up. "Trust me, you do."

"Go to hell."

"This is too important."

"I said go to hell, Zach." Athan's march grew quicker. "I didn't need you earlier today, so I don't need you now."

"What? I got you out of there. I broke you out of gaol!"

"No you didn't. *Emma* did."

"Who do you think paid the kid? Who do you think convinced Emma to go in there and get you?"

"Because you wouldn't do it yourself?" Athan turned to

327

face Zachary.

"Do you really believe that?" Zachary asked. "Do you?"

"I don't know what to believe anymore. Or who." Athan's shoulders slumped and the anger went out of his voice.

"I know you're tired, but right now, we've got to run."

"No," he shook his head.

"We must."

"I can't." Athan leaned forward slightly, looking to the ground.

"We—"

"They'll catch us." His eyes snapped back to Zachary's. "They know who they're after. They know *us*. They're looking for you, and they *had* me! It's over."

"Not yet."

"They have everything. It is over!"

Zachary took a step closer. "I can make this right." He stepped up to Athan and put a hand on his shoulder. "You need to trust me, Athan. Please, just one last time. Just trust me."

The night was silent and cold. The clouds obscured the moonlight as they both stood in the forest together, and Zachary could no longer read the expression on Athan's face.

In the distance, they heard the hollow whistle of a train.

328

The Earring
in the Blue Ribbon

"It's a piece of ribbon, Zach. So what?"

"Molly wanted me to give it to you."

"What? How—" Athan stopped walking, stunned. They were barely out of Oak Ridge before Zachary realized he was walking alone. He turned and sighed.

"I went to see her."

"I *told* you not to."

"I know, but I had to."

"You *had* to. I don't—"

"Look inside," Zachary insisted.

Athan wiped at his cheek. It still stung from Inspector Collins' blow. He unwrapped the ribbon and saw the glint of metal in the rising moon.

"Her favourite earring... Why?"

"Proof. That she still cares for you. She wants you back. She loves you and doesn't believe what the papers are saying. I'm taking you to her."

"No. I can't risk her safety."

"How could we possibly risk her safety just by going?"

Athan was about to tell him *exactly* how when Zachary's next words stopped him.

"She's in a terrible state."

"What do you mean?"

"She's running out of food, she has no money, she's thin.

And her mother...”

“Yes?”

“She's...”

“She's dead isn't she?” Athan's shoulders trembled.

“No, she's not, Ay. But she's...not to last. I promised Molly we'd be there by supper. You should've seen her eyes when I said that. She needs you. She's depending on us.”

Athan checked his pocket watch. “Zach, it's almost seven. We've missed supper by hours.”

“She's waited this long. A few more hours won't hurt, will they?”

“How long, do you think?”

“'Til what?” Edward was chewing his fingernail and his words were muffled.

“'Til they catch him.”

“Maybe they won't.”

“Look at all those dogs.” Douglas pointed to the street corner opposite where the bloodhounds strained at the leash, rising up and falling back as the constable held them. Five dogs, numerous police and half the bloody town. “They'll catch him.”

Edward frowned.

“What chance does that boy have?” He seemed to be speaking to himself, like he'd forgotten Douglas was there. He looked awfully pale, but Douglas pretended not to notice. Instead, he smiled.

“Better him than us, eh? Eh?”

“Shut up, Doug. I mean it.”

You do, too.

Douglas shrugged. “I was just—”

"Look at them." Edward pointing.

"Who?" Douglas' attention turned to the street below. He followed the line of Edward's finger.

Standing under a street lamp, Foster and Collins were talking heatedly with a young constable. Foster towered over him and Collins stood near his shoulder, blocking his escape as the young officer cringed away from the imposing Inspector. Foster was yelling, now.

"Seems our young escapee's not the only one with problems," Douglas said, wryly.

"I wouldn't like to be in that lad's shoes right now, either."

Foster was gesturing to the open door of the gaol house and the constable was pointing down the road. Collins cuffed the lad upside the head before stalking off.

The two men turned as Emma slipped inside, quietly shutting the door behind her.

"Nothing went wrong, I see? He got away, then?" Edward asked.

"Yes. They're both gone." She walked to join them at the window. "I also checked on Rose."

"And?"

"It's not her."

"So we're sunk," Douglas murmured.

Emma nodded silently and leaned against the sill, her back to the window. Edward edged away from her slightly and folded his arms across his chest.

"You're *sure* it's not her?" he asked.

"She has no images in her room, no frames. She has no..." She stopped and her stare grew distant.

"What is it?" Douglas turned from the window.

"Zachary. He had a gift wrapped up in a blue ribbon."

"So?" Edward asked.

"He must've given the ribbon to Athan," Emma said, continuing as if she had not heard Edward's question.

"So it's the boy, then?" Douglas felt a moment of intense sympathy for the young fugitive. To be accused of something he didn't do, only to fall victim...

"No it's not him, either. I saw a *woman*. And it was a woman's earring wrapped in the ribbon."

Confused, Edward turned sharply to Douglas. "We're not interested in ribbons though, are we?"

"We're interested in the metal inside, though, mate. Remember?"

"I saw the next victim wearing blue ribbons, Edward," Emma said patiently as she pulled on her gloves.

"Sweet lord almighty," Edward whispered.

Emma turned and strode toward the door. Douglas quickly opened it for her and Edward followed a little way behind.

"If they're on the run, how will we find them?" Douglas asked.

Emma smiled at him. "Oh, I think Rose will know where to find them."

Zachary knocked on the door three times before shoving his hand under his arm to keep it warm. Both men shivered in the chill.

It was almost eleven. The moon was high, bright; its light periodically obscured by the swift-moving clouds.

Silence.

They stood, stamping their feet for a while. Zachary crooked his palm against the glass to peer in the window. He straightened and shook his head.

"Maybe she's asleep," he suggested.

Athan was frowning. "No. She's a light sleeper." He leaned

forward and tried the handle. The door swung silently open.

"Molly?" He whispered, taking a step over the threshold. "Molly!"

They stepped inside.

"Moll?"

Zachary smelled it first. He stopped abruptly, surprised at how vivid the memories were that flashed through his mind. Memories of flesh and puddles and dull coins... His exhale became a low moan.

"What is it?" Athan stopped, concerned.

Zachary gripped Athan's arm, felt the muscles tighten, heard the sudden intake of breath.

He smells it, too...

"Don't," Zachary said, his mouth dry.

"Let go."

"Don't—"

Athan ripped his arm free with ease, turning to Zachary for a second before running into the house, disappearing into the blackness of the hallway.

"Athan!"

Zachary waited—wished—for his return. There was nothing for the longest time.

He slumped against the wall, his head dull and aching. "No. No, no, no..." He shook his head from side to side, his fists pushing at his temples. "No, no, no..."

From deep within the house rose a strangled, inhuman howl.

Athan...

Zachary pushed off the wall and took one step away from the door. Then another. Shaking uncontrollably, he stumbled down the steps and onto the path leading to the front gate.

He faced the house and crouched on the stones, his arms folded around his knees.

333

Cold Hands

They ran.

Heads down, watching their footing; their steps jarred with heavy and tired legs, the moonlit ground blurred.

The sound of their steps echoed around the black hills.

Finally Athan stopped.

Zachary ran on a few more steps before realising Athan was not by his side. "We have to keep going."

"Leave me alone, Zachary."

Athan was smeared with his wife's blood. He could see it when the clouds parted to reveal the moon high in the southern sky.

"No, come on." Zachary put a hand on Athan's arm. "We have to get back to Oak Ridge. Get back to Rose. She'll take care of us and then—"

"Are you *mad*?" Athan shook off Zachary's grip. "They'll hang us!" He almost laughed. He wanted this to end. He wanted to join Molly in Heaven, for that's where she'd surely ended up. But he didn't want them to hang him. Not for her murder or anyone else's. He wanted to die on his own terms a free man. An innocent man.

"We have to."

"She's—she was my wife. They're going to *love* that." Athan grimaced, then spat on the ground and swallowed a few times. He felt he had aged in the last two hours. Aged decades. "Why her?"

Zachary shook his head.

"Who did that to her?" Athan persisted.

"I don't know."

"Why would they... Why do...*that*? WHY!"

"I don't know! She was fine when I left. She was fine..." Zachary muttered.

"Yeah, when you left her." Athan rounded on Zachary, saw the smaller man flinch. "You went to her, then you left her. Christ Almighty, you led him straight to her!"

Athan could see Zachary wanted to deny it. But it was the truth. He'd led the killer to Molly. She'd been so close to giving up and then the killer moved in; preying on the weak.

"I'm sorry," Zachary whispered. "I just wanted to make it better."

He looked pathetic. After all this all he could come up with was an apology. Athan clenched his fist and felt Molly's blood pull at the skin of his knuckles.

Good old Zach. Stumbling through life like nothing matters.

"I had to see her—for you," Zachary said, a defensive tone creeping into his voice.

Athan didn't want to hear anymore. He closed his eyes and swung, his fist catching Zachary in the face. Athan felt the give of bone below Zachary's left eye and knew he'd broken something. The pain of the blow reverberated up into his shoulder as Zachary stumbled backwards and fell.

"And I told you *not* to go! You're as much to blame as the killer."

"What?!" The pain was in his voice, the shock.

"You damn as near murdered her yourself!" Athan screamed. "You led him there, you bastard! You led him to my *wife*. I told you I didn't want this butchery at her doorstep and you brought it right into her fucking house!" He took two steps toward Zachary, still sprawled on the rails.

"Get up! Get up, Zach!"

He could see the sunken part of Zachary's cheek, the swelling around the crushed cheekbone, the bleeding where his skin had spilt. Both eyes streamed with tears of pain. The moonlight disappeared, plunging them into total darkness. Seconds later it reappeared to reveal Zachary scrambling backwards.

Athan lunged forward, his hands grabbing and pulling at Zachary's hair.

"Get up, you bastard."

Zachary hit back, his arms and legs thrashing out, catching Athan in the shins and chest, missing their mark more times than they hit.

"Get off me!"

"You led him there."

"Athan, please. I didn't know!"

"You fucking killed her."

Zachary struck again, his foot connecting with the side of Athan's knee. Athan cried out and fell, the left side of his body jarring to the earth.

Zachary rolled, quickly and to the right, taking the few seconds he had to get away. He dragged himself to his feet, using the rails for purchase.

Athan watched, his knee hot and aching and useless as Zachary skittered back out of range.

Athan hauled himself to his feet and tested his knee.

"Athan, you *must* understand," Zachary said, between breaths. He lifted trembling fingers to the wound beneath his eye.

"No. You're responsible. My wife is *dead* because of you! And I'm going to kill you for it." He took a step forward.

Zachary turned and ran.

337

Athan tried to follow, but didn't make it more than a few feet before his knee gave way and he pitched forward. He caught himself with his hands, the sharp stones biting into the flesh of his palms, his cry of pain becoming a scream of rage.

As the breath left his chest, his head fell, heavy and aching. The stones and the metal rails came into sharp focus, glistening in the moonlight.

He tried to get his breathing under control, but his throat felt raw, painful.

He fell to his side and curled himself up, hugging his knees. The choking smell of his blood-soaked clothes, overpowered him. The grief washed over him and he let it. He was too exhausted to fight it.

From deep within his mind, the buzzing began—and so did the voice.

Zachary ran until he was sure Athan wasn't following him. Eventually, he stopped looking over his shoulder. His panic slowed with his steps.

He couldn't hear Athan anymore—just that one scream. He stopped on a rail tie and bent over gasping for air, his hands on his knees. Sweat from his forehead pooled and fell. As he watched, the rails seemed to disappear as the racing clouds covered the light of the moon. He closed his eyes tightly against the blackness around him and heard only the sound of the wind in the high trees. The injured side of his face pounded in agony.

Was this his fault?

He's wrong. It's the shock of finding her like that. I didn't cause her death.

Zachary opened his eyes and was relieved to see the clouds

had once more parted.

He would never lead danger to Molly. He only wanted to do what was right.

But did I?

Did I lead this killer to her? Did I lead him to Oak Ridge and Bronwyn?

To Rose?

He fervently hoped Sawyer was doing his duty and looking after Rose.

Zachary straightened and turned back in the direction from which he had fled. He genuinely thought Athan would kill him.

His left eye was almost swelled shut. Blood had dried to a crust on the skin of his neck. The pain throbbed in time with his heartbeat.

If he gave Athan time, the grief would surely leave him—or exhaustion would take over. Zachary crouched down and decided to wait a while. This close to Oak Ridge, Athan would have no choice but to head back to town and when he came back this way, Zachary would again try to make him understand.

Athan concentrated on his surroundings; the trees, the rails and the track, anything to stop the buzzing in his head. The ballast, the breeze, the trembling of his hands as they blurred at his side. His head was heavy with confused thoughts.

Did I hit it when I fell?

He concentrated on stumbling along, but his knee wouldn't support his weight properly. Certainly not enough to run Zachary down.

Will I really kill him? Why would I do that?

339

He stopped, swaying on the spot, confusion overwhelming him. His head was fuzzy with images and thoughts.

Who am I?

Athan. Athan Stowall; not-husband, not-father, not-friend.

He stopped and stumbled against the uneven rocks, his feet slipping on the railway ties. He wanted to tear his skin off to get at this buzzing.

Zach. What have I done?

His knuckles hurt. He knew exactly what he'd done.

He thought of his wife. How angry she'd be at him if he lost his mind down here in this forest. If he just fell apart after she was torn apart.

How beautiful she was when she was angry at him.

The buzzing increased. A fly? Wasp? In his head?

He wanted to see his wife again. He remembered her smile and wondered why she wasn't here with him.

He had no idea where he was. What had he been thinking two seconds ago? His brain slowed, but his surroundings moved fast.

He felt rage and fear; fear of being left alone, rage for what he had become. He hated being here and he hated the cursed rail line that had led him here. Not even thoughts of his wife could stop those feelings.

She was dead. Zachary was gone. Both in the space of hours.

He tripped again, the sharp tar-covered rock biting through and splitting the skin of his left hand.

There was no pain. It was surprising.

He turned his palm up. Blood.

So used to blood, now.

He fell against a tree to the side of the rails. Sucking in a breath, he tried to clear his head. He looked behind him to tell Zachary to hurry up. Because Zachary was the last face he remembered seeing.

Pale. Determined. Scared.

Scared of me?

Zachary was gone.

"Zach?"

Nothing.

"Zachary!" he yelled at the top of his voice. The plea echoing around him and disappearing into the night.

Damn!

He shook his head, swishing the thick swarm of bees around in his brain. It lasted mere seconds before they again settled down to their monotonous buzzing.

He looked at his pants and saw the smear of blood on the thigh from his cut hand. He wiped it again, spreading the stain.

Blood. Always the blood.

The buzzing wouldn't stop. It made him slump against the trunk, slam his head backward into the bark behind him. The bees didn't like that. They stopped for a second.

Only a second.

Clarity.

It had only taken a second for him to hit Zachary, too.

He saw that now, like it was happening again. He saw Zachary's head snap back.

"You killed her," he'd thought at the time.

No, he'd *said* it.

He saw himself threaten Zachary, watched him back away, then run from his words more than his fists.

One second was all it took.

The buzzing came back, angrier than ever.

Angry like he had been.

He slammed his head backwards again, felt the skin of his scalp split on the rough bark.

His head slammed back again and again.

Faster.

Stop the buzzing.

He wiped more blood onto his pants and looked down at his shirt where Molly's blood was still drying.

He slid down the trunk, hitting the ground hard, his eyes closed tight as his hands reached for his head.

"Shhhhh... It will be over soon."

A woman's voice soothed him. He opened his eyes and peered through the shadows. No-one was there. He kicked the embankment with the heel of his boot.

"Shhhh..." It soothed him and he let it. "I'll help you."

Athan gasped for breath, alone in his suffocating guilt.

He lifted his injured hand and watched it shudder and blur before him.

He sniffed the skin, sucked it, tasting his wife's blood and his own; a shock to his tongue.

He started to cry. Once more his head jerked backwards, pounding the trunk, trying to bash himself into unconsciousness.

"Shhhh... It's time to go. You want to go, don't you? Escape all this?"

Athan managed a nod. "Yes," he whispered.

God, yes...

Athan dragged himself upright, feeling almost as if hands were helping him on his way, cool and gentle. The back of his head and neck were wet with blood and it trickled, cold, down his shoulders and back.

He needed to find whoever did this to Molly, but he was so tired. He wanted to kill whoever made him hate his best friend.

Killing stopped the buzzing. Pain stopped the bees.

To kill. To be killed.

That's all he wanted, now.

A cold hand grasped his.

342

FAILURE

January 8, 1889

The chill night air had leeched into Zachary's clothes and skin and he shivered uncontrollably, staring down the track toward where Athan had yet to appear.

It had been too long. Athan, even limping on an injured knee, would have passed here by now.

Where is he? Waiting, like me? Waiting for *me?*

Zachary guessed it was almost 2am. He couldn't see the figures on the watch; his left eye was swelled fully shut. The air hung heavy with a wet, pre-dawn smell; thick and earthy.

Athan didn't really want him dead. Of that, he was sure.

His teeth ached with cold and he squinted in the dark. He couldn't leave Athan with the killer still out there. The rails were the safest route for anyone. Killer *or* victim.

He had to go back.

He waited for the moonlight to reappear before slowly trekking back along the rails.

Edward's horse nuzzled the ground and he jerked the reins sharply. Douglas shot him a look.

"At least we don't have to hold the door shut anymore, eh?" Edward smirked, half-heartedly.

Douglas ignored the comment. He didn't want to mention

that every house had a back door and their precious Emma could have finally taken her chance. He wouldn't blame her if she did.

The door to the house was open, a gaping black hole in the already-black night.

As he watched, he saw a light in that blackness, faint at first, but growing as Emma emerged, holding her small taper candle. He saw her shoulders lift and fall in either a sigh or fortifying breath.

Edward made a surprised sound, like he expected her to be hysterical as she had been the first time. But Edward hadn't ventured inside for Sacha or Bronwyn. Douglas was fast realizing the other man had no idea about Emma's strengths.

She made her way down the path and he could tell by her face that they were too late.

She looked sad, pale, but composed. Douglas wondered if she was getting used to it.

"Anything?"

"Nothing. It must be with the boys. They have been here. One of them laid her to rest on the sofa." She held up the folded remains of a blue ribbon. "It stands to reason then, that it follows them."

"You're sure?"

"I no longer sense a presence in the house." She blew out the candle. "And it is what I have seen."

Edward slumped in the saddle. "Don't be vague, luv. Just tell us—"

"When I read her palm I saw Athan, the man you *framed*. He was lying across the rails."

"Dead?"

"I can't be certain of that." Her voice dropped to a whisper.

"Bloody hell," Edward breathed.

"It wasn't your fault," Douglas said, quietly.

344

"I mean the rails, you twit!" Edward snapped. "What are *rails* made of, eh?"

Metal.

"Oh dear God." Douglas felt sick. They'd failed—they were *going* to fail.

"We have to go," Emma said, addressing them both. She mounted her horse and kicked its sides, spurring it into a gallop.

Zachary smelled blood.

He cautiously approached in the darkness, inhaling the wet, heavy smell of earth and blood like he was one of those police hounds, trailing the scent.

I didn't hit him that hard, he thought.

As the clouds cleared the moon, he saw a figure lying across the rails on the slow rise of the embankment. He stopped.

The cold wind, smelling of a slaughterhouse, wafted across his skin.

He realized how familiar he was with the odour. The numbness fled him as the bile pushed at the back of his throat and his chest shuddered with sudden panic.

"Ay?" His voice was weak and trembling. The figure did not move.

He took two more steps, clearly seeing Athan's blond hair, matted and spiked up in dark patches. Athan lay to the side of the rails, his arm flung out, his wrist lying across one rail, the copper bracelet resting against the iron.

His body was slick with blood, his skin was...

No. No, no, no, no, no...

Forgetting his fears, Zachary scrambled up the embankment and fell to his knees beside Athan. The clouds crossed

345

the moon and plunged them into sudden darkness. The fleeting glance of his friend's ripped body seared into his eyes like the flash of a bulb.

The wind swept through the trees as Zachary knelt, praying for the moonlight. He'd never been more terrified. This was worse than Sacha. He was out in the open and Athan was—

He looked to the right, his breath coming in gasps, now. In the darkness, he could hear the scratching of nocturnal creatures, the predators, the prey.

Which one am I?

The night remained black and he looked to the sky, seeing only the outline of the clouds.

I need to see.

But the clouds were full and slow. He reached out a fumbling hand to the body in front of him, feeling first the warm, wet material of Athan's shirt, then the pulpy moist flesh of his arm.

Forcing his fingers to steady, he felt along until he came to Athan's ruined neck. He pressed hard and leaned over until his ear touched Athan's lips.

No heartbeat. No breath.

Zachary jerked back, wiping his sticky hands on his pants, wanting to cry, but unable to make the tears.

Logic percolated through his intense grief.

The killer must still be here.

The sounds of the woods seemed to magnify and he looked from side to side, his one good eye straining, expecting to see the figure of the killer approaching, a shape blacker than the night.

His mouth went dry and he knelt there, penitent over Athan's body, waiting, listening, trying not to move.

A thump in the undergrowth made him shoot to his feet, ready to run.

And leave Athan?

I can't carry you, mate, he thought. *I can't bury you.*

The moonlight slipped across the body.

I'm sorry.

Zachary took two steps backwards and turned to leave. In the distance, he heard the whinny of a horse.

I have to keep running.

With one last look at his best friend, he slid quietly down the embankment and made his way to Oak Ridge.

MANY ABRUPT SHOCKS

Sawyer's stiff neck sent a stabbing pain down the left side of his back. He shifted slightly on the rocker and leaned forward to watch the voluminous clouds slowly track across the low moon. They were beautiful, really.

Sawyer looked at his pocket watch. 3.30am. He wound the watch with stiff fingers and stifled a yawn, peering into the garden for the umpteenth time from the porch. He hadn't told her about his late-night vigil, but it wouldn't matter. He'd be gone before she woke.

With a splinter from the porch rail, he picked the dirt from under his square fingernails.

He didn't feel tired. He *should,* given the many abrupt shocks of the last week, but sitting here gave him a purpose that not even fatigue could threaten. Rose was at the end of her wits, he was sure. She didn't speak of today's events, but he could see the change in her disposition.

The escape of Athan and the unknown whereabouts of Zachary had taken its toll. After the hours of questioning by Foster and Collins, Rose had allowed Sawyer to walk her home without complaint.

Sawyer had last seen the two inspectors meeting a score of reporters from London and trying to explain how it was that the second most wanted man in the country was once again at large.

He would do whatever was necessary to protect her from the killer.

As the clouds parted and the moonlight shone across the path, Sawyer spotted Zachary standing in the middle of the garden staring back at him.

From where he sat, Sawyer could see Zachary's heaving chest, his swollen eye, the dark smears on his clothes and hands.

Zachary took a faltering step forward.

Sawyer slipped from his chair, the blanket falling from his shoulders. He reached for the axe-handle and held it loosely in his hand. Ready.

Zachary moved closer, his face in shadow.

The man shook like he was ill. Sawyer swallowed hard, wondering if Zachary would attack him, talk to him or simply stand there like a nightmare in the dim light.

Sawyer held his breath and walked to the top of the small set of steps. He stood there, legs slightly apart, standing guard.

You know why I'm here. Leave.

The other man didn't move for the longest time. Then he shook his head as if trying to dispel a bad memory or clear his mind.

He looked up at Sawyer and opened his mouth to speak. Nothing came.

"Where is Athan?" Sawyer finally asked.

"Dead."

"Jesus."

Did you kill him?

"Athan's wife is dead. We found her. We argued. He...hit me and I left him for a while... He's dead." Zachary's voice rose slightly in panic.

Sawyer nodded slowly. "You can't see her."

"I need to."

"No." Sawyer's voice was still quiet, but firm. He thought about Rose asleep in the room upstairs.

Zachary paced unsteadily in front of the carpenter, his steps slow.

"Why is it everywhere I go people die? Everything I touch, everything I love, everyone who loved *me*... I need to see her. She'd want to see me, I *know* she would."

"No," Sawyer said, his tone guarded. "Look at you. You look like you've been dragged through Hell."

Part of him was relieved this confrontation had finally come to pass. Zachary was here for Rose. Sawyer's hand clasped the axe handle.

Just you try.

"Let me pass."

"Do you want her to die too?" Sawyer kept his voice low. "I don't. I've followed Rose home every day for over three months to make sure she gets home safe. I read the papers, I know what's going on in London. I can look after her better than you."

"*I* won't hurt her." Zachary stopped pacing and placed one foot on the lowest stair.

Sawyer tensed. "Don't."

Zachary took one more step, then stopped.

They faced each other, three steps between them. Sawyer breathed out slowly and fixed Zachary with a cold stare.

"Everything you touch dies, Zachary, you said it yourself."

The man seemed to crumble before him, his face creasing in silent pain.

Silence engulfed them. Neither moved.

Sawyer could see the splatter of blood across Zachary's cheeks and forehead. He started to breathe through his mouth when he smelled the sweat, sour and warm.

Then the darkness swallowed them.

Sawyer's fingers twisted around the smooth wood of the axe handle and sweat prickled his neck and armpits.

The stairs creaked.

He readied for an attack, but none came.

When the wan light returned, Sawyer was alone.

He heard footsteps running in the distance. Racing, stumbling, sprinting.

Sawyer stood, tense and ready for Zachary to reappear. He waited until his calf muscles twitched and his toes hurt inside his boots. He stared out into the night until his eyes ached from the strain.

Then he turned, walked back to his chair and picked up his blanket before settling where he belonged.

"God *dammit!*" Edward swore.

"What?" Douglas held the lantern up high, illuminating the rails and the body that lay across them. Edward opened his mouth, but Emma cut across him before he could say a word. She eased past Douglas and knelt next to Athan's corpse, holding her skirts just short of the carnage.

Douglas knelt beside her as she whispered, "Look at his hand. His bracelet."

His eyes followed hers. Athan's copper bracelet rested cold on the metal of the rails. Douglas straightened and looked from side to side. The line ran smooth and clear into the darkness on either side.

"It was here with him and not the other one?" Douglas asked.

Emma nodded, her eyes closed tightly as if she was trying to hold something back, some pain. "It murdered him and we were too late. What an awful way to die. Painful, full of fear, alone..."

"We'll find it, Emma," Douglas whispered. He thought about the terror of the man's last moments. Not an easy death.

None of them were.

Emma opened her eyes a moment later and carefully re-moved her wedding ring, placing it into a silk pouch at her belt. With sure fingers, she lifted Athan's hand from the rails. Douglas gritted his teeth as he heard the copper scrape against the iron.

Edward stood to his left and Douglas knew he had his hand on the wooden stock of his custom-made revolver.

Easy, Edward... It's gone. I'm sure it's gone.

Emma peered at the palm, her free hand gesturing for Douglas to bring the lamp closer. He did and looked at the blood that creased the skin of the dead man's hand, as if he could somehow see what she was seeing.

Cooling, dead skin was all he saw. He tried not to look at the rest of the body.

He watched Emma's face, her eyes darting as if tracking movement, objects and people that only she could see. A shudder ran through her and he placed a steady hand against her back in case she faltered.

He knew he shouldn't. He knew Edward would see and he waited for the sarcastic comment. None came.

After a short while, she blinked rapidly, her lashes glisten-ing with unshed tears. Douglas rubbed her back a little, knowing it was improper, but needing to do *something* for her.

She smiled at him and he stood with her as they turned away from the dead man. Edward came to join them in a small huddle, the lantern their only light.

Emma slowly breathed in and out. "West. Another man, this time. Young—younger than Athan." She smoothed her skirts with trembling hands. "He has brown hair and stands amid carcasses of...I don't know. Cattle... Maybe pigs?"

"West, eh?" Edward snorted. "Well, doesn't look like you'll be seeing that husband o' yours any time soon, eh?"

Emma slapped him hard. It was sudden. Violent. The sound of skin on skin was loud in the silence.

She glared at him, her now trembling hands feeling for the purse at her belt, taking out the ring and replacing it on her finger. Her eyes did not leave Edward's. Douglas saw the man falter and back down.

Well, I'll be...

"What about the other one, that Zachary fellow?" Douglas asked, his tone light as if nothing had transpired.

Finally, Edward broke the stare and turned away. Emma glanced at Douglas.

"He went east, back to Oak Ridge. He'll be saved if he stays in the town—people there will protect him. I saw it in his palm. He has a chance to be happy if he stays."

She looked up at the sky as it cleared rapidly of cloud, leaving the moon bright and high, the dawn sky beginning the break in the west.

"So, it starts again," Douglas muttered.

"Yes. Yes, I suppose it does." Emma gathered her skirts and walked back to the horses, leaving Athan on the rails behind her.

She paused and looked back. "Well, gentlemen?"

Douglas nodded and trotted to catch up.

Rubbing his cheek, Edward slowly followed.

EPILOGUE

Sacha Turgenev stood out in the night air for almost an hour, still as a statue.

If she didn't move, she wouldn't feel. She didn't want to feel.

Her eyes seemed to dry out as the sun dissolved behind the array of Oak and Birch trees near her cottage.

His horse didn't bring him back that night. Sacha pictured him riding away from her at great speed, his mount's hooves crushing stones on the road, the horse charging as its rider pushed it; the legs, the breath, the limits of its endurance. Pushed everything to get away.

Sacha breathed in, careful to keep her back steady so she wouldn't move or fall. Not an inch. The valley's autumnal mist hung still and it was thick on her lips and in her mouth.

She had shirts to wash that day, like every other day. She washed for the town; the hotels, the police, the butchers and the shopkeepers.

The money was enough and the work was solitary.

There was nothing else for her to do.

Just before dawn the next morning, Sacha moved her stiff legs, and turned to walk back into the cottage.

It was an unfamiliar place that morning; not hers, not a stranger's.

It was quiet and otherworldly. Simply walking from room

to room was a test of strength.

It came to her when she had washed and ironed the first two sacks of shirts; she did nothing else *but* wash shirts and talk to Richard, cook for Richard, laugh at Richard's jokes.

She didn't *want* to do anything else.

She had no friends. She had no parents. She was like a child who had just been abandoned but was very aware of the circumstances.

That first day after Richard left her, Sacha fell into a sobbing heap in the shirts and aprons from Riley's Bake House. Her chest trembled like something was trying to get out.

And maybe it was.

Maybe it was just too painful. Maybe her soul wanted to get out and fly high, where it could fall back down, dashing itself onto the rocks of her little hometown.

Or maybe fly off never to return.

Just like Richard.

Anything, just as long as it could get away from this body that suddenly hurt so much.

She clawed at her clothes, but exhaustion overtook her and she was forced to simply lay there.

The next night she spent on the floor of her empty home. She lay in the middle of a pile of towels where she shook and twisted and shuddered so much she thought she was going to break apart.

She didn't. But neither did she sleep.

For the next six months, Sacha tried to find a reason to live; any reason. She tried to enjoy the simple things like refreshing cold water from the stream, the frayed embroidery from her mother's chair, her dolls, the taste of lamb and rosemary.

She took off her wedding ring for one day, but became afraid he would find out, so she replaced it that night. She watched sunsets, read books she'd never taken time to read, fished, played in a storm of butterflies, spun in a wheat field until she was dizzy and fell down, laughing despite herself, even when black field crickets crawled over her arms.

She pretended she was a fish, or a part of the river, or one of the children playing around the breaking carts, watching the young horses, the wheelwrights and farriers.

She scored her name into a tree. She carved Richard's name into the dirt and pissed on it, squatting over it, her face blank, her eyes dull.

She tried drinking herself into a comfortable vagueness, but it required going into town and seeing people.

People who knew...

She didn't have the energy to succumb to alcohol. She had her poppy seeds, but, after making her wonderfully insensible to her grief, they made her sick.

At the end of the year, to the very day, Sacha was dead.

Nothing made her happy, nothing filled the hole inside her, formed by a single farewell that had hollowed her out like a gourd.

It was a brief moment of sharp despair that allowed it to happen. She had been playing with the coins in her jar, running them through her fingers, listening to them clink on her wedding ring.

Her whole worth in one small jar.

Had she thought more about it, maybe she wouldn't have even started.

But a murmuring, a whisper compelled her, coaxed her, promised peace if only she'd pick up the knife.

"Pick up the knife...escape."

Sacha stood in her kitchen, looking, as she did every night,

out the window to where he used to park his carriage before he sold it. There was always noise when he was here; matches lighting, footsteps, breathing, or the clumsy tuning of the old upright piano by tired fingers.

Now, the silence made her ears feel like she had gone into the mountains or beneath the waves. Everything was muted. She would move her jaw up and down for hours trying to clear the blockage.

The house was cold and dead. She was the only living thing. She'd given up feeding the dog; it was too much of a chore. Even the mice had stopped coming.

Sacha didn't realize it at first, but a buzzing started in her ears.

Her skin itched, her fingers were restless, shaking, twisting. Tears welled in her eyes, but couldn't fall.

The voice promised peace.

Sacha had just turned nineteen and she had to get out, she had to run.

And she did.

It was almost over before she realized what she had done. A paring knife, her nails, her teeth; she used it all. She ripped herself free from the skin that did nothing but wash shirts, grow cold at night and curl up in their bed like a dead bug.

It hurt her, but she saw flecks of white—

My soul, my spirit?

—glimmering under the bright red of her blood. She laughed as she dug deeper, her skin coming off, slapping wet against the cotton of her dress.

Her face, her arms, her legs, her stomach.

The last thing would be her hands. The knife became hard to hold, so she abandoned it, flinging it into the living room where it landed near the fireplace. There were enough tears in her flesh for her nails to gain purchase.

Tiredness began to overtake her and she struggled to stand.

"Not yet... Not yet!"

She wasn't finished.

She had to get out.

Her blood made the floor slick and she slipped, knocking the table.

The oil in the lamp sluiced in its glass reservoir. Her jar of coins teetered and fell, smashing on the cobbled floor, sending glass shards and coins across the dark stain below her.

She followed, crumpling to the ground, slamming one skinned elbow onto the stone. The grating sound loud in the silence.

"That's it," the voice whispered. "It's almost over. And then you can rest. Escape. Be free, child."

Her hands grew weary and her eyesight began to fail. Sacha smiled and nodded slowly.

She heard the sounds of the horses racing towards her, but she knew they weren't outside. They were in her mind, racing for her. Hooves on the cobblestones, the wheels of the carriage clattering forever nearer.

Racing to save her. To take her away from the misery and pain. To make her happy once more.

She closed her eyes.

All her pain was gone, but sleep was coming up fast.

She whimpered, ripping and tearing with a new burst of energy, a new frenzy. She watched blood arc and splatter onto the ceiling like crab tracks in wet sand.

Red tracks on my pretty white ceiling.

She dug deeper. She ripped harder.

Trying to get out before she fell asleep.

ABOUT THE AUTHORS

Steve Gerlach is one of Australia's few thriller writers. Born and bred in Australia, Gerlach's fast-paced, cut-to-the-bone style is a refreshing voice in the dry, barren Australian literary scene.

Steve's background includes many varied roles. He has worked as an editor for a book publisher; as the editor-in-chief of an Australian motorcycle magazine; editor and publisher of an international crime magazine, Probable Cause; a researcher and columnist for a major Australian daily newspaper; a Technical Publications Officer in the security industry; marketing executive for an international telecommunications software company; a writer for Australian Defence training and software producers; and currently works in the field of major infrastructure procurement and delivery.

He was also the Historical Advisor on the Australian film, Let's Get Skase, and has been a student of the Jack The Ripper crimes for more than a quarter of a century.

Steve Gerlach lives in Melbourne, where he is currently working on a new novel or two.

Amanda Kool is a mild-mannered technical writer by day; dark, seedy novelist by night. She majors in history, mythology, religion and crime and is a prolific researcher in all periods of history. She has written four novels, one of which she co-authored—this one. Her novels cover the gamut of crime thriller, post-apocalyptic epic and supernatural thriller. She never shies away from the big stuff. As well, Amanda has written a number of short fiction pieces and has worked on many collaborative projects in both the publishing and computer gaming industries. She has four pets: two dogs, one cat, and the author Steve Gerlach.

Lightning Source UK Ltd.
Milton Keynes UK
UKOW041815160113

204979UK00001B/48/P